FAITH

GREATER HEIGHTS

JULIE MURPHY

BALZER + BRAY
An Imprint of HarperCollinsPublishers

Also by Julie Murphy

Side Effects May Vary
Ramona Blue
Dumplin'
Puddin'
Pumpkin
Dear Sweat Pea
Faith: Taking Flight

Balzer + Bray is an imprint of HarperCollins Publishers.

Library of Congress Control Number: 2021941522
ISBN 978-0-06-289968-2

Typography by Jenna Stempel-Lobell and Catherine Lee
21 22 23 24 25   PC/LSCH   10 9 8 7 6 5 4 3 2 1

First Edition

For Natalie, who literally saved the day

She needed a hero, so that's what she became.

1

"I really have to go first?" I ask again.

Ches nods with certainty. "You're the most likely to back out, and there's no way Matt and I are getting matching BFF tattoos only for you to chicken out at the last minute."

I hold one hand up. "I'll remind you both that I've run into an actual burning building to save puppies."

"And people," Matt adds.

"And people," I confirm. "I am the definition of 'not a chicken.' Besides, having a fear of needles is totally normal."

Ches takes my hand. "We know that you're not actually a chicken. Just when it comes to needles."

"This the one you want?" Matilda, the petite tattoo artist with pink spiky hair, asks. Her voice is more gravelly than her appearance would lead you to believe. Her makeup is dark and dramatic and completely hides the person underneath. I wonder for the thousandth time on this trip if this is what happened to Colleen after the fire. Is she somewhere out here hiding beneath pink hair and bold makeup? Would I even recognize her if I saw her again? I hope so. And I hope she's okay, wherever she is.

Matilda waits for my answer as she holds a stencil of the wings the three of us picked from the wall of designs. Not quite angelic enough to be angel wings, but strong and powerful still.

I nod. "Me first, I guess."

"Let's see your IDs," Matilda says, and for the first time in my life, I realize that my ID is about to open a door that has been shut for all eighteen years of my life. A door of needles and permanence.

We each dig into our pockets and proudly hand them over. I'm pretty sure that getting matching tattoos with your high school best friends ranks high on the list of regrets for many people, but after last semester and all that the three of us have been through, I can't see myself regretting this. I just wish someone would knock me out for the whole needle-poking-my-skin-over-and-over-again part.

"You know," I say, "it's not too late for us to just get those matching buttons at the Spam Museum instead. Buttons can be forever too. . . ."

"While I do indeed heart spam," Matt says, "I think I'm ready to commemorate our friendship in a slightly more permanent way—and one that will make my mother say, 'Matthew James, what in God's name did you do to your body?'" His voice goes comically high and sounds nothing like Mrs. Delgado.

I snort as I glance at my phone. "I should check in with Grandma Lou."

Ches grips my wrist. "You called forty-five minutes ago and she was just as fine then as she was forty-five minutes before that."

This was, of course, Ches's idea in the first place. When Matt finally turned eighteen on Valentine's Day, she said we should get ink to bind us together before we all head off in different directions next year—even if I don't quite know what direction I'm heading. Spring break was the natural time to do it. Our epic plan was to road-trip—a visit to all the great roadside attractions Minnesota has to offer. It would be our first sort-of grown-up expedition without any adult supervision. And because I am definitely a chicken, I've been putting off our date with a tattoo gun until our very final day.

"Faith?" calls Matilda from her station, where she's suiting up with black latex gloves as she snaps them against her wrist like a war doctor going in for battle. "You're up, babe."

"Can my friends come with me?" I ask, eyeing the little gate separating us from the actual tattooing section.

"Normally just one at a time, but what the hell? You three get back here." She waves us through the gate and into an Actual Adult Decision.

The three of us shuffle in and I sit in the tattoo chair,

which reminds me of the dentist, which is . . . not good.

"I'm scared of needles," I blurt.

Ches sits on the opposite side of me and takes my hand. Her long, bony fingers weave through mine and her grown-out bob tickles my cheeks as she places a quick kiss on my forehead.

"You and a third of the population," Matilda says. "Just don't look. It makes a major difference. And you got your besties to distract you. I can stop at any time. Just say so." She holds the stencil up. "Now for this part I need you to look. Where is this beauty going?"

I point to the exact spot on my forearm where I want the tattoo.

She presses the sheet down so that the outline can transfer. "The skin is a little more tender here, so just remember to breathe." She pulls the sheet back. "How does it look?"

There on my pale inner arm just below my elbow crease is an outline of wings no larger than a silver dollar. A constant reminder of my life-changing ability. The wings were Matt's idea. I protested, saying if it was going to be something we all shared, it should be something we have in common. Not only about me. He smiled simply and said, "Faith, we were helping each other fly long before you became a psiot and did it for real."

I'm still getting used to my best friends even knowing what a psiot is, let alone using it in reference to me. It was over Christmas break when I finally revealed the secret I'd been holding on to for months: that after undergoing an activation procedure, I was identified as a subspecies of humans with advanced abilities that manifest in many different ways. For me, it was flying and eventually learning that I can (sort of) control the force field that surrounds me.

But Matt was right. He and Ches had been my best friends since long before I even knew what a psiot was. I don't know what I would have done without them over these last few months with Grandma Lou's health declining, thanks to her Alzheimer's diagnosis last fall. Then there's the ever-elusive Peter going MIA yet again. Peter might have saved me from Toyo Harada and his Harbinger Foundation last summer when my power was activated and I was very nearly turned into another one of Harada's psiot pawns. And the only evidence that Dakota Ash was ever actually a part of my life are the handful of leaked episodes of *The Grove* that were filmed in Glenwood before the whole show was put on hiatus when Dakota and the showrunner-creator, and my former idol, Margaret Toliver, got caught up in a drug ring right here in Glenwood and vanished soon after I caught both of them. I wouldn't have made it through any of that without Ches and Matt. They're not just my friends. They're my family. My wings.

"How does it look?" I ask them, holding my stenciled arm out for inspection.

Ches squeezes my hand and Matt nods eagerly.

I lean back and close my eyes. "Do it," I tell Matilda.

"Ches, read the care instructions once more," I tell her, as Matt pulls off the highway exit for Glenwood.

Each of us wear our bandages proudly. Matt on the interior of his wrist, Ches just below her collarbone, and me on my forearm.

"You need to chill," Ches says. "It's not going to get infected. It's like you overcame your fear of needles only to discover a new thing to obsess over."

Matt eyes me in the rearview mirror. "Warm water, unscented soap, and moisturize as needed. Let it flake off. No picking," he recites from memory.

I exhale deeply and dig around in the back seat for more trash to throw away. After a week of roadtripping in Matt's car, it definitely has a specific smell—old fast food, gas station air fresheners, and the caramel latte Ches accidentally spilled on the floorboard. It probably doesn't smell great to someone who hasn't lived in it for the past week, and I don't know what it says about me that I actually like it, but I do. I'm a little sad that it's all coming to an end.

"I wonder what Grandma Lou is going to say."

"That you're a badass," Ches says, full of confidence. And I think she's not wrong.

As we roll into my driveway, I notice a shiny red Cadillac

parked on the street, with a large magnet on the car door advertising Cedar Hills Retirement Community.

"Did Grandma Lou get a new ride?" Matt asks.

"Uh, no. She's on strict orders from her doctor not to drive." I look down at all the trash still in the back seat, panic sinking in my chest. I shouldn't have gone. She was too quick to say yes. I should have known she was up to something.

"Go," Ches says, keying in to the dip in my mood. "I'll help Matt get all this stuff cleaned up."

I nod quickly and fish my duffel bag out of the trunk before taking the front steps two at a time. Sparing my friends a quick wave, I open the front door and dump my bag on the floor. "Who the heck is parked outside our house?" I demand.

Sitting at the kitchen table across from Grandma Lou and Miss Ella, my grandmother's longtime best friend and nosy neighbor, is an older man with narrow eyes and bushy gray brows. He smiles widely at the sight of me, and I know it's meant to be a warm gesture, but something about his exaggerated features reminds me of a caricature at a carnival.

"Well, you're just about as polite as a stampede of elephants, aren't you?" Miss Ella asks with a dry smile.

"Oh, Faith, you're home early! Come, come." Grandma Lou pulls out the chair beside her. "This is George from Cedar Hills. He came by to talk to us a little about their assisted living facilities."

"Without me?"

Miss Ella and Grandma Lou share a look, like they've been caught. And they have been! There's no reason for Grandma Lou to be looking into assisted living. This wasn't supposed to happen until after graduation. It's too soon. She's still so much . . . herself. And more importantly, *I'm* still here. With her.

"Nice to meet you, Faith. I've heard so much about you." George stands. "I was just finishing up, actually. Lou, I'll leave you with plenty of literature. We'd be happy to set up a tour for you and Faith as well." He turns to me. "We have a really lovely facility. She'll never want to leave."

"Said every villain ever," I say without thinking.

"Faith," Miss Ella chides. "Manners!"

"George, thank you so much," Grandma Lou says. "I'll give this a think."

I don't take my eyes off him as Miss Ella walks him to the door. He's too tall, too smooth for a man his age. Everything about him is suspicious.

"Well, tell me all about your great big trip," Grandma Lou says, trying to change the subject.

"You can't move," I say, and I'm surprised to find that even though I'm angry, my voice sounds sad. Betrayed.

Grandma Lou sighs, frowning regretfully. "Faith, darling, it's time. I know it's hard to think about, but you're grown enough now to finish out your senior year on your own, and Miss Ella will be right next door. You can visit me as much as you want and—"

"What about a live-in nurse? One who could come during the day when I'm at school, and then I'll be here at night." Even though I know how poorly the interviews for a daytime home care nurse went when we tried to hire one back in December.

"Listen to the woman, Faith," Ella says, abruptly reentering the room. She gathers the coffee cups and takes them to the sink.

"Is that all I'm supposed to do? Listen? Don't I get a say?" Anger boils up in me. At both of them, because they did this on purpose. They cut me out. "I can't believe you went behind my back and did this!"

"Faith . . ." Grandma Lou's voice is thick with hurt.

"Now wait a minute." Miss Ella spins around and flips a dish towel over her shoulder. "This woman has sacrificed so much for you over the years, and now she's decided how she'd like to live out her remaining years while she still has the mind to do so. The least you can do is respect that and show a little gratitude."

"Ella, that's enough," Grandma Lou says with a soft sternness. "I'll see to those dishes. You head on home."

Ella throws her arms up, like she's washing her hands of us. "I've said my piece."

Once she's gone, Grandma Lou stands carefully and

makes her way to the sink. I watch her like I've never watched her before. Looking for signs I might have missed. But she's just like I remember her: a little hunched, a little slow, and a little ornery.

"You should go and unpack," she says, taking over the dishes Ella left behind. "We can talk about this again a little later. I want to hear all about your trip when you've had a minute to settle back in."

I nod, my gaze unmoving from the stack of pamphlets George left behind. And even though she's standing right here, in her cozy little kitchen, the house already feels entirely too empty.

2

Grandma Lou goes to bed early, and after the nonstop pace of my spring break road trip with Matt and Ches, I'm feeling a little deflated in the same way I do after Christmas every year. I'm obsessed with the frenetic energy that comes with the holiday, and I love diving into the parade of parties and giftings and sheer joy that radiates off every candy cane I pass. It's not that I'm obsessed with the holiday itself. It's that for those few days, I can forget all the little and big things I don't want to think about.

Now that I'm sitting here alone for the first time in a week, all I can think is: three months. Or, three months and nine days. It's been three months and nine days since everything blew up in my face. Since my town was ravaged by a designer drug called A+ and people and animals started going missing. Since Ches was framed and kidnapped. Since my former idol, Margaret Toliver, disappeared in a fiery blaze along with my celebrity and IRL crush-slash-girlfriend, Dakota Ash. Since I ran inside a burning building and was nearly consumed by the flames. Since fire became the thing that haunts me in my nightmares. And suddenly it's just all too much.

Carefully, I tiptoe down the hallway to where Grandma Lou's door is cracked open. On the other side, old seasons of *The Great British Baking Show* take the place of white noise, and she's soundly asleep.

Downstairs, I triple-check that the doors are locked and that I haven't left any car keys or house keys out where Grandma Lou might wake up and find them. Since she wandered out and got lost just before Thanksgiving, she's only had two other big episodes. Thankfully, she didn't make it very far either time, but I'm not interested in tempting fate. I just need a little fresh air.

Still, leaving her alone in the middle of the night feels like abandoning a sleeping baby. It could be fine. She could stay sound asleep. Or it could be catastrophic. But I haven't flown in a week, and there's an itch in my bones that can only be satisfied by the wind burning my cheeks.

Once I've secured the house like Grandma Lou is the queen of England and I'm whoever makes sure the queen doesn't go on a midnight walk through Piccadilly Circus, I draw a breath deep into my lungs and push away from my backyard. My body rises, air sweeping between my feet and the grass as I climb higher into the night sky. There's the familiar sensation of something warm tingling in my skin that I can only describe as magic. There and gone again so quickly that sometimes I miss it. Not tonight. Tonight, I feel everything. From the gradual shift in temperature as I fly high above the choruses of barking dogs and televisions flickering inside homes like fireflies, to the wind ripping through my hair and snaking down the back of my sweatshirt.

At first, after everything happened, I patrolled the skies of Glenwood through the freezing winter nights, soaring above rooftops as I searched for something. Anything that would help me piece together the puzzle that was the first half of my senior year. Any sign that it had actually happened or was real at all! But there was nothing. Margaret. Dakota. Colleen. Peter. Everyone had just vanished. My life was flipped upside down and the only remaining evidence was my ability to fly.

But it couldn't be that simple. There was too much on the line for Margaret to just disappear or for her to let Dakota off the hook without any consequences. Dakota had let me go the day when the paper mill went up in flames, when she knew Margaret had capital-*P* Plans for me. I should have died there, but I didn't. That makes me a loose thread, and if I know something about Margaret from years of obsessing over her storytelling prowess on *The Grove*, it's this: the woman doesn't do loose threads.

I know I should hate Dakota. I should despise her for lying to me and using me. And I did for a little while. But every night when I fall asleep, just at that moment when I lose control over my own thoughts, I can't help but think of her. I wish I could hear about her day and how her rescue dog, Bumble, is doing. I wish I could *see* her.

All the official reports said Dakota Ash died in the fire. But that's just the story. I know better. They didn't find her or any remains. Even before she sent Ches a stack of cash to take care of her legal woes, I went over to her place in case she'd left Bumble behind, but he was gone. His food bowl, leash, and toys too. The whole house was just as she'd left it, with the exception of those three things, and that's when I really knew. She'd gone without leaving me even the smallest sign.

For the first month or so after the mill, it was all anyone could talk about. Gossip magazines and websites constantly reported on conspiracy theories and potential sightings of Dakota Ash and Margaret Toliver. There was even a televised candlelight vigil with the whole cast on a studio lot in Los Angeles. I'll admit that I followed along obsessively, hoping for just a glimpse of Dakota. But every tip or sighting was easily reasoned away. Until Evansville, Indiana.

Only a few of the online gossip columns picked it up, but someone in Evansville snagged a blurry photo of a young woman dressed in head-to-toe black playing with her dog in a dilapidated snow-covered park. I didn't even have to see Dakota to know it was her. I recognized Bumble immediately.

So she's out there. Somewhere. The girl who sold me out to my apparently villainous former idol is out there. The girl who was my first kiss. The girl who I have such deep, conflicting feelings for that it scares me. She's out there.

And I have no idea what to do with that.

Matt's street passes far beneath me and I swoop down low, aiming for Cedar Hills Retirement Community. The air is brisk and tinged with the hint of sweet spring flowers coming into bloom. It's cold enough that a person who wasn't also a psiot might be blinded by tears, but it turns out I'm more than just a flying fat girl, I also have a force field that bends around me like a bubble. A bubble I can control. Or, that I'm getting *better* at controlling. For now, it shears the wind away from my face just enough that I can fly without goggles. Because, let's be real, goggles really aren't part of the vibe.

Below me Cedar Hills comes into view, and it's also kind of like a bubble. The whole complex is designed in concentric circles like a Russian nesting doll. I know from George's oh-so-helpful pamphlets that the apartments lining the outermost edge are for independent seniors. The next ring of buildings are smaller clusters, with multiple people who require slightly more assistance living in each building. There are pools and gyms and rec areas, but at the very center of the property is the assisted living building, where I'm sure Grandma Lou would have to be so that she could have round-the-clock care.

Cedar Hills has been around since just before I moved here. It's the kind of place adults talk about as saving the local economy. Families drive from all over the state to bring their aging loved ones right here to Glenwood. In fact, the only reason Matt's grandmother isn't also here is because it's too expensive.

It all looks perfectly fine. Nice, even. Now that I'm not so mad about being cut out of the process, I know all the logical reasons why this is a good idea. Grandma Lou can ease into life there now while she still has the mental fortitude to create bonds and connections. I'll be able to graduate and go to school . . . or go wherever flying fat girls go after high school. And I know I can always visit her. But in a way I'm too scared to admit out loud, I can't help but wonder if she'll forget me sooner than she would if she stayed in her own home with me.

Most selfishly of all, I'm not ready to be on my own. I'm not ready to be the adult in the room. I already do so much. In the last few months, I've taken over keeping up with the bills, and I drive anywhere she needs to go. If not me, Miss Ella. But there's still something comforting about knowing that she's there and if I need her, *she'll* be the adult in the room . . . if she can.

I slow, coasting down to get a closer look at the independent living buildings, and I spot an older man as he leans over the edge of his balcony. One minute everything is fine; the next, he's tripping forward and dropping his phone from his fourth-story apartment. I swoop down, making a wide circle in the dark courtyard. Then, faster than he can possibly see, I dart toward the phone, catching it up in my force field like a fish in a net an instant before it collides with the paved walkway. Faith: Defender of the Smartphone.

With the phone in hand, I glide up toward his balcony.

"Damn it," he mutters, turning around to grab a flashlight.

While his back is turned, I lay the phone on the side table next to his rocking chair and tap the screen once so that it lights up. Then I duck back out of sight.

"Well, wait a minute," I hear him say.

There's no stopping my grin. In the last few months I haven't done anything as flashy as stop a bank robbery or rescue kidnapped babies, but there have been plenty of these moments. One dash of superpowers from me and I can turn someone's day around without them ever knowing. If "Guardian Angel" weren't so cliché, it would be a front-runner for my code name, but even though it feels much too cool and sleek for me, Zephyr is the name that swirls in my head when I glide through the sky. Peter says psiots don't have superhero personas, but when I charged into that warehouse last fall to save Dakota and get to the bottom of what was happening in Glenwood, I needed a name. Someone I could hide behind. And Zephyr felt right.

I aim for the main building next and watch through a window as the glowing light of a television illuminates the face of a sleeping woman. A tall man in scrubs with a bushy beard walks in, and the second before he turns the television off I see a hollow, exhausted expression on his face. He leaves, shutting the door behind him.

I wonder about the woman and her family, about how they made the decision that this was where she'd spend her final days. I wonder if, when she lived in the warmth of her own home, she preferred to leave the television on while she was sleeping. If perhaps it was comforting. Maybe her family knew that she liked it that way . . . but in this place, with a constant rotating staff of orderlies just trying to do the best they can for total strangers so that they can go home to their own families, no one truly knows this woman. No one knows her tics and preferences and quirks.

No one would know that suddenly turning the television off startles Grandma Lou when she's sleeping. No one would know that she only likes pepper on very specific dishes or that the smell of patchouli makes her break out into a fit of sneezing or that she keeps a separate drawer of single socks, in the hopes that one day she might find their lost mates and that her socks will have their own sock reunion.

No one would know Grandma Lou. No one would know her like I do.

As I shoot higher into the sky and aim for home, I have another really horrible thought. Without Grandma Lou around, who will know me like she does?

 **3**

"Your chocolate milk, milady," Matt says with a curtsy as I get out of my car on Monday morning.

He and Ches are waiting for me. He leans against his driver's-side door, and she sits on the hood of the car with her legs crossed.

I take the chocolate milk and have a generous swig. Why does it taste so much better than real milk? Oh, that's right. There's chocolate in it. "Well, don't you look lovely," I tell Matt. Today he wears the custom lavender boiler jumpsuit with his initials embroidered over his heart that he ordered from some plus-size boutique in Portland with his initials embroidered over his heart. The color is absolute perfection against his soft brown skin, and his hair is perfectly styled into dark, luscious waves. Like me, Matt is fat, and I love seeing him in clothing that turns my pupils into pulsing hearts. He's my number-one reminder that fabulous is one size fits all—and it doesn't hurt that we can occasionally share clothing.

"Thank you, thank you," he says before he turns to Ches. "If the shape of your ass is permanently dented into the hood of my car—"

"You'll remember me forever and ever while I'm living it up at the University of Chicago," she finishes for him.

"School policy is that we not gloat about what fantastic universities we've been accepted to," I playfully remind her.

"Well, school policy also dictates that there be no smoking on campus, and no one seems to care about that." She motions to two faculty members walking into the building right past two seniors splitting a joint.

"Maybe the parking lot doesn't count," Matt says.

"Or maybe our teachers smoke as much weed as everyone else," Ches offers.

I sigh. "I've never smoked weed."

Matt chuckles. "You don't need to smoke weed. You can fly."

Ches slides off the hood. "He's not wrong. That's a high all its own." She loops an arm through each of ours. "Remind me how I'm supposed to even care about the rest of this school year when I've already been accepted to my dream school."

"Excuse you," Matt says. "A few of us are still trying to make our own magic happen and come up with a better plan than Glenwood Community College."

"GCC is perfectly respectable, and you'll get to hang out with me," I tell him.

He turns to me. "I still can't believe you're not applying anywhere else."

"What's the point? Grandma Lou is here, so I'm here too."

Matt opens his mouth to protest and give me the same lecture he's given me for the last three months. "Wait. Whose car was that in the driveway?"

I shake my head. "Some awful salesman from Cedar Hills. I guess Grandma Lou is thinking of moving into assisted living sooner than I expected."

"That blows," Matt says. "If it helps, my grandma's assisted living complex is, like, super rowdy. They even had some kind of STD outbreak."

I cringe. "That doesn't really help at all."

Ches jumps in. "Matt, my darling, I agree with you that Faith should dream big, but this is her life and she gets to make her own decisions—just like the time you decided to ditch us on Faith's birthday eve for Rowan."

Matt narrows his eyes. "This again? It wasn't even your actual birthday. And I'd just spent an entire week without him!"

"Really?" Ches askes innocently. "Felt like he was with us the whole time . . ."

Matt blushes. So far, we haven't been allowed to meet the mysterious Rowan who has swept Matt off his feet, but that hasn't stopped Matt from talking about how amazing he is at every opportunity. We know that Rowan has beautiful eyes, a high school degree, an older sister, and an inexplicable affinity for Swedish Fish, but if he was standing right next to me, I'd never know, because I have no clue what he looks like beyond perfect.

We walk in through the main entrance just as the first bell rings, and I leave Matt and Ches to their bickering while I head for the journalism room.

Every time I walk into this room, I expect to see Colleen sitting behind Rebecca. The way she did every class period before everything changed. Hair hanging in front of her face, gloves on her hands, shoulders a little hunched like she was always afraid something was about to land on her. Of course, eventually something did.

But she's not here. Her desk has been empty since she disappeared. I think everyone feels a little too weird to use it, so instead it just sits there empty. Haunted.

I settle in at my cubicle and am immediately assaulted by the smell of my two-week-old lunch molding in my trash can. I threw it out before spring break, and the custodial staff must have missed it when they did their rounds, but there's no missing it now. This is a smell that could conquer nations. Galaxies, even.

"Does anyone smell that?" Johnny asks. He's a little tanner than he was two Fridays ago. Even though I spent the last three years crushing hard on Johnny, all it took was developing real feelings for Dakota for me to realize that crushes definitely come in varying levels of intensity.

23

Rebecca makes a noise that's a cross between gagging and coughing. "It smells like fermented egg salad sandwich and a half-eaten pickle."

"You have a very acute sense of smell," I tell her, raising my hand hesitantly. "My lunch from two weeks ago is the culprit."

Johnny walks over and takes the trash can. "I got this," he says, two fingers pinched around his nose. "I'll take it to the guys' bathroom. No one will know the difference between this and the usual smells in there."

He returns a few minutes later, my trash can still in hand but blessedly empty. "Thank you," I tell him.

And then, like he's suddenly remembered that we're supposed to be deeply awkward toward each other since I very much chose Dakota over him, he nods sheepishly and returns to his desk.

"Where's Mrs. Raburn?" Rebecca asks. "The woman has never missed a day of school in her life."

The final bell rings, and the sound of someone loudly clearing their throat silences us.

A tall man with deep black hair and peppery stubble lining his jaw stands in the doorway. He wears dark, distressed jeans and a black leather moto jacket. A pair of Ray-Bans completes the look. Whoever this guy is, he is way too cool to be standing in the halls of East Glenwood High School.

Mystery Man lets out a low whistle. "This place hasn't

changed a bit." And then more quietly, he adds, "I don't know if that's comforting or depressing."

Rebecca sighs. "I find it rather depressing."

"Uh, and you are?" Johnny asks.

"Liam Hollis. Your new journalism teacher." He walks in and sits in Mrs. Raburn's chair, kicking his feet up on her desk.

He's pretty hot for an old guy, but I honestly feel like the feet-on-desk thing is a little disrespectful.

"What did you say? Where's Mrs. Raburn?" Taylor asks from behind me.

Mr. Hollis opens Mrs. Raburn's drawer and sifts through it a bit. "Good ol' Raburn went skiing over spring break, and like the overachiever she's been since we were in school together, she broke not one, but two legs."

Johnny's jaw drops. "Wait. You're *that* Liam Hollis. As in the most successful journalist to come out of Glenwood . . . ever? W-what are you even doing here, Mr. Hollis? Shouldn't you be reporting on civil unrest in Turkey or, like, Russian intelligence or something?"

Mr. Hollis laughs dryly and scratches his brow, which has a deep scar running through the center of it. "Everybody's gotta come home eventually, right?"

Johnny nods like he feels this sentiment deep in his bones. "You said it, man."

Rebecca rolls her eyes. "The longest you've ever been

away from home is when your family went on a three-week Alaskan cruise for your grandparents' anniversary two summers ago, Johnny."

"We were in St. Croix for spring break," he mutters defensively.

"Mr. Hollis, did Mrs. Raburn leave you any sort of instruction for what we should do this week?" Rebecca asks.

"First off, call me Mr. Hollis one more time and I'll send a scathing email to the head of admissions at University of Minnesota about how ineffective you are as a human being."

"How did you know I applied to U of M?" Rebecca asks.

"It's a state school. You all applied. At least as a safety. Go Golden Gophers! And second of all, Raburn is out for the rest of the year. She called me this weekend and asked me to finish up the semester for her."

I raise my hand. "Excuse me, Mr. Hol—Liam . . . Mr. Liam?"

"Just Liam will do."

I nod. I can't think of anything more awkward than calling an adult by their first name. "Liam. If you're this hugely successful journalist, what are you even doing in Glenwood? Did Mrs. Raburn, like, save your life in a freak accident and now you're duty bound to help her or something? I don't get it."

Liam kicks his feet off the desk and braces his hands against the chair's armrests as he leans back, like he's trying to escape this tiny classroom. "I was already in town . . . on my own business."

And that piques my interest. "What kind of business would bring you to—"

"Faith," Johnny says, quietly admonishing me. "What's the big deal?"

I shake my head, trying not to feel stung. "Right. Sorry. Not my business."

"It's okay." Liam gives me a soft smile. "Just some family stuff."

I nod, and my cheeks begin to warm. I think I have a crush on a teacher, and I don't know what to do with this feeling. At least he's a substitute, I guess.

"So anyone want to show me the ropes around here?" Liam asks. "What kind of reporting is the great *East Glenwood High Telegram* getting into these days?"

Johnny stands, his shoulders squared back, and his smile is one that says, *I'm trying really hard to look confident and not goofy.* "My name is Johnny Leonard. I'm the student editor in chief, and if it wasn't obvious before, I'm a big fan of your work. Like, the biggest fan."

Johnny proceeds to introduce all of us and the various things we cover, and when he gets to me, he says, "Faith's done some solid exposés for us, but she really shines at creating great content, like quizzes, or sometimes she'll help me with a snarky letter from the editor. Honestly, she can do it all."

Liam nods. "Fluff."

"Excuse me?" I ask, sure I heard him wrong.

"Fluff," Liam says again. "The quizzes and stuff like that. It's fluff. It's not a bad thing. Fluff is what keeps people going. It's important stuff. It softens the blow of the more hard-hitting reporting."

Johnny nods. "Totally. Give your audience the information they need, but also provide them with content that keeps them coming back. You could say Faith is the backbone of this newspaper."

I smile at him wearily. Johnny's barely acknowledged me this whole semester, and suddenly I'm the backbone of the journalism department the moment Liam shows up. "Thanks," I tell him.

After journalism, I take the long way to sociology—another class I share with Johnny this semester—to avoid having to walk too fast or too slow in a sad attempt to keep my distance from him. I'm still not sure what to make of his overly enthusiastic compliment earlier.

I hate this. I just want to talk to him so things can get back to normal, and we can go back to being friends again. Friends who sometimes flirt.

The downside of taking the long way is that I have to pass Colleen's locker. It's become a shrine to her, even though no one here knew her that well to begin with. When she and Gretchen Sandoval went missing, everyone thought that whoever took Gretchen was also responsible for Colleen's disappearance. But after Gretchen (who made a full recovery and returned to school in January) mysteriously reappeared inside the Halloween corn maze, a lot of people started to wonder if Colleen had just run away and if her disappearance was just a coincidence.

Technically, the authorities still consider her to be a missing person, but her family has tried to make peace with the fact that they might never see Colleen again.

I don't know who started it or how it began exactly, but Colleen's locker is covered in sticky notes. Most say generic things like *You are loved* or *We miss you*; a few even say *RIP Colleen*. Every time I see the notes, I can't help but want to tear them all down. All these people are praying and hoping for Colleen's miraculous return, but they don't know the truth. They didn't see what I saw—a girl frightened out of her right mind, a ragged hospital gown fluttering around her legs, a man erupting in flames at her slightest touch. If Colleen comes back, she'd probably burn this place and everyone in it to the ground.

Her return is the thing that keeps me up at night, the thing that haunts my dreams.

It's the last thing they should be praying for.

4

After school, I call to check in with Grandma Lou. "How was your day?" I ask.

"Well, Ella's got me on a short leash. Wouldn't even let me go to the dairy section on my own, but it was fine. I set up a walk-through tour at Cedar Hills for this weekend. You're not working, are you?"

"Uh, I'm on my way to work right now. I can check when I get there."

"I've got your schedule right here," Miss Ella calls from the other room. "Saturday and Sunday, *off*."

"I . . . guess I'm off then."

And just like that, we're taking a tour of Cedar Hills. I can't wait.

At All Paws on Deck, I clock in and get to work setting up our makeshift photo-shoot backdrop so we can post cute pictures for the website. One of Dr. Bryner's cousins is a photographer, who donates his time to help us take photos of all the animals available for adoption.

The best part about the last three months is that my internship at the shelter has turned into a paid position. The hours are limited and the pay isn't much, but just the idea that someone is paying me to spend time with rescue animals feels like an achievement all its own.

Once the photo shoot is set up, I do my rounds, inspecting each crate for food and water. I check on Molly, a poodle mix who arrived at the shelter so neglected and unkempt that she had to be shaved entirely just so we could examine her. She's aggressive and constantly growling, and honestly, the kind of dog that we might never be able to adopt out. But she's my favorite.

I don't know what she's been through, but sometimes when her lip gets caught on her jagged bottom tooth, it looks like she's smiling through the sheer discomfort of being alive. And that is highly relatable content, if you ask me.

Molly pushes her nose through the grate of the kennel. It's not exactly friendly, but this is new territory for her, and I reward her with a treat.

After checking on everyone and doling out a few bonus treats, I settle in at the front desk with my notebook and attempt to write a quiz for next week's paper. But it feels so minuscule and unimportant when real-life dilemmas are pulling at my brainpower. What's a quiz to discover which

Taylor Swift song you are to the fact that my grandmother is very likely moving out and I'll be on my own before I've even graduated high school? Not much.

A small voice in the back of my mind whispers, *Filler. That's all you contribute. Pointless filler.*

Filler.

Fluff.

"Faith!" Dr. Bryner screams from the back of the clinic, interrupting my thoughts. "Faith! Come quick! Bring the fire extinguisher!"

I scramble out of my chair as fast as I can, and it takes me a whole ten seconds to remember where the fire extinguisher is because I've never had to use it here before.

And then the word hits me. *Fire.* Oh my God. There's a fire. And all I can see in my head is the billowing smoke from the old paper mill, the sound of sonic screams shattering glass all around me as I rush through the back rooms to find Dakota. Except it's Dr. Bryner standing at the back door.

She grabs for the fire extinguisher and dashes into the alleyway. White foam arcs toward flames lashing at the air from the dumpster.

A shock of laughter escapes my mouth and I have to clap my hands over my lips to keep it in. A dumpster fire. An actual dumpster fire is raging behind All Paws on Deck. And here I thought dumpster fires were just internet meme fodder.

"Should I call 911?" I finally manage to ask like the total noob I am right now.

"Um . . ." Dr. Bryner looks frantically at the dwindling fire. "I think I've got it under control. I mean, it's contained. How bad could it get?"

I step closer to get a better look at the smoldering heap inside the dumpster. "Who would even do this?"

She shakes her head, eyes blank and brow furrowed. "I . . . have no idea. . . . Probably just some teenagers, I guess. . . ."

Colleen. My chest tightens a little at the thought. I don't know where she is or what she's doing . . . but I can't help thinking of her as a wounded animal, and in a way, it makes sense that after being aimless for so long, she might try to return to Glenwood.

Dr. Bryner aims the nozzle and hits the ashes once more with a spray of foam. "I think it's pretty much dead. We'll check on it again before we leave, and I'll call the landlord to see if he's got security cameras back here."

"Oh. There are cameras back here?" I ask, suddenly remembering all the time I've spent with my feet off the ground back in this very alleyway.

"I didn't say they work," Dr. Bryner scoffs.

Even though I normally close up on my own, Dr. Bryner stays late with me to make sure whoever set our dumpster on fire isn't lurking in the shadows.

I say one more goodbye to Molly and give her a treat to

hold her over until the night staff comes in.

As Dr. Bryner is locking the door, she says, "I haven't gotten any reference checks yet on your college applications. Are you sure you put my information in correctly?"

"Oh . . . um . . . I'm staying here . . . for a while, at least. Just going to take a few classes at Glenwood Community College."

She nods slowly. "Nothing wrong with that. GCC is a great little place, but have you really given this a lot of thought? Are you sure?"

I take a deep breath. "I want to be here for Grandma Lou. She was there for me when my parents died, and now it's my turn."

She looks me right in the eye. "Faith, I know your grandma Lou, and I can say with absolute assurance that nothing about raising you was a charity case. You're nearly a grown woman. I won't tell you what to do with your life, but I can say that martyrdom is a waste on someone like Grandma Lou."

Martyr. My nose turns up at the word. Martyrdom feels so performative. I'm not doing this so that anyone will look and see what a selfless granddaughter I am. I'm doing this because it's the right thing to do, and after everything I thought I knew has been turned inside out, this is one circumstance where I'm sure what the exact right thing to do is and I'm going to do it. "I feel good about my decision," I tell her, refusing to let my voice waver.

She nods. "I'm glad. And you know you'll always have a place here."

The panicked half of my brain nearly shouts, *OKAY, GOOD BECAUSE I MIGHT JUST LIVE IN GLENWOOD FOREVER.*

As I open my car door, I glance down to see a matchbook on the concrete. I pick it up and find that every single match has been torn out except one.

"What the . . ." I peer over my shoulder like I might magically find some dumpster-fire-lighting pyromaniac waiting there. But I'm alone.

"Everything okay?" Dr. Bryner calls from her car.

"Oh yeah!" I say, forcing a smile. "Just dropped my keys."

"See you tomorrow!" she says, waiting for me to get into my car and start the ignition.

I tuck the matchbook into the pocket of my jean jacket and follow her out of the parking lot. It could be a coincidence, but something about it feels intentional. Ominous. Like whoever lit that fire is toying with me.

A few months ago, I might have stuck around to investigate, but tonight I just don't have it in me to face the darkness on my own.

 5

When I get home, Miss Ella is sitting in the living room by herself, which is a bad sign.

"Where is she?" I ask, a knot forming fast and hard in my guts.

Miss Ella stands, slowly stretching. "Upstairs. Asleep. We were at Green's Produce, and I turned around and she was gone."

I can feel my whole body jump into action like there's something I should do or somewhere I should be. I rush toward the stairs.

"Now just hold it for a minute," she tells me. "The woman didn't make it far. She was just out in the parking lot, looking for her car. After a minute or two of talking to her, she started acting a little foggy, like she'd just woken up."

My lips quiver, searching for a response. "Is—is she okay?"

"Faith, she's fine for now, and—" She sighs heavily. "Lord knows I hate to see you have to deal with this at your age, but she needs more attention than either of us can give her."

"I'm sorry. I know it's been a lot for you," I tell her, "but if you can just hold out for a few more months, I'll—"

She steps forward and touches my hand where it rests on top of Grandma Lou's recliner. "It's time to think long-term." She pulls her purse over her shoulder and fishes out her keys. "I brought you some chicken-and-rice casserole. Just pop it in the microwave for a few minutes and you'll be all set. I checked on Lou just a few minutes ago, so she oughta be fine for a while longer. Call me if you need me."

She steps out the front door, and I follow her. "Miss Ella?"

"Yes, dear," she says as she walks down the steps.

"Thank you."

She doesn't turn around, and I think it's to save both of us from any tears. "She was my best friend before she was your grandmama, you know. This isn't easy for me either."

"And the Boss Girl purse organizer can be yours for the low, low price of fifty-nine ninety-nine!"

I crack my eyes open enough to see the glow of the television. After I ate dinner and checked on Grandma Lou, I sat down in her recliner and promptly passed out. Now the only thing keeping me company is the late-night hostess on the Home Shopping Network.

As I roam around the house, turning off all the lights, I notice that the flag on the mailbox is up. I don't know why, but it strikes me as odd.

I go out barefooted and let my toes just skim above the cold pavement. Flying has become so much a part of my life that I sometimes wake up levitating, and sometimes it feels like it takes more energy to keep my feet on the ground than off.

Still half-asleep, I hover in front of the mailbox and open it. Inside is a gas station receipt folded in half. On the back in a scratchy handwriting, it reads:

in the backyard

And I'm awake. My heart skips a beat as I look around the dark street, searching for the author of the mystery note. My first thought is Dakota. *DakotaDakotaDakota.* But why wouldn't she just ring the doorbell? And then Colleen, but I decide a note isn't Colleen's style.

I ball up the receipt and shove it into the pocket of my jeans. If some creep is waiting for me in my backyard, I plan on surprising them as much they're trying to surprise me.

After a quick glance around to ensure that every window on the block is dark, I push off from the ground and soar to the roof. I perch there, toes steady against the peak, my body obscured by the chimney. And there, in one of Grandma

Lou's rickety old lawn chairs, a hooded figure sits with a cigarette dangling from their fingers. The tip glows deep orange against the dark.

I spread my arms out for balance as I descend from the roof, the tips of my toes grazing the grass as I land directly behind them.

"Show-off," a gravelly voice says.

A gravelly voice I know. "Peter?"

He reaches over to stub out his cigarette on the patio pavement and tosses it in a very dead potted plant that Grandma Lou neglected.

"Have a little respect for my grandmother's garden, would you?"

He laughs dryly, letting his hood fall back, and even though it's hard to see, I spy dark circles beneath his eyes. "She might have better success as a gardener if she had fake plants."

I give him a pointed look and cross my arms over my chest.

"Fine." He fishes the cigarette out of the pot and puts it in the pocket of his hoodie.

"That's actually kind of gross, but thank you." I sit down on the other chair beside him. "Way to be cryptic with that note, by the way."

"It's for your own safety," he says firmly.

My own safety? Yeah, I don't buy that for a second. Peter

has a lot of things going for him, but a high level of regard for the safety of others doesn't seem to be one of them. I can't believe it hasn't even been a year since I first met Peter when I was lured into Toyo Harada's underground laboratory and my latent psiot abilities were activated under questionable circumstances. And I was one of the lucky ones. I walked out of there—or rather, flew out of there—with the help of Peter, when he decided he was done being one of Harada's pawns. Our dramatic exit from Harada's Harbinger Foundation ruffled some feathers. Maybe it was the whole part where we ran from the guards and I dove off a building for the first time in my life?

"I haven't seen you for months, by the way," I tell him. "You said you'd be in touch and then radio silence."

"That wasn't my intention. I'm—I'm sorry. I didn't mean to leave you in the dark."

He seems genuine, which doesn't really make me feel any better, but does make it hard to stay mad at him.

"So, why are you here now?"

He studies me for a moment, and there's a shadow in his expression. Whatever it is that brought him back, I'm afraid it isn't good.

"Faith," he starts, a sigh falling from the end of my name. "I—Psiots are dropping like flies."

"What?" Panic pounds in my chest. "Like, there's something wrong with us? We're getting sick?"

"No, no, that's not—Someone is taking us . . . and changing us. And it isn't, well, it isn't good."

There's so much he isn't saying, and something tells me I don't want to know more. "Do you know who's doing it?" I ask.

Peter shakes his head, his mussed brown hair falling limp. "I don't know for sure. I just . . . I thought that if they knew where I was and I reached out to you, they'd find you, too. I didn't want to risk that. I didn't want to bring that to your doorstep."

"And why are you here now? Did you k-kill them?"

"I wish," he says bitterly. "No, but I have a lead. So, I'm going to go dark again while I chase that and take care of some personal—"

"Faith?" Grandma Lou's voice calls from inside. "Faith?"

"Just a minute," I call before turning back to Peter. "No! You can't keep popping up and leaving again! I—I don't have anyone else like me, and I—"

"You're right."

"I—I'm what?" I stop.

"I'm starting to think we're all safer together than we are on our own." He runs his fingers through his hair. "We're just too vulnerable spread out like this. I'm not much of a people person, but I'm hoping to gather up a group of psiots. I've got a few in mind and I want you to join us."

"What—like, now?"

"Faith?" Grandma Lou calls again.

"I'll be right there, Grandma Lou!"

"No, not right now," he says. "Like I said, I've got to take care of a few things, and we need to get you across that graduation stage first."

I can hear the floorboards of the steps creaking inside the house. I have so much I want to ask him. So much I *need* to ask him. How many more psiots are even out there? Are they cool? Would they like me? Could I still go to college? Do I even want to go to college?

Are we in danger?

But Grandma Lou's in the kitchen already.

"Wait," I tell Peter. "Please, don't go. I'll be right back."

He smiles with his eyes. "Think about what I said, and keep your head down, okay? Just keep your head down and you'll be fine."

"Faith?" she calls again.

"Hang on, Grandma Lou!" I call back.

"Are you outside, dear?"

I turn back to Peter. "Stay right here," I hiss.

"Faith! It's too chilly to be out there without a jacket." Grandma Lou's voice is right at the back door.

"Keep an eye out for friendly faces, Faith." Peter's smile turns tired.

Grandma Lou pushes the screen door open.

I jump up, hoping I can block Peter from her view. "Oh,

Grandma Lou, let's get you back to bed."

"Me?" she asks. "Let's get you back to bed. What in the Hades are you doing out here?"

"I was just talking to—" I turn around to introduce Grandma Lou to the strange man lurking in her backyard, but he's gone. Of course he's gone. "Stargazing," I say as disappointment crashes through me. "I thought I heard something about Jupiter doing something with its moons or . . . I don't know. Let's go to bed."

Confusion settles into the creases of her forehead, and I can tell that she's trying to decide which one of us is actually losing it at this precise moment.

And the truth is I don't know.

6

On Friday, we spend all of journalism class listening to Liam's stories about the time he was mistaken for a senator's son and taken hostage in the Czech Republic. Despite all the twists and turns, the most shocking part of it all is that someone this fascinating is from Glenwood. It takes me until the end of class to realize . . . I can fly, and I am also from Glenwood. But I don't think of myself as fascinating. Most of the time, I still feel like the same person I've always been.

Then again, most people don't have psiots showing up for clandestine conversations under cover of night. Peter's offer has been ringing in my head for days. If he comes back and asks me again, would I go with him? Would I join forces with Peter and his other psiot friends? Maybe then I'd be just as fascinating as Liam Hollis.

But that would involve leaving Grandma Lou, which I just can't do.

When the bell rings, and we've accomplished exactly none of the things we need to do to complete the next issue of the paper, I slide my notebooks in my backpack and head off to my next class.

I only make it a few feet out the door before Johnny sidles up alongside me. "Hey," he says. "Mind if I walk with you? I meant to talk to you about prom coverage, but Liam's story was too intense to interrupt. And he left us on a cliff-hanger!"

I laugh. "Well, it wasn't much of a cliff-hanger if you consider the fact that he's here and alive."

Johnny shrugs. "I guess I hadn't thought of it that way."

We round the corner and hit a traffic jam. The entire hallway is clogged with people. I try to spot the cause, but whatever it is, I can't see it. "So what about prom coverage? I thought Rebecca was taking the lead on that."

"She was. She is," Johnny corrects himself. "But I was thinking we could do little features on all the prom court nominees when they're announced, but maybe it could be quirky in a good way. Most embarrassing moments. What they'd do if they won the lottery. That kind of thing. You know, the stuff you're good at."

"I like that idea," I tell him, thinking on it. "Make the cool kids seem normal."

"Because they are normal," he says, sounding like he's trying to convince himself more than me.

"According to who?" I ask, but my question gets lost in a sudden surge as the crowd shifts and we're drawn inside it like ants into a puddle.

I try to get my bearings and figure out what's going on. It only takes a moment to realize what the horde of people are surrounding. But I still don't see the reason why.

Johnny peers over the shoulder of the tall guy wearing a letter jacket in front of him. "Is this . . ."

"Colleen's locker," I finish. "I wonder if the school cleaned up the shrine or something."

"They could have at least done it over spring break while no one was here," he mutters.

I strain to get a look, but there are too many bodies between me and the locker.

"She probably did it all for attention," a petite girl in front of me whispers to her friend.

"If attention was what she wanted, that's what she's getting," the other girl replies with a flip of her braids.

"Excuse me," I say, leaning forward. "Could I get through?"

The petite girl looks up at me. "Uh, no one is budging, if you can't tell."

The next bell rings, and beside me Johnny shakes his head. "We gotta get to class."

"Excuse me," I say again, but this time more cheerfully.

The two girls squeeze together as I pass them, but they

close ranks again before Johnny can get through.

"All right." A decidedly adult voice rises above everything else. "Time to get to class. There will be plenty of time to catch up later. Everyone, scatter."

I continue on, snaking through the crowd, which is no easy feat as a plus-size girl. This is one of those times when I deeply resent not being able to use my abilities in public. Flying would make this a breeze. So would my force field. Just a little nudge and I could part the seas in front of me.

"Excuse me," I say once again, pushing past another letter jacket.

"I just really needed to get out of town, ya know," a soft voice says. "I didn't mean for, like, people to freak out."

I stop dead in my tracks.

"Come on, people!" The administrator's voice is amplified by a bullhorn, and it aggressively fills the hallway. "Move it."

The crowd begins to clear, and I finally see her with my own two eyes.

Standing in front of her locker, carefully collecting every Post-it note, dried flower, and stuffed animal, is Colleen Bristow.

The Colleen. As in siren-screaming, flame-shooting, vanished-after-some-fairly-traumatic-shit Colleen.

Her big doe eyes land on me and she pauses mid-sentence. "Faith?"

I stumble backward, my instincts taking over. Every muscle in my body tenses, ready to fly, to fight, to protect all the students still in this very narrow hallway.

"Colleen," I say cautiously. "Just stay right where you are."

The third and final bell rings overhead.

Colleen turns and carefully puts everything she's been holding into her locker, then swivels back to me with a sympathetic smile. "Trust me. I'd like to, but I have to go to class. I've—well, I've got a lot of catching up to do."

All around us, the hallway is emptying and classroom doors shut one by one.

Colleen takes a step toward me.

My chest tightens.

She takes another step. The smile on her face stretches a little too wide.

My breath hitches.

"That's close enough," I say firmly, suddenly aware that we are the only two people left in this hallway and I am alone with Colleen.

Our last encounter plays in my mind in violent flashes of flame and shadow. The only reason I got away was because she was distracted. The truth of the matter is that I am no match for the likes of Colleen Bristow. Or for her powers.

I barely manage not to flinch as she reaches out and cups a hand around my shoulder. "Faith, we should really talk. I'm sure you have a lot of questions about me running away. It was a selfish thing to do. And you were always one of the few people here who even talked to me. It wasn't fair for me to just disappear like that. I see that now. I hope you'll consider forgiving me."

Words fail me. I try over and over again to respond, but before I can say a word, she pulls her messenger bag over her shoulder and walks down the hallway.

At the last classroom on the left, she pauses with her hand on the doorknob. She glances back with that same glossy smile on her face and waves at me.

Part of my brain screams at me that this is a threat. That she's about to go into that classroom and incinerate everyone, but at the same time, I'm too stunned to move.

Facing the door again, she steps inside, and from where I stand, I can hear her say, "Hi, my name is Colleen and I'm so sorry I was tardy. It won't happen again."

 7

"Okay, so are we getting paid for this?" asks Ches, snarling down at the black vest we've all been forced to wear, a far cry from the usual dark, flowing skirts and crop tops that typically suit her tall frame and ivory complexion.

"For the millionth time, Ches, we are helping Rowan out of the goodness of our hearts." Matt looks in the rear-view mirror once more, fixing his already perfect hair.

"I've never worked in food service," I say, trying not to sound overwhelmed. "Does it require any kind of formal training? Do we have to take some kind of food safety class?"

"You just walk around!" Matt says as we get out of the car. "You just walk around and give the tiny egg rolls and mini sandwiches to the old rich people. That's it."

"Maybe Colleen's memory was wiped," I say, mentioning her for the millionth time since yesterday.

By the time we got out of school, local news crews had

gotten wind of her return, and the administration had to escort her out to her sister's car. Colleen waved sheepishly at the cameras and simply said, "I'm so thankful to be home."

"I don't know how you forget about fire shooting from your hands," Matt says.

"I wish you could have seen it," I tell him.

He thinks for a minute, then shudders. "Nah, I'll just take your word for it."

I smile limply. The only evidence of the warehouse fire is Ches's broken memories of being drugged and chained to a pipe, and after yesterday, even I am starting to wonder if everything I experienced that day was as real as it felt or if maybe something more sinister was at play.

Ches sighs dramatically. "This is not how I imagined meeting your secret boyfriend for the first time."

This morning Matt called me and Ches and explained that he was ready for us to meet the mysterious Rowan, who doesn't even have so much as an Instagram profile. Admittedly, we were both excited, especially since Ches had once or twice speculated as to whether Rowan even existed. Matt then added that the reason he was ready was because he had sort of kind of promised Rowan he would save the day and find a waitstaff for his catering gig. Hence the black vests and tiny food.

"He's not a secret. He's just . . . busy with school and work . . . and his boss is losing it because half their waitstaff got food poisoning from that sushi buffet on Gordon Avenue." He turns back to us, his lips twitching. "But I like him a lot, okay? And I know he'll like both of you, too, especially since you're here volunteering your time."

"Out of the goodness of our hearts," I confirm.

"I just don't get it," Ches says. "They were going to pay someone anyway. Why not pay us? I put on pants for this! Pants with a button and a zipper!"

Matt lets out an exasperated groan.

I touch his shoulder. "We will be super polite and wonderful and the best free labor of all time, I swear. Right, Ches?"

She claps a hand on his other shoulder. "Right. He already has a million reasons to adore you, because you're perfect boyfriend material, but we will be two more outstanding reasons. And on our best behavior."

Matt smiles half-heartedly. "Thanks. Let's get in there and serve some tiny food."

"The tiny food musketeers!" Ches says as she charges ahead into the back vendor entrance of Glenwood Springs Country Club.

Inside, people are either in chef jackets or head-to-toe black. We blend in seamlessly with the latter. The only difference is everyone else seems to know exactly what they're doing, and we're hugging the wall.

"Are we just supposed to stand here?" Ches whispers.

Matt nods as an event planner whooshes past us. "Until we are summoned, yes." He gives a covert wave to a tall Black guy with springy honey-blond curls. "And we have been summoned."

"You're here!" the guy says as he rushes across the room. "And you brought reinforcements!" He doesn't miss a beat as his gaze slides from Matt to us. "You must be Faith and Ches."

Ches's stunned smile turns into a stutter. "You—you're r-really lucky to have our very best friend Matt as your arm candy." She curtsies awkwardly.

I offer a short wave, happy to look like the normal one among us. "And we're so excited to finally meet you!"

"You're excited?" he asks. "I'm excited. I was starting to think Matt was embarrassed of me."

Matt elbows him. "We talked about this."

Rowan smiles at us. "You're both angels," he says.

"I wouldn't go that far." Matt turns to me and Ches. "Ches, Faith, meet Rowan. Officially."

"Please call me Row," he says with a charming smile. "Matthew thinks calling me by my full name is . . . I don't know . . . cute?"

"You started it by calling me Matthew," Matt says.

I let out a little giggle. "Honestly, Matt has called you Rowan for so long that I don't know if I can reprogram my brain at this point."

"While this is deeply adorable, could you show us what exactly you need us to do?" Ches asks.

Rowan squeezes Matt's hand once before leading us around the prep room and explaining that all we have to do is circulate through the clubhouse with trays of hors d'oeuvres. When we run out, we come back for another tray.

"Whatever you do, don't make small talk," Rowan says. "The events coordinator at this place loses her mind when she sees me say more than three words. I think she'd like it better if we were just little robots zooming around."

"Well, doesn't she sound charming," I say.

Rowan snorts. "Yeah, at least she's not your sister."

I cringe a little. "Oh, I'm so sorry."

"No, no, no. She likes to pretend we're not related. She doesn't want people to think she gives me special treatment, so she goes out of her way to treat me like trash."

"I don't treat you like trash," says an equally tall Black girl in her early twenties with her hair slicked back into a bun, as she speed-walks past us. "Look alive, people! Guests are arriving."

"That's Katelyn," Rowan says. "She even talks to our parents like they work for her."

A large man with a crate full of champagne glasses grunts. "That's because we do. At least for today."

Rowan rolls his eyes and smiles. "Have I mentioned that my parents own the catering company where I work and not only did you save me, but also my mom, who was this close to asking my brother's stoner roommates to help us out for the day?"

"Anything for moms," Ches says.

Matt confirms, "Anything for moms."

With that, a tray of very fancy-looking pigs in a blanket is foisted upon me and social time is over. We spend the next hour and a half circulating through the clubhouse and being as invisible as we can possibly manage. I honestly feel like Thing from *The Addams Family*. Just a floating hand carrying tiny food. There are a few kids from Shady Oaks Prep, and even though I've seen them around town often enough to recognize them, the way they treat every waiter and country club employee (myself included) puts a bad taste in my mouth. They give more respect to the food on the tray than they do to the person holding it.

"This place is so weird," I whisper to Ches and Matt as we hover at the back of the room, waiting for fresh trays.

"What do you mean?" asks Ches.

"It's like we're the help or something. These people don't even acknowledge me when I walk up to them," I say.

"They're rich," Ches says simply. "They don't need to acknowledge you."

Glenwood has never felt like the kind of place where you were either a rich kid or a poor kid, but I guess I've never been to the country club or places like it. Maybe it's different for people like Ches, though, who live in Old Glenwood. Maybe they see the differences between us all in ways that I don't.

"We're up," Matt says as Rowan signals from the kitchen that more appetizers are ready to be served.

This time I'm given a tray of bacon-wrapped avocado slices, and it takes all my willpower not to try one myself. "Would it be too much to ask for these as payment?" I ask Ches.

"As much as I love an avocado," she says, "it's not the kind of green payment I prefer."

I think I see someone wave me over, so I weave through the crowd to deliver the deliciousness on my tray.

As I approach, I hear someone say, "Did you hear that missing girl just showed up again out of nowhere? She looked like a ghost on the news."

"Stupid girl ran away for attention and probably got herself into some bad situations," someone says in response. "Now she's trying to erase it all with her miraculous return or whatever. She probably wants to get into an Ivy League with her sob story."

I can't help myself. I pause, utterly shocked by the depth of their bias and just plain nastiness.

A petite girl with sleek brown hair shimmering beneath a velvet headband spins around. "Uh, I think we're fine here," she says like I'm about to rob all of them.

"Talia, chill." A lanky white guy with a single dimple in

his left cheek turns to me. His rumpled button-up with a crooked collar complements his shaggy blond hair. He's not dressed in flat black or chef white, which means he's probably here to eat tiny food instead of serve it. "Is that bacon?"

I nod. "Bacon-wrapped avocado, actually."

"Hold the phone," he says before popping one in his mouth and scooping the last two up in his hand using a cocktail napkin. "Don't mind Talia. She's like a kid who doesn't like different foods to touch on her plate."

"So what does that make me?" I ask. "The mashed potatoes or the turkey?"

"Neither," he answers seriously. "You're the mac and cheese."

Someone calling me mac and cheese has never made me blush before, but here we are.

Behind me, Katelyn clears her throat, and even though I've just met her, I can easily picture the look on her face.

"I better go."

"Come back with more snacks," the prep school boy says.

Unfortunately, I don't come back with more snacks. While Matt and Ches are put on dessert duty, I'm tapped to help clean up the kitchen. Rowan joins me as I load the dishwasher with glasses.

"This was really cool of you and Ches," he says.

"Oh, it's no big deal. What else am I going to do on a Saturday?"

He snorts softly. "I could think of plenty of things."

"So . . . are you planning on asking our dear Matthew to prom?"

He tilts his head from side to side. "Does Matt even want to go? He doesn't strike me as the type."

"Everyone wants to go to their high school prom," I tell him.

"Well, I guess I'll have to think about it." He inhales deeply through his nose. "I was honestly sort of scared to meet you two. I thought maybe you both were really mean or that Matt was hiding me."

I shake my head. "I don't know what his deal was, but I promise we're the nice ones."

Rowan grimaces. "I kind of get the feeling that I was asking him too many questions . . . about Dakota Ash." He sighs and bites down on his lower lip. "I'm sorry, I'm sorry. I was just such a fan of the show and was sort of obsessed with trying to see the cast around town while they were filming. I was shocked when Matt said you knew Dakota. What was she like?"

I nod. "Oh. Um . . . there's not much to know." I'm sure Rowan is great and trustworthy, but if I've learned anything this last year, it's that you can't be too sure.

"You don't have to tell me all the details, but like . . . he just clammed up every time I brought it up. I just can't believe you dated a famous per—"

"I don't know that we really dated."

He starts back in on his work. "You don't have to answer if you don't want to, but were you there when the warehouse caught on fire?"

The question hangs in the air for a second too long until suddenly Rowan's dad barks out, "I need help on trash!"

"I can help!" I call over my shoulder, and then to Rowan, "Could you finish these up for me?"

I don't wait for him to answer and instead walk with purpose toward the piles of trash bags waiting to be rolled out to the dumpster.

I have no clue where Dakota is or what she's doing, and I'm still so mad at her it makes my teeth hurt, but I won't forget what she did for Ches. Not only did she run back into that burning building to help me save Ches in the first place, but later she sent enough money for Ches to hire an incredible lawyer and still squirrel some away for school. After nearly losing everything last year, that alone was enough to get things back on track for Ches. And that matters to me as much as any of the bad stuff.

One of the cart's wheels spins out of control as I push it to the dumpster, persistently veering off course like it's got a mind of its own.

"Should you be operating heavy machinery?" a voice asks.

I peer over the mountain of trash bags to see the rumpled

boy taking a drag from a cigarette. If I had to guess, I'd say he's not much older than me, but he looks, well, intense is the only word I can think of. He slouches against the wall in that classic way, one foot up, one braced against the ground, head ducked for maximum drama. He looks mysterious, and I have a bad habit of getting caught up with mysterious people.

"Should you be smoking that?" I ask.

"Just don't tell my mom," he says, lazily plucking a white earbud from his ear and cupping it in his hand.

I can't blame him for choosing the alley instead.

"Would she be disappointed?" I ask with a grunt, forcing the cart over a crack in the pavement.

"Only that I was smoking without her."

I can't tell if he's joking or not, so I say, "That's . . . interesting."

He shrugs. "Can't beat 'em. Join 'em."

"Is that what you're doing out here?" I ask. "Looks more like you're abandoning them."

He shrugs, and the gesture is somehow both fluid and stilted. Like I hit close to a nerve.

"Well, if you're going to smoke back here, make sure you take that butt with you." I heave a trash bag over the lip of the dumpster and get a whoosh of rotten air as a reward. Delightful. Matt really does owe us for this one. "These things are more flammable than people realize."

"Sure thing, Miss Goody-Goody."

I throw another bag into the dumpster. "Actually, I'm Faith."

"I know," he tells me, a small smile playing at his lips.

In a flash, I think of the last dumpster I had a close encounter with and the strangely threatening matchbook left by my car. Does he know who I am because he set that fire? Because he's been watching me? Is he a dumpster-obsessed pyromaniac?

"How do you—"

He cuts me off, pointing to the sticker on my vest that reads *Hello My Name Is Faith*.

I blow the stray hairs from my ponytail out of my face and try to ignore the way my pulse is pounding. "Oh."

"I'm Benji." He smiles, but it doesn't reach his eyes.

"Well, Benji, I better get back in there." I drag the cart away from the dumpster, all too aware that things just got awkward. "Be good to your lungs."

He almost laughs at that. "It was nice meeting you, Faith," he says, then stuffs his earbud back into his ear and leans his head against the wall, shutting me and the rest of the world out.

 **8**

The next morning, Grandma Lou is at my door with two cups of coffee. The aromatic scent slowly brings me to life, and I can hear Grandma Lou laughing as I hold two grabby hands up.

"What did I do to deserve coffee in bed?" I ask groggily. After she went to bed last night, I took what was supposed to be a very quick flyover of Colleen's totally normal and not-at-all suspicious apartment complex. But just because I didn't see anything suspicious immediately didn't mean there wasn't anything suspicious going on, and I ended up circling and, okay, spying—until well after midnight.

I can admit that it was perhaps not the best use of a Saturday night.

"Well," Grandma Lou says as she sets one of the coffee cups on my nightstand. It's my favorite and a gift I gave Grandma Lou last Christmas, a bright yellow mug with a rainbow handle that reads, I Am a Ray of Effing Sunshine in tiny adorable letters. Grandma Lou laughed so hard when she saw it that she snorted. "It's less about what you've done and more about what we've got planned for the day."

I scoot up in bed and rub the crusties out of my eyes, racking my brain for what I've clearly forgotten.

"We're . . . going . . . to . . . ," I start, but I'm still not finding it.

Grandma Lou sits on the edge of my bed and takes a sip from her mug. "Take a tour of Cedar Hills," she finishes gently.

I take a swig of coffee and let the heat burn down my throat until it spreads through my chest. "Right. That."

"You don't have to come," she says. "But I'd like it if you did."

Grandma Lou is a determined woman. I know this better than anyone else. She'll do this assisted living thing with or without me, and I guess I'd rather it be with me.

"Okay," I finally say. "I'm in. I'll be down in a minute."

She stands and places a kiss on my forehead. "And you can quit with hiding the tattoo already. I noticed it the moment you came home from spring break."

"What? How did you even . . ."

"I may not be as sharp as I used to be, but I've still got my grandmotherly intuition."

———— ✲ ————

When we pull up to Cedar Hills, we're greeted by a gate and a guard sitting in a little stall. He checks Grandma Lou's name against his list and instructs us to follow the round-abouts to the main building. Much like the country club, I've never given much thought to this place, because I've never had to, but in the light of day, Cedar Hills Retirement Community and Assisted Living could pass for a resort. Huge palm trees that defy my knowledge of local horticulture shade the road as we pass tennis courts and seniors zooming by on golf carts.

"I guess these are all the people who live in the apartments and condos," I say.

"I've gotta say, Faith, this might be the fanciest place I've ever had the chance to live in. It's a shame I won't remember much of it," she says with a chuckle.

That sucks the air right out of me.

"Lighten up." Her voice is gruff but soft. "If anyone can make jokes about my memory loss, it's me."

"Fair," I concede.

The road takes us straight through to the main building, which looks like some kind of Utopian complex with a huge, shaded carport and rows of sleek modern-looking rocking chairs lining the entrance like it's the porch of the future. A few residents sit outside, all of them wearing pastel outfits that seem to coordinate. Despite it being the warmest day of the year so far, some have blankets draped over their laps while nurses or maybe orderlies in sharp white outfits stand and sit alongside them. Many converse with the residents, laughing and even holding hands in one case.

It's not the kind of scene I was expecting, and even though I am still very firmly in the anti-assisted-living-for-Grandma-Lou camp, it's reassuring to know that the place she's considering is bright and soothing.

I wish I were a famous journalist or a successful . . . anything . . . just someone who could give Grandma Lou the life she deserves, especially as her world is shifting so quickly. But I'm only a high school student with little to no money to my name. If I can't be physically present for Grandma Lou at all times, the thought of her being here makes me feel slightly less awful.

At Grandma Lou's insistence, I bypass the valet attendant and park in one of the visitor spots.

Waiting just inside the front door is George, the man who was at our house with all the Cedar Hills pamphlets when I got home from my road trip, and even though I've had a lot of good thoughts about this place since passing through the gates, seeing him again darkens my mood.

"Faith, Lou, it's so good to see you both again," he says. Now that he's not invading my home with sinister designs, I can see that he's tall with a defined nose and strong jawline. His broad shoulders slope as he leans down to hug Grandma Lou, and she gives his cheek an air kiss. Definitely not the formal greeting between a potential resident and assisted living sales rep.

He walks us to the front counter and says, "Cecilia, could I get two guest passes for Lou and Faith Herbert?"

The plump middle-aged secretary with soft brown curls bounces to life. "Oh, Mr. Aldrich! I didn't see you on my books today."

George chuckles. "Just giving a private tour to an old friend."

Uh, yeah. Because it's his job.

We take our badges, and George leads us around the main building, where the residents with the highest needs live. I expected it to feel like a hospital, and in some very slight ways it does. Employees doling out medicine, a few glossy-eyed residents, and wheelchairs lining the halls. But it also feels like a really nice apartment building that just so happens to have handrails lining every corridor.

George takes us to an empty efficiency-style room on the fourth floor with a wash of natural light cascading across the bed. There are fresh flowers on the small dining table for two and one of those fancy one-cup coffee makers that I know for a fact Grandma Lou hates.

"Well, isn't this lovely," Grandma Lou says, her voice not fully sounding like her.

"It's so . . . plain," I say.

"Faith," Grandma Lou chastises me quietly.

"Well, I always liked the idea of residents being able to add their own touches to their space if they so choose." George perches on the edge of the bed. "When I was a young man—not much older than you, Faith—I remember visiting my grandmother in her assisted living home. It was a dreary place." He laughs cheerlessly. "Everyone there was old and dying, but it was almost as if the administrators went out of their way to make it look and feel like that too. My father passed when I was a boy, and my mother worked two jobs. Having my grandmother in assisted living wasn't a choice. It was a necessity. And I just remember this ridiculous painting of Pegasus on the wall. When we weren't there to keep her company or walk her around the grounds, Gram was left alone in that room, staring at that awful painting she didn't even choose herself."

I look from George to Grandma Lou. A hollowness expands in my chest. "Was that supposed to somehow make me feel better about dumping my only living parental figure in this place?"

"I'm not being dumped," Grandma Lou says sharply.

George shakes his head. "That's what makes Cedar Hills so special. It's everything my gram's experience wasn't. Life is filled with tough decisions, including how we spend the last chapter of our lives. Cedar Hills doesn't make the decision any less difficult, but we do try to ease the burden in what ways we can. It's an option I wish had been available to

Gram, but I'm grateful it was here for my mother when the time came."

I nod slowly. "So, Grandma Lou won't be, like, confined to this room all day by herself, will she? I'll be here as much as I can, but I'm pretty sure she would kill me if I skipped school to watch *The Price Is Right* with her."

Grandma Lou narrows her gaze on me, a playful smirk curling her lips.

"Lou would have no lack of activities at her fingertips. We like to give our memory-challenged residents as much freedom as we can. The complex is built in a series of rings, each of which is guarded, so everyone—residents and staff included—passes through those checkpoints. As an added measure, all residents wear a life monitor band." He holds his wrist up. "Think of it like an Apple Watch on steroids."

"You track people through those things?" I ask. The idea is both appealing and startling.

"Only when we need to. Our life monitor bands are mandatory for all residents. The privacy agreement our residents sign is very thorough and clearly states that we will only activate location tracking if and when a resident's well-being is in danger."

Grandma Lou looks to me. "You can't say you wouldn't slap one of those things on me in a heartbeat if you could."

My mouth twitches into a slight smile. I absolutely would.

Grandma Lou loops her arm through mine. "George,

this was lovely of you. I think Faith and I have a few things to discuss."

"Of course," he says. "But I'd be happy to give you the golf cart tour of the rest of the facility."

She smiles, and I swear she's blushing too as she turns to me.

I shrug. "A quick zoom around the place couldn't hurt."

On our way to the elevator, I notice a room with a door standing wide open. Inside, a white man with papery, thin skin and dots of blood bruises peppering his forearms sits perfectly still in his recliner, staring at a television that isn't even turned on.

"Is he okay?" I whisper.

George follows my gaze and then nods. "That's Augustus. He's well taken care of."

It's like he tries to sound ominous and vaguely threatening.

Grandma Lou nudges me toward the elevator, and I attempt to push back the feelings of dread seeping through my rib cage.

After showering us with complimentary baseball hats and sunglasses, George escorts us to the Rolls-Royce of golf carts. I mean, the thing has a built-in refrigerator stocked with brand-name bottled water. He and Grandma Lou sit up front, while I slide into the back seat.

I can't hear much of what they say, but the two of them

laugh as their shoulders knock together, and every once in a while George talks over his shoulder to point out the pool or the rec areas or even the movie theater. This place is its own little universe, built with an aging population in mind. If I'm honest, it's pretty incredible, and I can't believe it's right here just outside Glenwood.

After our tour, George delivers us directly to our car.

"Here," he says as he hands me a business card. "I've written my personal cell phone number on the back. Faith, you can contact me at any time with whatever questions or concerns you might have. My priority is your priority, which I'm guessing is Lou and her happiness."

I loop my hair behind my ear and take the card, studying it for a moment. *George Aldrich, Cedar Hills Owner and Founder.* "Oh. You—you're . . . this is all yours."

He nods. "I think we both know what it feels like to wish you could give the world to your grandmother."

Tears sting behind my eyes as I give him a half-hearted smile.

The thing is, I just never thought the world would mean being away from me. But here we are.

 9

We drive in silence past the roundabouts and through all of George's very safe, very secure security checkpoints until finally we're back in the real world, and nothing is quite as bright or clean or smooth.

"Grandma Lou?"

"Yes, dear." She's looking out the window, one hand wrapped around the door handle like always.

No part of me wants to let go of moments like this, but I guess if I'm going to learn how to be *the* adult in the room, I'd better start by practicing being *an* adult in the room. Or car, as the case may be. I take a deep breath. "That place wasn't so bad."

"No," she says in a sort of satisfied voice I've never heard her use before. "It wasn't bad at all."

But there's one question that's been nagging at me ever since I stopped being flat-out angry and started reading the pamphlets. "I just don't know how we can afford a place like that."

"We can't," she says simply.

"But then . . . how—why would we even take a tour?" Grandma Lou doesn't believe in window-shopping if you're not prepared to make a purchase. She's not the kind of person you can polite-guilt into anything, even if that person is an "old friend," as George claimed. We do okay on her social security and Grandpa Fred's pension, but it could never be enough to maintain the house and pay for a place like Cedar Hills.

Grandma Lou shifts in her seat. Like she's nervous. It's so uncharacteristic that I take my eyes off the road long enough to say, "Grandma Lou?!"

"There's something I should tell you . . . ," she starts. "About George."

"Okay . . ."

"I've only been in love twice in my whole life, Faith. The second time was your grandfather. I miss that man every day. But my first love was George Aldrich."

I can't hide the shock in my expression as my jaw drops. "George? As in George Aldrich, the man who just spent his afternoon showing us around his old folks' home?"

She grins. "The one and only."

Ahead of me, the road is far too long and far too dangerous. I pull over onto the dirt shoulder and turn on the hazard lights. Because if ever a moment called for hazards, it's this one.

"Grandma Lou! Oh my God! Tell me everything," I say. "I want the full story."

"There isn't much to tell," Grandma Lou protests, but she's smiling, and I know she's going to spill. "George was my high school sweetheart. He was so smart. The top of our class. His parents had a farm outside of town. His dad died when he was just a boy, and even though everyone told his mom to sell the land and cut her losses, she kept the farm." Her eyes drift out her window into the wide, open pasture running alongside the road. "George was working in the cornfield before he turned ten. I never got to know him very well until one night I got a flat tire on an old farm road. I walked and walked toward the only light I could see until I found myself knocking on a stranger's door, only to find George Aldrich on the other side."

"Did you know him from school?" I ask.

"Vaguely. The kids who lived on the farms outside of town kept to themselves mostly. I'd always thought he was cute, but he never said much and honestly, everyone treated the farm kids like they were stupid. A ridiculous notion. Anyway, I asked George if he could give me a ride home. Instead, he drove me back to my car and taught me how to change my tire. After that, we were joined at the hip. We'd drive up and down these roads, talking about owning our own slice of land one day. Having our own cornfields and our own family. Until one day, George broke the news that he'd been accepted to the University of Illinois."

"What? And he never told you he was even applying? What about the farm?" I ask, even though I already know how the story ends.

"I was so angry at the time. It took me a long time to understand. Wanting big things is scary, but admitting you want them is even scarier."

"So did he just go to college? Without you?"

She nods. "He wanted me to go, but . . . those were never plans we made together. I—I felt like an afterthought. So he left, and not long after, I met your grandfather. We got pregnant with your dad and got married. I didn't see George again until he came home to help his mother when his grandmother fell ill. By then he was working his way through the business world."

"Wow." In a way, I wish I could have known Grandma Lou back then. It feels somehow unfair that I only get to have her for this very specific time in her life. "Do you ever wonder what would have happened if you'd left for Chicago with George?"

"Only a very little bit," she says, and though it's such a rare thing, I can tell she's not telling me the entire truth.

"Did you two keep in touch?"

"I've followed his career. It's hard not to, with him buying up just about all the land surrounding Glenwood. When I knew I wanted to start . . . making some decisions about what comes next, I called George. I knew I could never afford Cedar Hills, but maybe he could refer me to another facility." She shakes her head as she knits her fingers together in her lap. "But he was adamant that I consider Cedar Hills. He said we'd work something out, and by that I fear he means I'm his charity case. But I also want to be in a place where I know I'll be taken care of—and one that you feel confident in. George understands that."

"Is he married still?" I ask.

She scowls at that. "Trust me, I have no mind for romantic entanglements at the moment."

I roll my eyes. "That's not why I was asking."

"His wife passed away thirteen years ago," she continues. "Not long after your grandfather."

"And you never called good ol' George up?" I ask, thinking of all the time they still could have had together.

"Well, it's like I said. Wanting and wanting out loud are two very different, but very daunting things."

I sigh deeply and sink back in my seat. A heavy, unspeakable sadness for Grandma Lou settles in my lungs. Maybe if she'd never had to take me in, things would have been different and she might have taken the leap. Maybe she would have made the same decision regardless. I'll never know.

"What's done is done," she finally says. "And I'm

starving. Let's get home and make some lunch. We can talk on full bellies. I never make decisions on an empty stomach."

I pull onto the road and Grandma Lou flips through the radio stations before settling on the classic rock station. Stevie Nicks's melancholy voice croons through the speakers as we drive home, *"And the days go by, like a strand in the wind."*

And I know even before we get home that we've both already made the decision.

Grandma Lou is moving to Cedar Hills.

 **10**

"So Greta and I started sidebarring on our own thread because neither of us even knew what to say to Kimber." Ches bites down on a piece of watermelon jerky with a sigh as the cafeteria roars all around us.

"I mean," she continues, "it's likely that Kimber and her boyfriend will break up before the three of us even move into the dorm in the fall, so it probably won't even be a problem, but I'm just not cool with her boyfriend crashing with us on the weekends whenever he wants."

Over her shoulder, I watch as Colleen steps into the lunchroom and heads slowly begin to turn. She wavers for a moment, her sack lunch dangling from the tips of her fingers, before charging into the fold of tables and students. As if on cue, Austin Snyder stands from his table of loyal friends and followers and waves her over.

Austin is *that* guy. The guy everyone knows. He's

charismatic and friendly to just about everyone. Even though I've only had him in one class and interviewed him a few times for the paper, I can personally attest to the fact that when he speaks and you listen, the only word you can use to describe the feeling is intoxicating. Matt swears some secret cabal is grooming him for politics. I'm inclined to believe— or maybe hope—that he's just that nice.

When Austin approaches Colleen, her chin dips down shyly and her cheekbones flare with color. Fiery pink.

"What do you think I should do?" Ches asks. "Faith?"

I shake my head. "Oh, um. I think it's best to be honest. You're going to be living with these girls for the whole year. It might be uncomfortable at first, but I think it'd be for the best."

Ches nods slowly. "I know." She motions to her phone sitting between us as she swipes back and forth between two pictures. "I meant, what do you think about these two tarot posters? Do I go with the Sun or the Empress?"

"Oh! Oh! I'm sorry. Totally the Empress."

She pulls the phone back and squints at the picture. "I'm feeling the Sun."

As she zooms in and out, I watch Colleen sit beside Austin. For a moment, she glances up, and all the way from the other side of the lunchroom, I swear she meets my gaze and holds it for a second, then two, before laughing coyly at whatever charming thing Austin has just said and looking away.

After I finish eating, I leave Ches for the library to study for my quiz next period on the Stanford prison experiment. I swing by my locker for my psychology notes and find Liam's classroom door open. I'm not trying to be a total snoop, but it's impossible to ignore the single tear streaming down his cheek as he bites on his knuckle, watching something on his phone.

"Um, sir? Is everything okay?" I ask from the hallway.

He shakes his head and then nods and waves me over. "You've gotta see this, Faith. Come here a sec."

A little bit of uneasiness crawls up my neck as I step into the empty classroom.

He waves me closer. "You gotta see this video. The feel-good news sites get me every time."

I step behind his desk so I can watch over his shoulder as he replays a video of a tabby cat stuck in floodwaters. I clap a hand over my mouth, horrified. "Oh my goodness. That sweet baby!"

If I were there, I know exactly what I would do. I'd fly right over those waters and pluck that cat from certain death, then nurse him back to health. I begin to suspect I'm about to watch this cat give up all hope and pull an Ophelia in the river, but then out of nowhere, a girl on a makeshift raft appears on-screen. She's headed straight for the cat, the unforgiving waters rushing beneath her. There's no way she'll be able to stop long enough to grab the cat. She'll have to snatch it as she races past. Which means she'll only have one shot.

"Does she save it?" I whisper.

"Just watch," he says.

I don't want to watch, and I can't look away. The water tosses the raft back and forth, threatening to pull her off course, but the girl dips an oar in at just the right moment, angling straight for the cat. The camera shivers, blurring for a split second. When the picture comes back, the girl is there. She scoops the cat up by the scruff just in time, clutches it closely to her chest, and shifts her weight so the raft stays upright.

I let out a victory whoop as the video fades into a picture of the girl and the cat—both healthy and clean as they cuddle on a couch together.

"Doesn't that just give you faith in humanity?" Liam asks.

I swipe a finger under each eye, pushing the tears back. "It really does."

"It's not something you see very often," he adds.

"Drowning cats?"

"No." He smiles and looks straight into my eyes. "Someone who's willing to risk everything for someone else."

He stares at me like he knows, but that's impossible. Right? Unless he's one of the friendly faces Peter told me to watch for. But surely, if that were the case, he wouldn't be so cryptic. Or be a substitute teacher.

"I—"

Liam's expression changes suddenly. His brow furrows and his nose wrinkles. "Do you smell that?"

At first, I shake my head, but then the crisp smell of something electrical smoking infiltrates my nostrils. I nod hurriedly. "Fire." My thoughts immediately turn to Colleen.

We hurry into the hallway and silently agree to go in opposite directions.

It's not long before I know my way is the winner. "This way!" I call.

Liam rushes to meet me, and as we turn the corner, we see the source. Smoke seeps out from beneath the closed door of a janitorial closet. The smell of something on fire is already thick in the air.

"Go get help," Liam and I tell each other in unison.

"Faith," he starts, but this is no time for teacher-student arguments.

"You pull an alarm and I'll clear the hall," I tell him. "We have to warn the school before it gets out of control."

"Okay, but you meet me outside," he says, expression firm.

I nod. "We'll meet up outside."

He takes off in the opposite direction, stopping only to pull a fire alarm. Immediately the emergency lights begin to pulse, and the speakers wail.

I watch until I'm sure Liam hasn't doubled back, then move toward the smoking door. I can't leave until I know everyone is out, but in spite of the growing heat, I'm shivering. All I can think of is the last time I came face-to-face with a wall of fire. How helpless I felt. How useless I was, but that doesn't change anything.

My pulse pounds as I pull my sleeve over my hand and reach for the doorknob.

A low hiss slips through my clenched teeth. The doorknob is hot to the touch, and I have just confirmed once again that I am not fireproof.

A voice comes over the intercom. "This is not a drill. Please walk in an orderly fashion to your nearest exit and meet your homeroom teacher in Lot D."

Without a second thought for who might see me, I push off from the ground and glide down the hallway, checking every room, but it looks like the fire hit at exactly the right time. Everyone was on their lunch hour and they're already halfway to Lot D by now.

I double back, but the smoke is getting thicker. It coils in dense clouds along the ceiling, heat gathering along with it, which I take as my cue to leave, but just as I pass the electrical closet for the last time, I hear a faint cough coming from inside.

Not good.

"Hello?" I call.

The only response is a soft thud.

"Shit," I whisper.

Every muscle in my body tightens at the thought of opening that door. I don't know much about the mechanics of fire, but I do know that opening doors is a big no-no. The second I do, whatever fire is on the other side could get exponentially worse. Me and whoever's on the other side of that door could have mere seconds before the entire hall is engulfed in flames. Or it could be just a little smoke from a frayed wire.

My eyes burn and I feel my lungs protesting with every breath. Okay, so, not just a little smoke.

I try to reach out for the knob, but my body is frozen. My arm feels like lead.

And suddenly, I'm back in the warehouse. Fire consuming everything in sight. Glass shattering above me. The knowledge that Ches was somewhere inside, unable to help herself. She was the cat in the water, and I was the girl in the raft. I was so fearless in that moment. The danger didn't feel real, and maybe that was because I'd never known true danger.

But I do now. And it's terrifying.

Help will be here soon, I tell myself. *Help will be here soon.*

But not soon enough.

I pull my sleeve down over my fist and grasp the doorknob, twisting it as quickly as I can. Searing heat penetrates the thin cotton of my long-sleeve T-shirt, but I grit my teeth against the pain.

Smoke floods around me like water, and a small body hits the ground with a thud and a groan. Inside the closet, hidden in curtains of dark gray smoke, I spot the orange flicker of a flame, and I have no interest in waiting around to see if it has friends.

I stoop to find that the body is Mrs. Sullivan, one of the custodial staff members. "Mrs. Sullivan," I say, "can you stand?"

I don't give her a chance to answer. Instead, I say a quick prayer of thanks to Grandma Lou for insisting I take first aid training from the Red Cross and lift Mrs. Sullivan in a fireman's carry.

There's no time for anything other than flight, so I push away from the ground, and it's as though I'm swimming through the smoke.

I hear Mrs. Sullivan gasping for breath, small moans escaping from her lips.

"We're almost there," I tell her.

I reach the nearest exit just as a crew of firefighters rush through the doors. Immediately on their heels, Coach Grant and Liam, his hair tousled and his eyes wild with concern, appear with paramedics in tow.

Seamlessly, they transfer Mrs. Sullivan from my shoulder to a stretcher.

I cough into my elbow as a woman with curly blond hair ushers me out to an ambulance. "Let's get her some oxygen," she calls.

I feel a firm hand on my shoulder and hear Liam's voice as he says, "Faith, I should have sent you for help. I'm so glad you're okay."

I nod through the coughs as my lungs endure the familiar burn of smoke inhalation, however brief it was.

The whole school is out here. I spot Ches standing at the farthest edge of Lot D, waving down Matt, who must have just returned from his off-campus lunch with Rowan, and right behind them, standing near her new friends with a serene smile creeping along her lips, is none other than Colleen.

 *11*

I plop down in the back seat of Matt's Jeep, and Ches hands me a chocolate milk and a Pop-Tart. "Your sustenance, milady."

Matt glances at me in the rearview mirror as we take off down the street. "And by the looks of it, you need it. Did you even sleep last night?"

"On the couch," I say through a yawn.

It's been days since the fire at the school. The first day, no one was allowed back, but by the next it was business as usual. All classes in session. The hallway where the fire took place is partitioned off with big plastic drapes while the district works to repair all the damages, which meant a handful of teachers had to double up on classrooms. And that was it. The proper authorities determined it was an accident and that was that.

But I can't shake the feeling that it wasn't an accident at

all. First there was the fire behind All Paws on Deck, then Colleen's miraculous return, and now this? Peter's warning about someone picking off psiots is a constant alarm in my head, but that also doesn't quite track. Something is going on here, I just don't know what. And until I figure it out, it's nightly patrols for Faith. Flying endless circles above Glenwood in search of . . . who knows what. Fire? A flashing neon sign that says, *Trouble Over Here*?

Ches wiggles around in her seat, straining against the seat belt. "Faaaaaaaith, you can't keep skimping on sleep. You'll rot your brain."

Matt pats her thigh. "That's TV." He pauses. "And tablets and phones and screens in general."

"And staying up for hours on end searching for an elusive pyromaniac," Ches says. "We're going to come stay with you if you keep this up. We'll each take a watch and make sure you get a full night's sleep."

"I'm fine," I tell her. "I promise. I'm getting enough sleep."

"Faith," Matt says, his tone suddenly earnest. "Have you thought about my mother's offer to stay with us?"

It takes all my self-control not to sigh visibly. When Matt's parents first heard that Grandma Lou would be moving to Cedar Hills, his mom called immediately and offered to let me stay with them for the rest of the school year. It was really, really sweet, but I just can't.

"I really appreciate the offer, Matty, and I'll definitely take her up on dinners every once in a while. But I think it's better if I stay home."

"My name's not Matty," he says with a smile. "I just hate to think of you alone."

And while I hate to think of me alone too, Matt's mom is a smother mother in a way that I don't need, especially with everything going on right now. Plus, if I'm going to be sad, there's something to be said for moping in your own home.

"Just because I'll be living alone doesn't mean I *am* alone," I tell him.

At school, we're halfway to the front entrance before I realize I left my backpack in Matt's car. "Shoot. Can I borrow your keys? I'll get them back to you after first period."

Matt drops the keys attached to his lavender fur pom-pom key chain into my hands and I double back to the car. I grab my backpack and the rest of my Pop-Tart, lock the doors, and am cutting back through the faculty lot when someone yells, "For fuck's sake!"

I spin toward the sound, all senses on alert.

"That was never part of the plan." It's the same voice, and this time it's low, dangerous, definitely not the kind of tone I'd expect for a typical schoolyard disagreement.

I follow the sound to a black Dodge Charger, which is parked with windows open. Inside, I make out a dark silhouette in the driver's seat, and I manage to duck behind a minivan just before he turns his head a few degrees and I can clearly see it's my journalism teacher, Mr. Liam Hollis.

"I won't save you this time," he says. "There's only one rule: don't make a mistake. I made a mistake the first time I saved your ass, but it won't happen again." He pauses for a moment, and I realize he's listening to someone else speak. "It's not our job to ask why. Or any questions at all. Our only job is to do what we're told, and I won't go down because you're getting careless. We've worked too hard for someone like you to mess things up."

I see him hang up the phone and step out of the car. I duck. I don't know why I'm hiding exactly, but that sounded like the kind of conversation I wasn't meant to hear, and I have enough problems right now without adding him to the list. Plus, he could have been talking about anything. He's a well-known journalist, and I'm sure it had to do with a story he's been working on for a long time. If someone was about to wreck my story, I'd probably talk to them like that too.

Of course, the problem with accidentally spying on my teacher is that I have to give him time to get ahead of me, and by the time I make it to journalism, I'm officially tardy.

"Sorry I'm late," I say quickly as I take my seat and shove the last bite of Pop-Tart into my mouth.

"Listen, you're all on your own today." Liam's cheeks are flushed, and he looks just as agitated now as he was in the parking lot.

"Do you have an appointment?" Johnny asks with concern.

"Uh, no, I'm not going anywhere." He sits back and kicks one foot up. "But I've got a few things to handle, and you all seem perfectly capable of self-starting, so just pick up where you left off last time, and if you have any questions about your assignment, check in with your editor in chief. Treat this place like the newsroom it is, people. There's no hand-holding in journalism."

Liam turns his attention to his phone, and I'm itching to know what this big story is he's working on. Maybe it's even something happening right here in Glenwood. Of course, something is happening right here in Glenwood. Something is happening right here in East Glenwood High, and maybe I've been going about this the wrong way. Maybe instead of patrolling the skies, I should be thinking like a journalist. A journalist who writes more than fluff.

Just about the whole staff lines up in front of Johnny's desk, with Rebecca holding everyone up with her endless questions and musings. I wait until everyone has had a chance to check in, and it's clear that Johnny is riding the high of self-importance. For the last two years, his job as editor in chief has been nothing more than a title, but suddenly he's radiating with Chosen One energy. Good. Maybe that will work to my advantage. Ever since we came back from spring break, things have been a little better between us.

Now is a good time to ask for something different.

Once the queue has cleared, I make my approach. "Hey, Johnny, do you have a sec?"

He clears his throat into his fist. "Uh, sure."

I sit down on the exercise ball he co-opted from the phys ed department's discards and nearly lose my balance. Very smooth. "Have you given any thought to doing a piece on Colleen?"

"Bristow?" he asks, but it's not really a question. "Well, I mean, I have, but . . ." He hesitates, and suddenly everything is so awkward. "That's just not really in your wheelhouse."

"I know, I just thought it could be a nice moment to try a new direction," I say. "We all remember Colleen from last fall, right? She used to be shy and such a wallflower, but now she's back and she's so transformed. Plus, I'm sure we all know what it feels like to be on both sides of that coin. To want to just disappear and to also feel completely invisible to people."

"I guess you know a thing or two about that," he says dryly, obviously referring to how I chose Dakota over him.

And suddenly all the guilt I've felt over hurting him vanishes like a puff of smoke.

"Are you going to make me pay for this forever?" I ask in a whisper. "Because I didn't sign up for that. Johnny, I can't fully explain what happened last fall, and even though I wish I could, I don't know that I would have done anything differently now. But if you're going to let this hang between us, then what's the point? I care for you. You're one of my oldest friends. And yeah, things got messy last fall, but can't we just go back to how it was?"

He turns back to face me, and for the first time in months, the facade of indifference has melted, and I can see what he's been hiding underneath. Raw hurt. Instead of answering me, he says, "Rebecca is covering the Colleen story. It was a good idea, but just stick to your beat, Faith. It's what you're good at."

That stings. I don't want him to know how much, so I stand to leave.

"Faith," he says. "I know you wish things would go back to how they used to be . . . but feelings don't work like that. Once they're out of the box, you can't just coil them up and stuff them back inside. I'd liked you . . . since middle school. And I never thought you would like me back. Those few days when I thought that our friendship had finally turned into something more . . . I would take them back if I could. Only because it hurts too much now. It hurts more to have something you can't keep than to never have had it at all." He pauses briefly, and when he speaks again, his voice is thick. "Because now I know what I'm missing."

He reaches for my hand dangling at my side, and I'm glad we're at the back of the room where no one else can see us, because even though I want to pull away, I can't.

Johnny is . . . Johnny is everything my life should have been before Peter and Toya Harada, the maniac behind the Harbinger Foundation, and flying and Margaret and Dakota. The moment I was activated, my life changed course. Dramatically. Painfully. Like a set of train tracks that had been welded to the earth was suddenly ripped up and pressed back down in a different direction. Here with Johnny, our hands gently linked, it feels like how things were before, and I want to live here for a moment. Just a moment longer.

I look down at his fingers before taking a step back. "I wish we didn't have to change."

His voice is so quiet I can barely hear it. "Yeah, me too."

12

Instead of pretending I have a story to write, I decide to take the direct approach.

I drop a note in Colleen's locker that simply reads:

Can we talk? I'll be in the journalism room after school. —Faith

I can't say that she's been avoiding me, but every time I try to catch her in the hallways, there's someone around, one of her many new friends who needs her attention for something, and we can't talk. I mean, really talk.

If she doesn't show today, it will be an obvious red flag. One to add to a growing pile of red flags.

Not only is her return suspicious, but Colleen's locker is only half a hallway away from where the electrical fire took place. The hallway is still taped off with plastic while crews work overnight on getting it back to fully functioning. Until then, teachers have had to shuffle in and out of rooms and share classroom spaces. Of course, no one has any reason to suspect Colleen except for me, which is a really good reason for her to avoid me.

I've been waiting here for fifteen, almost twenty minutes now—and the school is so eerily quiet that I'm about to call it.

I reach down for my backpack and sling it over my shoulder. I told Matt and Ches to go on without me and that I'd get a ride home, which actually means I'm flying home.

The door creaks open and Colleen stands there. She's dressed in a plain maroon shirt tucked into jeans, her hair swept back in a perfect ponytail. Noticeably absent are the gloves she wouldn't have parted with for the world last year. Which is honestly kind of terrifying, because it means she's so much more in control of her abilities than she used to be.

"I would have come sooner, but I've been staying behind to catch up on all the work I missed while I was gone." She shrugs and smiles like everything is completely, 100 percent normal.

"Oh," I say, unable to help the sympathy I already feel for her. I can't imagine missing that much school and trying to rebound. "I'm sure that's been pretty difficult."

She steps into the room and perches lightly on Liam's desk. "It's pretty weird to be back in here."

"I was wondering if you were going to come back to journalism." I gesture toward her still-empty desk.

"Electives aren't really the priority right now," she explains. Again, totally, 100 percent normal.

"Makes sense."

"So what did you want to talk about, Faith?"

I cross my arms over my chest, then think better of it and slide my hands into the pockets of my jeans. If I want answers, she's going to have to feel comfortable. "Johnny says that Rebecca is doing a story on you."

"Yep," she deadpans.

"That's great. I think a lot of people would like to hear what it was like for you when you . . . um, you know."

"What are you getting at, Faith?" She taps her fingers on the desk, making no effort to hide the fact that her patience is dwindling.

Okay, enough with the subtle approach. "I want to know what the heck you're doing back here in Glenwood."

Her whole body reacts in shock. "What do you mean? I was alone and it sucked. I came home. End of story."

"We both know that's not true, Colleen."

"Okay then, Faith, what's the real story?" She pushes away from the desk with so much confidence that I take a step back. "What do you think you know about me?"

I throw my arms up. "The last time I saw you, you were shooting fire out of your hands and shattering glass with your scream and you were hell-bent on killing me. And now you're just here like none of that even happened, and what I want to know is: Why?"

Her eyes go wide and distant for a minute, and I can't help but recall the way she looked that night in the mill. Like she'd lost the part of her that made her human.

Something inside me shivers, but I hold my ground.

"Faith," she says carefully. "Do you hear yourself right now? I don't know what you're talking about, but you're really scaring me. I ran away. It's that simple. I ran away and got involved with some bad people and I did some bad things, but the things you're describing . . . those aren't even human things. . . ."

"What do you mean by 'bad things'?" I demand.

"I was so confused after . . ." She shakes her head and begins to walk out the door before turning around and saying, "I had nowhere to go, so I just went anywhere. I dabbled in drugs. I don't know. Hooked up with a few people. Everything's foggy. But I had to get out of it. So now I'm back, okay? And I just want things to go back to normal. I used to be invisible, and it turns out that being unable to disappear is worse than being nonexistent." Tears well in her eyes; she is the very picture of a recently traumatized girl.

I shake my head, guilt clawing at my chest. "Colleen, wait," I say.

But she's already gone.

The hurt lingers behind her, and I start to wonder if I was wrong to confront her. Maybe she's exactly what she says.

A girl who found herself in a few bad situations and is just trying to make the best of things. Maybe when she says she doesn't know what I'm talking about, what she means is that she wants to forget. And maybe she should be allowed to.

Still, something about all this doesn't feel quite right, and I can't help but feel like I'm being gaslit here.

Colleen may not have chosen to be part of Margaret's ill-fated experiment, but I also can't ignore the havoc she caused.

I'm even more confused than I was before.

The second I'm out of the building, I circle around to the wooded area out back and shoot off from the ground. Wind shreds through my hair and rips at my clothes as I push faster and higher until I'm just a speck in the sky.

Colleen had one thing right. There's something comforting about being able to disappear.

 *13*

It takes me, Miss Ella, and Grandma Lou five days to pack up the items Grandma Lou wants to take with her to Cedar Hills.

I didn't realize how much of packing would require me to go through stuff that belonged to my parents or Grandpa Fred. And then Grandma Lou wanted to go through as much as she could herself to decide what should be donated or what I might want to keep for myself.

That in itself was like going through an emotional spin cycle, but the hardest part was when Grandma Lou pulled me aside and showed me where she keeps all our important documents. The deed to the house, birth certificates, death certificates, social security cards, passports, insurance paperwork, wills, and anything else a human adult might accrue over a sixty-seven-year-old lifespan. It all felt like so much. Like over the course of a few days I became the woman of the house.

I can't help but wonder if it's like this for everyone else or if most people experience change in slow, unsuspecting moments. But life has never afforded me that luxury. Change has always surged through my life all at once. A car accident. An experiment. And now Grandma Lou. The dementia might be slow and unforgiving, but the decisions we've had to make because of it feel too early and too quick.

In the end, all that sorting and emoting and packing boiled down to four suitcases, which are scooped up by a young man in a slate-gray uniform the moment we arrive at her new home.

Grandma Lou and I spend Saturday afternoon in her room hanging up pictures and putting away clothes and a few dishes and coffee cups in her small kitchen, which has just enough room for a coffee maker and toaster, while Miss Ella brings by every employee she can find to personally introduce them to Grandma Lou, like this might somehow score her some preferential treatment.

I'm in the middle of checking a framed band photo of me in seventh grade with a level, when someone behind me says, "It's a shame you're holding the hat and not wearing it."

I spin on my heel to find a lanky boy standing right behind me, one who I last saw loitering around a country club dumpster with a cigarette dangling from his fingertips. "Benji? What . . . are you doing here?"

He stands a few feet away, his tall frame filling the doorway. "Well, I work here, and I just so happen to have a special delivery for a Ms. Louise Herbert."

"You have a job?" I ask quietly just as Grandma Lou pokes her head out from the closet.

"For me?" Grandma Lou asks.

Benji strides across the room, which up until this moment seemed so much more spacious than I thought a room at a place like this should feel, but now feels no bigger than a matchbox. He holds out a hand. "Your life monitor band in sage green."

"There are colors?" I ask.

"Sixteen, to be exact. And yes, I do have a job."

I squint at his name tag. "Benjamin Aldrich?"

Grandma Lou's jaw drops as she fixes her fists to her hips. "Little Benji?"

"Um, excuse me?" I ask. "Little Benji?"

Grandma Lou grins. "I doubt you remember me, but we met a few times when you were just a wee thing. You certainly did inherit your grandfather's height."

The puzzle pieces click into place and I realize who exactly Benji is. "You're George's grandson?" I ask.

"But you've got your grandmother's nose," Grandma Lou tells him.

"You knew my gran too?" he asks, his voice free of all pretense and calculation for just a moment.

"Only as an acquaintance," she says. "But she was such a generous woman. Faith, you must know Benji from school?"

I shake my head.

"I go to Shady Oaks, ma'am. But Faith and I met in front of a dumpster a week or two ago." He smirks and side-eyes me.

She snorts quietly. "Now that's a story I have no interest in hearing."

Benji bounces on his toes, like he has an overflow of energy that could spill at any moment. It's a gesture I find so at odds with everything about him that I wouldn't be surprised if I was gawking. "Well, if either of you need anything, just pick up that phone and hit zero. Ask for Benji. I'm here most days after school."

Once he excuses himself, Grandma Lou says, "Pretty cute, if you ask me."

"I didn't ask you," I tell her.

Miss Ella walks in and, with a thumb over her shoulder, points in Benji's direction. "Were the boys that handsome when we were that age, Lou?"

She chuckles. "Not that I can recall. Evolution at work, I suppose."

After we finish unpacking, Grandma Lou leads us to the cafeteria, which is a cafeteria in theory only. This place is more like a luxury food court with a sushi bar and a juice bar and a pita bar and basically every other kind of food with the word *bar* after it.

The three of us eat a buffet of pasta, egg rolls, and tacos. (Decision overload, if you know what I mean.) Miss Ella even wraps what leftovers she can in paper napkins and puts them in her purse. After the most awkward, almost emotional but definitely not-emotional-at-all goodbye ever, Miss Ella heads home with plans to pick up Grandma Lou tomorrow to go shopping.

I follow Grandma Lou back to her room, and we watch TV while she sits in the recliner and I sit on the edge of her bed. I'm not ready to go. I don't know if she can feel me grasping at this moment desperately, begging it to never end, but she doesn't say anything either. We watch TV together as though it's something we do every night, when I really should be doing homework.

"I guess it's time to go," I say, realizing how much darker her room has gotten.

We've done a good job of making this place feel familiar. Of filling it with all the things that will remind Grandma Lou of who she is. And for a few moments at a time, it's easy for even me to forget that we're not home, and that I won't just say good night and shuffle down the hallway to my room.

"Faith. Sweetheart," she says. "Be sure to check in with Miss Ella."

I nod into my chest. "Okay. Okay. I will."

She stands before me and rubs her hands over my shoulders like she's warming me up, just like she used to that one winter I took swimming lessons. It was indoors, of course, but I'd run out of the pool despite the lifeguard blowing their whistle at me for not walking, and I'd fall right into the open towel she held out for me. Then she'd warm up my shoulders just like she is now.

I stand and pull her into my arms, enveloping her completely. I always forget how small she is. I've got nearly half a foot on her, but I only seem to feel it when we embrace.

"You lock the doors," she tells me, her voice wavering a little. "Call me every night when you get home. If you don't call me, I won't be able to sleep. And we'll have a few weekend slumber parties here. The refrigerator is full, and I left a list of groceries I normally buy on my notepad. Miss Ella should be stocking you up every week, but just in case."

It takes everything in me not to ask all the questions I've already asked time and time again. Why do we have to do this so soon? Why can't it wait? Why can't I be the one to take care of you?

But all the questions come down to one indisputable answer: this is Grandma Lou's decision, and she's asked me to respect her decisions for as long as she can make them.

So I do just that. I hug the last remaining parental figure in my life as tight as I can, and I put on a brave smile. I promise to call and not to stay up late and to do my homework and wake up on time for school. And then I walk out of her little matchbox room and out to the car. I drive past the security checkpoints and back to the house where I now live all by myself.

 **14**

When I get home, both Matt and Ches are waiting for me on the porch.

"What are you two doing here?" I ask as I slam the car door shut.

"You didn't think we'd leave you all alone on your first night as woman of the house, did you?" asks Matt.

"Well, technically, I'm spending the night and Matt is cutting out a little later to rendezvous with Rowan," Ches says.

They stand and follow me inside.

"Only if it's totally okay with both of you," he clarifies.

I cozy up to him a little. "I hope you both have a magical night."

"And I already said I don't care," Ches tells him.

"Are you sure?" he asks. "Is Future Ches going to hold this over my head?"

"No," says Ches as she rolls her eyes. "For the millionth time. No."

Honestly, even I'm not sure if I believe her. Matt has never dated anyone this seriously before, and even though Ches has big future plans to look forward to, she's really struggling with not being Matt's first priority.

"We're good," I tell Matt. "We'll just watch scary movies that you don't even want to see, anyway."

He nods after a moment. "I still hate missing out. Only do and talk about things I don't care about after I leave. Deal?"

I laugh and Ches rolls her eyes again as they flock to the kitchen for drinks and snacks.

The three of us pile up on the couch and watch TV while we zone out on our phones. It's the exact kind of company that I need right now. I'm physically present with people I love without having to be emotionally available.

After the first movie, Matt heads out, and uses the cover of spending the night with me and Ches to stay with Rowan, who lives in the apartment above his parents' garage. I know alone time like this is limited for them, and Matt's been feeling anxious about having so many parental rules in his life while Rowan is pretty much free as a bird—or as free as a first-year community college student still living with his parents can be—so after he leaves, the horror movie marathon can safely begin.

"I don't know how this is physically possible after all the popcorn we've already eaten, but I really want more popcorn," Ches muses as we lie flat on our stomachs in bed, Pennywise's eyes glowing from a storm drain on the television screen.

"I'm out of the microwavable stuff, but I might have a solution," I tell her. "I'll be right back."

Downstairs in the kitchen, I grab a stovetop popcorn from the back of the cabinet—a favorite of Grandma Lou's—and get the stove fired up. While I wait for the popcorn to heat up, I wander toward the front of the house, where today's mail sits stacked up on the console table in the entryway. Even upstairs with Ches watching *It* in my room, the house feels thoroughly empty. It's hard to get over that feeling.

And yet, underneath all the sadness and confusion and fear, a small part of me feels like there might be something thrilling about living alone that I have yet to discover. No more sneaking out to go flying, no more worrying that Grandma Lou might walk into my room in the middle of the night and find me hovering three feet above my bed, no more parental supervision.

Mail, however, is not one of those things.

She only moved out today, but already I'm overwhelmed by the prospect of opening adult mail with things like bills and tax notices. As the popcorn begins to slowly pop in the kitchen, I sort the stack into three separate piles: mine,

Grandma Lou's, and junk. To be fair, much of the mail that is for me should be in the junk pile. Mostly unsolicited college catalogs and a postcard from the coast guard about enlisting.

I'm midway through the strangely enticing note from Captain Caledonia Styx when I catch a scent on the air. One that has become all too familiar in recent weeks. Something is burning.

I drop the postcard, my blood running cold in an instant. A single thought is screaming through my brain: my house is on *fire*.

"Are you burning the popcorn!?" Ches calls down from my room.

Popcorn! Right. I was making popcorn. Now I'm burning popcorn.

"Accident! I'll start a new batch." I shake my head, relief washing through me as I walk into the kitchen to find the popcorn still popping and not even a whiff of smoke in the air. "That's weird," I say under my breath.

My relief vanishes, but I try not to completely freak out. It could be anything. Absolutely anything. And my job as a totally capable semi-adult who lives on her own is to figure it out and take care of things before I burn the house down.

I move back to the front of the house, where the scent is stronger. Maybe it's a bad outlet or a next-door neighbor having a late-night barbecue mishap. The smell is strongest by the front door, which is honestly a relief, but I won't feel better until I see it with my own two eyes, so I slip my feet into my Vans and walk outside.

There on the sidewalk in front of my house is a small fire. "What the hell?" I step closer, trying to decipher what it is, hoping that it's not an animal or some other precious thing, but when all I can make out is a hunk of plastic, I run back inside for the fire extinguisher Grandma Lou kept under the sink.

Ches meets me at the bottom of the stairs, dressed in her black cat onesie pajamas and looking completely bewildered. "What's going on? Is everything okay? Is that the popcorn?"

"Something's on fire outside," I tell her, and dash back out the door.

"Should I call 911?" she asks, trailing close behind.

I shake my head as I rip the pin from the extinguisher and take aim. A burst of white smothers the flames almost immediately, and I cough into my elbow.

Ches waves her arms to try to clear the smoke and fumes. "What—is that a dollhouse?"

Together, we crouch down in front of the melted lump. Yellow and pink drip down the sides of what appears to have been a plastic dollhouse. Inside, the walls are slashed with black, their painted designs completely burned away. The floors droop now and the windows sag open, giving it the gruesome appearance of a very creepy Halloween mask. Worst of all is that in one of the bedrooms is a single doll with half her face melted off. There are no other dolls in any of the rooms.

And I can't help but compare it to my own house. Where I live alone.

"I think it was."

"That is so creepy. And so random," Ches mutters, scowling down at the house. "Not to mention rude. This is definitely going to leave a mark."

I look around over my shoulder and down the street for a sign of anyone or anything. It is definitely creepy, but it doesn't feel random to me. It feels like a threat. And I don't have to try too hard to imagine Colleen lurking in the shadows.

"It was probably just some loser kid trying to get back at his little sister," she says. "Or brother. Gender is a construct, even when pyromaniacs are concerned." She takes my hand and picks up the fire extinguisher. "Come on. The popcorn's going to get cold."

"Oh no! The popcorn!"

"I'm on it!" Ches shouts, charging ahead of me with the fire extinguisher.

This time, the popcorn is definitely the source of the burning smell, but thankfully, it doesn't require the extinguisher.

We set the singed popcorn on the back porch to cool, then make a fresh batch and head upstairs once more.

I triple-check all the locks and windows before curling up with Ches in bed. Neither of us mentions the fire again, and we finish *It* while Ches falls asleep with popcorn in her hair.

Sleep doesn't come so easily for me. I flinch at every random sound the house makes, even though I can catalog them all. I'm too on edge. Too convinced that the dollhouse was a very specific threat. Colleen may be acting innocent to my face, but she's clearly playing at something more. I only wish I knew what.

I'm so angry at myself for how scared I am. Not just because of the dollhouse, but because Grandma Lou isn't here. It's not like she could ever protect me or that I would ever let her try, but something about living in the same space with her felt sacred. Like, surely anyone who might be looking for me or other psiots would at least consider my home a neutral zone for as long as Grandma Lou was here. No one would hurt her or me . . . at least in front of her. Right?

In a matter of months, I feel like I've turned into someone I barely know. Where's the girl who flew into a burning building? Or went searching for missing people in dark, unknown places?

The beginning of the school year is so distant and murky in my memory, but despite having just been dropped into this world of psiots and activation camps, I was still me. I was still Faith Herbert. Mega fangirl with my loyal blog following. Painfully optimistic.

Now the girl in the mirror is a stranger.

Behind me Ches rolls over on her side and nuzzles into my back, and just that small touch is enough to soothe the anxiety rampaging inside me. I let my eyes close and sleep wash over me.

I dream of flying. My body buoyed by air and soaring over my house and neighborhood, my school, and then the now-familiar sight of my entire town from above. These skies have become a part of my home, in a way they never were before. I drift and dive and suddenly Dakota is there beside me. Our hands locked together, a wide grin on her face.

"I'm like your little rain cloud," she says, laughing. "But you know what rain does?"

"What?" I ask.

And before I can do anything about it, her hand slips from mine. "It falls," she says, expression stony as she begins to plummet toward the earth.

I gasp, covering my mouth, as I rocket awake, the sky outside that milky in-between color before sunrise.

At first, I'm convinced it was just the dream that woke me up, but then something creaks inside the house.

"Faith?" Ches mutters, still mostly asleep.

"Sorry," I say quietly. "Just a bad dream. Go back to sleep."

She snuggles into her pillow, black eyeliner smeared all the way from the corner of her eye to her temple, and doesn't move again.

I take a deep breath and tell myself to do the same, but then there's another low creaking sound. This one is slower and definitely downstairs.

This is *not* a drill. I scoot toward the edge of the bed and scoop up the sweatshirt on the floor. Then I levitate down the hallway. At the top of the stairs is the metal baseball bat Grandpa Fred always kept there in case of an intruder. Grandma Lou left it there, too. Not because she had any intention of using it, I think, but mostly because it reminded her of him. I grab the bat in my fist, fully prepared to use it.

I drift downstairs, careful to stay a few inches off the ground. I guess it could just be Peter again, but last time I saw Peter he made it very clear that he wouldn't be around for a while, and for all his faults, he doesn't strike me as the breaking-and-entering type. No, if the burning dollhouse was the threat I think it was, then there's a good chance this is Colleen coming to make good on it.

A clattering noise comes from the garage, and I race to the door as fast as I can, flipping on the lights and brandishing the bat like it's freaking Excalibur.

One of the garage windows is open and the recycling bin is toppled over on its side. Pushing themselves up from the ground is the last person I expected to find breaking into my house in the middle of the night.

Our eyes lock and my heart flutters.

"Dakota?"

 **15**

It's her. Dakota Ash is standing before me. And my brain is making the *AAAAAAAAH* noise internally.

I've dreamed of this moment. Of seeing her again. Of her coming back. Of our tearful reunion. But now that she's standing in front of me, I'm a very complicated tornado of every emotion I've ever felt and a few I'm pretty sure are new, and I don't know what to pick first, but anger seems like the most uncomplicated option.

"What are you doing in my house?" I demand.

"I'll be gone by this evening," she promises, glancing over her shoulder to the open window.

I walk past her and slam it shut.

"You can't be here."

"I know," she whispers. "I'm sorry. I'm so sorry. I just needed a place to sit still for a minute, and I thought you might not even notice me."

"So not only were you going to break in, but you were going to leave again without saying anything?" Anger sweeps through me like a fire, but she winces, and for the first time, I really look at her.

Her eyes are wild with adrenaline and her hair is pushed back into a stiff mess. Her jeans are grease-stained, and her denim jacket is buttoned all the way up like she's protecting herself from something. The circles under her eyes are dark and there's a deep cut under her eye, dried blood crusting it shut.

And all at once it hits me: she's hiding from something. Or someone.

"Oh my God, are you okay?" I ask, concern brushing straight past anger. My instinct is to reach out and touch her, to tug at the hair that's at least two inches longer than it was the last time I saw her, but I remind myself that I can be concerned and angry at the same time and hold myself back.

"I'm—well enough," she says. It's obviously a lie, but I don't push her. "I just needed someplace safe."

My heart squeezes at that. Even after everything, I'm still her safe space.

"Where's Bumble?" I whisper.

Wordlessly, Dakota turns around and opens the window again. She reaches down to help the dog up, and Bumble immediately uses her shoulder as a platform to launch into my arms.

"Oh, sweet girl," I whisper as I stumble backward. "I've missed you so, so much."

Well, I definitely can't kick her out now. Not if she has Bumble with her.

I sigh. "You want to come inside? Ches will be up in a few hours, and then we can have breakfast and you can tell us everything."

Dakota glances nervously at the door, then back to me. She shakes her head. "It's probably best if she doesn't know I'm here. The fewer people in the loop, the better. Besides, I don't want to cause you any trouble. If you can just give me until tonight, I'll disappear again."

I swallow hard. Just because I'm still furious with her for disappearing in the first place doesn't mean I want her to disappear again. Especially not if she needs help. Which she clearly does.

Outside, the sky is beginning to lighten as the sun thinks about rising. Ches won't be far behind.

"Wait right here."

I run back inside the house and grab some chips, extra dog food I keep for strays, water, two bowls for Bumble, blankets, and pillows.

When I return with my arms full of supplies, Dakota is pacing and Bumble has made herself comfortable on the cold concrete, using her paws as a pillow.

"This should hold you over for a while," I say. "I'll try to get Ches out of here as fast as I can, but the girl believes in extravagant weekend breakfasts as much as she does smudging every night before bed."

As if on cue, something thunks above our heads as Ches rolls out of bed.

"I can't thank you enough," Dakota says softly.

"No," I tell her. "You really can't." And even though I can't ignore the tingling in my stomach every time she looks up at me from under her heavy lids, I keep my expression hard. I won't let her forget what she did to me. I won't let myself forget.

Ches stumbles down the steps still in her pajamas, letting out a huge yawn, and I'm already making Grandma Lou's homemade waffles.

"Hey, you!" My voice is thick with cheer. "Breakfast is almost ready. How about you go upstairs and get dressed? We can eat and then I can take you home."

"Oh," she says with a pout. "Well, what are you doing all day?"

"I've gotta run up to All Paws on Deck for a few hours," I lie through my teeth.

She nods groggily and trips back up the stairs. "Okay, yeah."

After we eat a feast of waffles and hash browns and eggs, Ches takes my plate from me. "What should I do with all these leftovers? You cooked for an army."

"Oh, don't worry about all that. I'll get it when I get back."

She wrinkles her nose. "Please say you're not going to start living like a slob just because you live alone now. If I come over and find, like, old food in the sink, I'm going to tell Miss Ella and then I'm going to do a cleansing ritual in your kitchen."

My jaw drops in mock horror. "I would never. No, I'm just in a hurry to get to the rescue, so you ready?"

She nods impatiently. "Yeah, but are you?"

I grab my keys and put my plate in the sink. "Let's go."

"Are you forgetting something?" she asks. "Maybe your work uniform?"

I glance down at my striped T-shirt tucked into my jeans with holes in the knees. "Right. Work. Uniform. Got it."

After I drop off Ches, I even drive in the direction of All Paws on Deck, because I really hate lying to my best friend, but I would really, really hate to get caught.

When I get back home, I stand at the front door and take a few deep breaths.

"You okay over there?" Miss Ella calls from where she's kneeling in her flower beds.

"Yes, yes, I'm fine!" I call back to her.

"I told your grandmother I'd be checking up on you,"

she yells over her shoulder, "so don't be alarmed if I swing by unannounced."

"Got it," I say, and step inside, closing the door behind me and heaving a sigh of relief as I turn the dead bolt.

Bumble races up to me. "Hey, sweet girl, I've missed you," I say. "Hello?"

She follows close on my heels into the kitchen. "Dakota?"

Feet pad down the steps as Dakota appears in a waffle-knit robe I bought Grandma Lou for Christmas one year that she never wore. In fact, the tag still hangs underneath the arm.

"Sorry," Dakota says with a sigh. "I had to choose between eating and showering, and I figured you might prefer if I chose the latter." She gingerly touches the cut under her eye and a shallow one on her cheekbone. "I cleaned it as best I could." Her damp hair is brushed back, and I can see now that some of what I thought was dirt were actually bruises. My stomach twists. I hate knowing that someone hurt her like this.

"I hope it's okay that I grabbed this robe," she continues. "I saw it hanging on the back of the door, and I really need to wash my clothes, if that's okay."

"Yeah, of course." I can feel myself gravitating into her orbit. "Let's get you some food and I'll clean those up a little more. Then you can tell me exactly what you're doing here."

She nods, and I can't help myself. I lunge forward and

give her a brief but suffocating hug. "Don't take this to mean I'm not mad at you. I'm still very mad, but I'm happy you're alive."

"Me too," she whispers.

 **16**

Dakota eats her hot sauce with a side of eggs and hash browns and abides by the same philosophy when it comes to her waffles and syrup.

"So, I guess you could start with the nasty gash on your face," I say once her pace has slowed. I don't mention the bruises on her arms and dotted across her chest, only visible now that she's not wearing her jacket like armor, but I didn't miss them either.

She leans back in her chair, holding her now-full stomach. "It looks like I've been in some kind of biker brawl or something, doesn't it?"

"I don't know if you're cool enough for that," I tell her.

She holds a hand to her chest and pretends to be offended. We're both working hard to lighten the mood, but her shoulders slump and her expression turns serious once more. "I've been trying to work with my manager back in California to get me a new identity."

"The hair is a good start." I gesture at the locks now curling around her cheekbones as I attempt to make light of what is a very serious situation. "This is basically soccer mom compared to what it was before. No one would see it and think Dakota Ash."

Dakota makes a face at that, then shrugs. "Yeah. Well, it turns out that Hollywood managers aren't as well versed in crime as the movies might lead you to believe. So while my manager, Holly, has been chasing leads on procuring fake identities for months, I've been lying low in small towns between here and the Canadian border."

"Who exactly are you hiding from?" I can't help but think of my spring break road trip with Matt and Ches and how I looked for Dakota without meaning to. In passing cars. The dark booth at the back of a restaurant. The reflection in the glass door of a gas station drink freezer.

"Well, I thought I was on the run from Margaret and the people she works for."

"You thought?"

She nods. "For a while, Bumble and I holed up in the country on this lady's property. Her name was Martha, and she let me rent a trailer from her and didn't ask a lot of questions, but one night I came outside to see my truck on fire, so she drove me and Bumble into town—"

"Wait. It was just on fire?" I ask. "Like, was it a mechanical issue or . . ."

"I don't know. It could have been something with the truck. It was on its last legs when I bought it, to be honest, but I'm pretty sure it was someone sending me a message."

That sounds a little too familiar to be coincidence, but it's clearly not the end of the story. "What did you do after that?" I ask.

"Martha helped me find another car but told me she couldn't risk renting to me anymore. I couldn't blame her. So, after that, Bumble and I just skipped around from motel to motel. Not staying anywhere for more than a few days. I was passed out in a crusty motel room in Bigfork when two goons—two very familiar goons—unceremoniously let themselves into my room and used their fists to send a message from their boss."

My eyes trace that gash beneath her eye, and my blood goes cold thinking of her trapped alone with two men easily twice her size.

"Do you mean Margaret's bodyguards?" I ask.

"You know the ones," she confirms. "Those two bald barbarians, Remi and Nigel. They wanted to know where Margaret was. This whole time I thought they worked *for* her. I didn't realize they were babysitting her. As you can see, they had a similar, if more violent, misunderstanding about me. I'm just relieved they didn't hurt Bumble."

Bumble perks up at the sound of his name and hurries over to Dakota's side. He's probably hoping for scraps, but it also warms my heart to see the trust in his eyes when he looks at her. Aaaaaand, I'm officially jealous of a dog.

"And then you came back here?" I ask.

"I've been in and around Glenwood for a few days. I . . . I've just had a hard time sleeping, and Holly's not returning my calls anymore. I can't go home. Half the country thinks I'm dead. The other half thinks I'm some underground crime boss, but if I go home, then I'm everything my family predicted I would always be."

I want to tell her that this is no time to cling to her pride, but if I'd had the type of family life Dakota did, I don't think I could go back.

"Where'd Grandma Lou go?" she asks.

And so I tell her. I tell her about Cedar Hills and George, about how strange it is to live alone, even though it's been such a short time, and how it also makes me feel so grown-up. I tell her about nosy Miss Ella and the casseroles Matt's mom sent over last night to keep in the freezer. "So, I guess we're both on our own," I say before realizing what an idiot I sound like and that our situations aren't at all alike. "I mean, not that I have it as bad as you do . . . or that it's some kind of competition. I just meant that—"

She grins into her coffee. "I get what you mean." She takes a long sip before adding, "I'll be out of here by this evening. I just . . . I don't know. I needed to regroup, I guess. Figure out what comes next."

I want to take her at her word. To show her just how angry I am by letting her leave when she so clearly needs help. But that's just not who I am. Maybe it's Bumble or because Dakota looks so exhausted or because I'm not ready to say goodbye again. Maybe it's because I want answers to questions I don't know how to ask. Whatever the reason, I say, "You don't have to go. In fact, you should stay here for as long as you need."

"Faith, I really don't mean to intru—"

"You're not intruding," I say, even though this is the actual definition of intruding. "I'm not letting you go back out there to live on the street. Not while you have Bumble."

She almost smiles. "Thanks," she says.

"I'm still mad at you, though. That hasn't changed," I say as I take her empty plate to the sink.

As I glance back, I don't miss the way regret perches in her eyes when she answers, "Fair."

Dakota falls asleep on the couch around seven o'clock that night, and she doesn't wake up again until seven the next morning. Bumble guards the door, and I sleep in Grandma Lou's recliner, because if anyone followed Dakota here, I want to be here to greet them.

Once she's up and fed, we get our story straight. Bumble is an adoption failure with severe separation anxiety. I've agreed to foster her until she can be adopted again. Miss

Ella buys it, and so do Matt and Ches. In fact, there was some kind of wager going between the two of them on how long it would take me to bring home an animal from the rescue, so they seem pretty pleased with themselves. I'm just glad neither of them remembers Bumble well enough to spot the lie.

Dakota isn't so easy to explain away, so we decide she has to be a ghost. No one can see her or suspect there's anyone at the house but me. And because I am certain Miss Ella will notice if even the smallest thing is amiss and immediately report it to Grandma Lou, I come up with a few ground rules:

House Rules for Ghosts

- No answering the door.
- No messing with the lights unless I'm home.
- No talking/TV/music unless I'm home.
- No noises in general.
- Bumble can go out in the backyard by herself
    ONLY through the doggy door.
- Don't be seen by anyone.
- Especially Miss Ella.

After reading over the list, I add a few hearts and stars to lighten the mood. I don't think it helps. Thankfully, the doggy door was a leftover from the previous owners and something Grandpa Fred never got around to replacing (to the annoyance of Grandma Lou).

"We'll be fine," Dakota assures me for the millionth time as I leave the paper for her on the coffee table.

"Miss Ella is like a one-woman neighborhood Crime Stoppers. I don't want to risk anyone finding you because she can't mind her own business."

"I'll be quiet as a mouse," she promises.

Last night, Dakota and I went out and picked up the Toyota Camry Martha helped her buy after her last truck went up in flames. It was parked a few blocks away, but we both agreed that was too close for comfort and decided to drive it out into the country and hide it in some neglected cornfield.

On the drive back, Dakota quietly asked, "Is Ches okay? Was she cleared of all charges? I'd been watching the local news and figured it was a good sign when I hadn't heard anything about her."

"Yeah, she hired a real sharky lawyer. She didn't even have to go to trial."

She nodded, staring into the darkness outside her window. "Good. Good."

"She's using the rest of the money for school. She's going to Chicago."

"She'll love it there."

"She's already connected with a group online called MidWitches, for witches from the Midwest. I guess a lot of them are in the Kansas City and Chicago areas."

We stayed quiet for a long stretch of road that was so dark, it felt like the pavement was swallowing the glow of my headlights.

"Would it help if I keep saying I'm sorry?" she asked.

"I don't know," I said. "I don't know."

 **17**

"I heard Colleen and Austin Snyder went on a date on Friday and then showed up to some party together," Matt says.

"I can't decide if I feel left out by the fact that our school has parties and we're obviously not on the invite list," Ches says as she rolls over on her side, tilting her wide-brimmed black hat to shield her eyes from the sun.

It's so nice today that I dragged the two of them outside to eat lunch on the grassy hill behind the school. Matt only complained about the grass tickling his legs for a minute before the warm sun outweighed the other inconveniences of eating outdoors.

"I just don't get what Colleen would want with Austin," I say. "Or what he would want with her. Before she went missing . . . or ran away or whatever, they didn't even exist in the same circles. He probably didn't even know who she was until he heard her name on the news."

"That's just it, though, don't you think?" Matt asks. "Girl disappears. Girl mysteriously returns. Girl is suddenly interesting and relevant."

I nod half-heartedly. "I guess so."

Down the hill, at the middle of the courtyard, I see Colleen with Austin and his circle of friends. The two of them sit with their shoulders pressed together. He leans over and whispers to her as a slow smile spreads on her lips.

"Johnny and Rebecca clearly thought she was fascinating enough for an entire article in the paper," Ches points out. "That interview was like a full center spread."

The really irritating thing is that the latest edition of the paper with her interview was our most popular in a long time. Not only has Colleen reappeared, but she's completely transformed. It feels like the entire school is a Colleen fangirl now, and I can't help but think she's got something huge planned. Something huge and definitely not good.

"Hey," Matt says, interrupting my doomsday thoughts. "What's the deal with your new journalism teacher anyway?"

I shrug. "He's a sub."

"Uh, only the hottest substitute teacher I've ever seen." Matt's eyebrows shoot up.

"Seconded," Ches says with a sigh. "I have him for study hall on B days, and let's just say I haven't done much studying. Also, he's, like, very charming and worldly. Last week, he told us about the year he spent living in Chefchaouen, Morocco, which is like this whole city full of artists, where all the buildings are different shades of blue, and he studied leather weaving under this guy whose family had passed down their craft for generations."

"It's so much easier when hot people are assholes," Matt says. "It's like you can admire them from afar without ever actually wanting to get involved with them."

"Yeah," I say, my thoughts drifting to Dakota. "That makes things significantly less complicated."

After school, I head right into work, and we're too busy for me to even spare a thought or worry for Dakota or Miss Ella snooping. There was a bad hoarding case over the weekend, with thirteen cats and nineteen dogs living in one house, so we're busy with things like flea baths, bloodwork, and heartworm treatments.

I'm supposed to visit Grandma Lou tonight, but after all the messy jobs I've done today at the rescue, I need to go home first and change, which is a good thing, because when I pull up, I find Miss Ella parked in my driveway, taking groceries into the house.

"Miss Ella!" I jump out of the car before it's even fully turned off.

"Well, there you are," she says. "Aren't you lucky? These are my last few bags to take inside."

Oh my God. Inside. She's been inside. She's through the door before I can stop her. I chase after her, hoping that Dakota is hidden away.

"You've got to let me get into this refrigerator to organize it," she says. "It's just a mess."

"Oh, I can do that," I tell her, frantically looking for any sign of Dakota that might be hard to explain away, but there's nothing. Not even a blanket out of place on the sofa.

Miss Ella sets the last of the groceries on the table and picks up a few boxes of pasta before heading for the pantry.

"Here!" I say. "Let me take those for you."

Her wrinkly lips curve into a suspicious frown, but she says nothing as she turns back to the table for refrigerated items.

I open the pantry to find exactly what I feared: Dakota holding her breath.

She holds a hand out for the pasta and puts it on the shelf. *I'm sorry*, I half mouth, half whisper.

"What was that, dear?" Miss Ella asks.

Dakota shakes her head and mouths, *It's okay*.

I shut the door and glance at the clock on the microwave. 5:58. "Oh my gosh, Miss Ella! Thank you so much. But look at the time. If you don't go now, you'll miss the six o'clock news."

She points to me and then snaps her fingers. "Shoot. You're right." She takes her keys and her purse, and I follow close behind. Just as she's about to step out of the kitchen, she turns back to face me, nearly running straight into my chest because I'm so close. "You never did help me set up my DVR like you said you would last Christmas."

"This weekend," I tell her. "This weekend. I promise."

She turns back around and makes her way to the door. "I'm holding you to it."

"Yes, ma'am," I say as she walks outside and down the steps. I wait until she gets into her car and reverses out of my driveway and then pulls into her own before I call out, "All clear!"

Dakota sighs behind me. "You never said Miss Ella had keys to the house."

"I forgot. I'm so sorry," I tell her. "You're sure she didn't see you?"

Dakota laughs. "Uh, I'm pretty sure if the head of the neighborhood's crime watchers saw a stranger in her neighbor's house, you would know."

"Fair," I tell her. "I'll figure something out with her and groceries."

Dakota picks up a gallon of whole milk from the table. "I wonder if it'd be too much to ask Miss Ella to get some almond milk next time?"

"I'll take care of the groceries myself from now on," I tell her. "Besides, I'm pretty sure Miss Ella would tell me that almond milk is nothing more than chalk water and there are only two kinds of nuts: the ones in your trail mix and the ones in your pants."

Dakota snorts out a laugh. "Noted."

 *18*

When I finally make it to Cedar Hills, I can feel myself dragging. This day has gone on forever and it's still only Monday. How can that be?

I check in at the front desk for my visitor badge and take the elevator up to Grandma Lou's floor. As I get off the elevator, I notice that the door to Augustus's room is shut and I can actually hear voices inside. A little bit of comforting warmth spreads through my chest at the thought of the lonely man finally having some visitors of his own.

At the end of the hallway, Grandma Lou's door is cracked open, like she left it that way for me. Rapping my knuckles gently on the door to announce myself before stepping in, I find her sleeping in her recliner with the television on. She's watching the seven o'clock news, which is just a rerun of the six o'clock news.

I sit down on the edge of her bed. I want to see her and

talk to her, but I also don't want to startle her.

On the television, the weatherman volleys back to a reporter sitting behind the desk. "Thanks, Germaine. Here's hoping for that warm front in time for the weekend. In local news, the Aldrich Group has just purchased several hundred acres of land neighboring the current Cedar Hills facility. No word yet on what this land might be used for, but as it is outside city limits, zoning codes do not apply. The Aldrich Group did not return a request for comment."

"The Aldrich family takeover. Watch out," says Benji from where he stands in the open doorway. The top of his hair is gathered up in a short spiky ponytail that shouldn't be cute but somehow is. "One acre at a time."

"Hi," I say, my voice tentative. "So, no comment, huh?"

"The official comment is no comment."

"Not even on the hair?"

He pats his little baby ponytail. "I've started to consider headbands, too."

"If it's in your way, you could just cut it."

"Ah, yes," he says, "but then how else could I piss off my dad every time he looks at me? Roger Aldrich hates nothing more than liberals and men with long hair."

"In that case, you should consider a few barrettes. In glittery colors."

That gets a smirk out of him. "I was just coming to check on Lou," he says. "Gramps instructed me to give her extreme preferential treatment, which is fine with me. Means I got to spend my whole shift in the mahjong hall."

"You probably made her day." A fact that makes me feel bad and grateful at the same time.

"Things like mahjong and chess and even bingo are supposed to help keep their brains sharp," he says. "You know, a few months ago, Gramps had an episode and we thought maybe it was dementia, but the doctors couldn't find anything. When he went in, they said he was sharp as a tack. But my dad became obsessed with making him do any kind of preventive things he could. Brain games. A brain-healthy diet. Anything."

I stand and make my way toward him, so we can talk in hushed tones and not wake Grandma Lou. "Well, I hope buying up all that property wasn't part of it. That would be a very expensive incident."

"Nah, that was all Dad. He's wanted to expand for years, but Gramps never felt like it was the right move. Then just last month, he changed his mind. I think he's trying to let go a little. Take a step back." He shakes his head. "I don't like it. I don't like to imagine him preparing to . . ."

"Die?"

He nods. "Yeah, I guess so."

"I know what you mean." From the sounds of it, Benji's parents are still in his life, but it seems like he and George might share a relationship like mine and Grandma Lou's, and it's not really something that many other people my age really understand. "The art of letting go," I say.

"I guess you heard all about him and Lou then, huh?"

I peer over my shoulder to where Grandma Lou sits with my dad's baby blanket on her lap. "I think they were really in love."

"I think they still might be."

I turn back to him. "What do you mean?"

"Gramps has been visiting her every night before bed since she moved in. The orderly for this floor told me earlier today. Sometimes he reads to her. Sometimes they watch television or just talk."

"Really?" I ask, my voice heavy with emotion. It's so sad to know this is how their story ends, and yet there's something really beautiful about it, too. Selfishly, it makes me feel less bad to know she has someone here who knows her. Who truly cares about her.

"Faith?" Grandma Lou's groggy voice calls.

"Hey," I say, turning back to her. "I heard you had a pretty action-packed day."

"From who?" she asks as she begins to perk up. "Can I get you something to drink?"

I glance over my shoulder to point to Benji, but he's already gone. "No, no, I'm okay," I tell her. "Tell me everything. I want to hear all the assisted living gossip you can spare."

Grandma Lou fills me in on a few of her neighbors as best she can, but some of the details are foggy. There's Eddie, who's next to Gladys, but then she starts talking about Miss Ella like she's here too. I can see the moments when she catches herself. The furrow in her brow as she realizes she's lost her train of thought or when she can't remember why exactly she's here.

Guilt tightens in my gut, like somehow I did this to her by letting her move in here. I wonder if perhaps she's taking a sudden turn for the worse and if being here caused it. There are moments when just talking to her feels like sifting through static, trying to find the right wavelength.

As I'm leaving for the night, all the doors on the hallway are shut and dark except for one, and I can't help but peer inside as I pass. And that's when I see him, hovering in the doorway like he can't decide if he wants to stay or go. I stumble back into the wall, making more noise than I intended. What is he doing here?

"Mr. Hollis," I say, because he's seen me staring and now it's too late to pretend otherwise and my brain wasn't quick enough to remember that he prefers to be called— "Liam, I mean."

Liam glances over to Augustus, sitting in a recliner identical to Grandma Lou's. His eyes are open, but unfocused, and out of nowhere I think of Gretchen Sandoval and the glazed look in her eyes when I found her catatonic in the corn maze last fall. The logical part of my brain knows that this is not the same thing, and yet I can't help feeling deeply uneasy. This man won't be jumping out of his chair to startle me anytime soon, but there's something about seeing him that makes me wary of the unknown. Of not fully under-standing where we go when we're no longer here, even when our bodies are. Thinking about it gives me a kind of vertigo.

"Oh, Faith." Liam sounds like he's just realized I'm here. "Could you sit with him here for a minute? I need to catch that orderly kid who was making the rounds."

I nod and step inside the room, which is completely bare in comparison to Grandma Lou's. No family photos or bed-ding from home. Just the standard-issue quilt and pillows and a mass-produced photo of the ocean hanging over the bed.

"I'll be right back," Liam says to the man, who doesn't flinch beyond a slow blink.

I sit down on the chair beside Augustus's recliner as he stares lifelessly at the television, which is tuned to a History Channel special about conspiracy theories and how aliens built the pyramids.

"So, you must be Augustus," I tell him.

But he doesn't move. There's a quickening in my chest, and I feel simultaneously ridiculous and guilty for being even a little bit scared of this man. There was probably a time in his life when he was full of laughter and vigor, but now he's just a shell. A lump in my throat forms as my mind begins to wander and I imagine what the future might hold for Grandma Lou.

I lean a little closer to the man and whisper, "I'm sorry. I don't think I'm scared of you. I think I'm just scared of seeing the people I love die and—"

The man's eyes dart to the side, his head unmoving, and slowly he lifts his arm until his finger is brushing my cheek.

My thudding heart has all but stopped.

He pulls his hand back to reveal one single eyelash balancing on the tip of his finger. My single eyelash.

"Okay, got that all sorted!" Liam says from behind us as he reenters the room.

I gasp so hard I begin to cough.

"Everything okay?" he asks.

A little startled and a little stunned, I bounce up to my feet as my coughing subsides. "Well, that was fast."

He nods. "Thanks for standing by. He's mostly fine on his own, but I didn't want to . . . I hate leaving him alone, which I have to do more often than I'd like to admit."

I nod knowingly.

"Let me walk you to the elevator," he says.

I follow him out the doorway, sparing one last glance at Augustus. A deep sorrow settles in my bones. For him. For Grandma Lou. For everyone I've said goodbye to and all the goodbyes that are yet to come.

Even though Liam is barely a teacher, it's weird to see him here outside of his element and in such a moment of vulnerability with the man who I'm guessing is his father.

He closes the door behind us. "You here visiting a grandparent?" he asks.

I nod. "My grandma. She's more like a parent, though. My, uh, last living guardian." I shake my head. "But I guess technically I'm eighteen, so I'm my own guardian now."

He cracks a smile and slides his hands into his back pockets. It's the kind of smooth move that could be the genesis of a serious crush if my brain wasn't in precisely one thousand other places, and if he weren't my teacher. "Man, if I lived on my own when I was your age, my place would be chaos central."

"Oh, trust me. My friends have big plans." And I can't believe I just admitted that to a teacher.

"What's your grandma in for?" he asks, like she's a prisoner, because she is, and I think he might actually get that.

"Dementia."

"Oof," he says.

"Is he your dad?" I ask.

He glances over his shoulder with a nod, as though he can see right through the door. "Dementia, too. And Parkinson's."

"I'm so sorry," I say.

He grimaces lightly. "It's okay. We've had a, uh . . . rough relationship."

I nod like I know what that must feel like—to have to tend to someone who you don't truly know or like—but he seems to appreciate the gesture.

"I better get back to him," he says as we step up to the elevator. "See you at school?"

"Yeah. I'll see you then."

As I drive home, I'm barely aware of each turn and stop. I'm on autopilot, unable to think of anything else besides how very still and detached Liam's dad felt.

And some small part of me is already screaming, because I don't know what I'll do if that happens to Grandma Lou.

 **19**

With the prom theme announcement just days away, I—
Faith Maker-of-Newspaper-Quizzes Herbert—am left with
the age-old question: If I were a prom theme, what prom
theme would I be?

The blinking cursor on my ancient journalism room
computer taunts me as the bell rings and I still have absolutely nothing to show for the last hour and a half.

All around me, everyone gathers up their belongings in
a hurry as they split off for their next classes. Liam sits back,
reclined as far as his chair will go as he intently reads something on his phone. He doesn't even flinch as the second bell
rings and the only people left are me and him.

When I showed up to class this morning, Liam didn't
acknowledge me, much less the fact that I'd seen him just last
night in the hallways of Cedar Hills. It's not that I expected
him to be like, *Hey, crazy seeing you last night in the old folks'*

home in front of the whole class, but maybe some small nod or smile or suggestion that we'd shared a moment that connected us outside this classroom. But there was nothing. And actually, it's better this way. I don't feel like explaining my whole life to the rest of the class, and I'm sure he doesn't either.

I clear my throat loudly. "Uh, hey, Mr. Hol—Liam?"

"Hmm?" He doesn't look up.

"I've got sociology after this period, and we're just watching a movie today. Would it be okay if I stuck around to finish what I'm working on? Maybe you could write me a tardy note?" That last part comes out like a question, because tardy notes are the ultimate special teacher favor and are rarely bestowed upon us mortal students.

"What?" He looks up from his phone, my words finally sinking in. "Sure."

"Thanks," I say in a tiny voice.

Prom themes, prom themes, prom themes. If I were a prom, what would my theme be?

I begin to type out a few ideas.

- Superheroes
- Retirement Community
- Good Guys vs. Bad Guys
- Having Too Many Crushes
- Adult Enough to Live Alone, But Not Adult
  Enough to Go Grocery Shopping

"That is, um, highly specific. Maybe try Under the Sea, Stars and Stripes, Masquerade, and Enchanted Forest."

"What?" I look over my shoulder to find Liam hovering.

"Prom themes," he says as he sits down beside me. "Those were the prom themes for all four years I was in high school. I don't think Having Too Many Crushes is as much a theme as it is a long-standing high school tradition. Superheroes is . . . well, that's a seventh birthday party theme, and I can't quite figure out what you were going for with Retirement Community. And the adult thing . . . well, shit if I know."

"It never hurts to think outside the box," I insist, even though I can feel myself shrinking with embarrassment.

"I can't argue with that."

"And besides," I say. "My excursions lately have been pretty limited. Sleep, school, work, Cedar Hills visits. Not a lot of inspiration to pull from."

He barks out a wry laugh. "I have way too much in common with one of my high school students."

"Those are all good themes for this quiz, though, so thanks for that."

"So junior-senior prom, huh? Do they still hold it here in the gym? I remember there was a big push to have it at the country club, but a bunch of rich people were really concerned about having public school kids too close to their precious green."

That gets a laugh out of me. "Yeah, it's definitely still in the gym."

He crosses his legs and raps his knuckles against my desk. "So, your grandmother . . . how long has she been at Cedar Hills?"

"Less than a week," I say. "I thought for sure she'd be home long enough for me to graduate, but—"

"Those things have a way of taking a turn." The tone of his voice tells me he knows from experience. "Trust me when I say this kind of stuff doesn't care about your hopes or plans."

"Was that supposed to be comforting?" I say with a laugh.

His phone begins to vibrate, and he slides it out of his messenger bag. "I've gotta get this," he tells me. "But hey, good luck with the, uh . . . quiz." He stands and quietly answers. "Hello? Yeah, yeah, give me a sec." He walks out of the room and closes the door behind him.

I lean back in my seat. I wish I could introduce Peter and Liam. Something tells me they'd really get along. Thinking of Peter reminds me of his offer, to leave Glenwood and join up with his group of psiots. I love Matt and Ches, and they'll always be my best friends. But it's hard not to feel a little alone—like there are certain parts of my life that they'll never be able to understand. The idea of being surrounded by psiots—other uniquely gifted or, heck, maybe even cursed individuals—is the kind of thing that almost feels like a daydream.

For now, though, I have a quiz that needs writing.

I turn back to my computer, delete my fake prom themes, and begin to type.

1. If you could watch only one musical for the rest of your life, what would it be?

A. *Into the Woods*

B. *Phantom of the Opera*

C. *SpongeBob SquarePants: The Broadway Musical*

D. *Hamilton*

I study the answers and feel a little too proud of the minimal amount of work I've done. Whatever. An easy win is still a win.

 **20**

At the end of the week, we're summoned to the gymnasium for the obligatory prom court nominations ceremony. I would skip except the journalism staff is required, by law, to be here.

"I can never decide if our mascot is meant to be satirical," Ches ponders as Walt the Bunny storms the basketball court behind Principal Peck, who stands at a podium in the middle of the gymnasium.

"I don't know. Bunnies can be pretty vicious," Matt says. "I mean they're essentially rodents." He shivers. "And then those red beady eyes . . . it's too much."

"Bunnies are not vicious." I shake my head vehemently. "But you can basically put the word 'fighting' in front of anything and it sounds like a mascot."

Ches nods. "Fighting artichoke. Fighting pickle. Fighting—"

"Banana slugs!" Matt interjects.

Ches checks the time on her cell phone. "I can't believe attendance is required at a pep rally."

Matt groans. "Why do we even need a pep rally for prom? Isn't everyone already pepped enough? It's essentially the moment the entire American education builds to."

"I think that's actually supposed to be graduation," I say.

He thinks on that for a minute. "Huh."

Natural light streams into the gymnasium from the windows dotting the roofline, and the strobe lights that have been set up are barely visible because of it. Small confetti cannons that are not nearly as big as the ones the football team uses spray puffs of confetti every thirty seconds, which is actually more depressing than no confetti at all.

"Students," Principal Peck says into the microphone, like she's hosting a wrestling match and not an attendance-required pep rally, when all of us could have just gone home early. "Before we get started today, it is my pleasure to unveil the theme for this year's prom . . ." She turns around and motions to one of her office aides, who tugs on a rope behind the podium a few times before, finally, a hand-painted canvas banner unfurls. In bright blue strokes, it reads: ON CLOUD NINE.

Matt shrugs. "Could be worse."

Principal Peck speaks into the microphone, her voice slicing through the commotion. "Thrilling, I know! I'm looking forward to seeing the prom committee bring this vision to life! Now, it is my pleasure to welcome our school paper's editor in chief as he announces our prom court nominees as chosen by you—the student body."

"Look at Johnny go," Matt says as Johnny walks toward the podium and then begins to jog as he realizes the applause will stop long before he reaches the microphone. "He's still cute. We still think he's cute, don't we?"

Ches nods. "For sure."

"Like maybe even cute enough to take to prom?" Matt asks as he nudges me in the ribs.

"Yeah, right," I say. "That ship has sailed."

"Hello, fellow bunnies," Johnny says into the microphone.

He's answered with total silence. Crickets. Except for Rebecca, who claps and hoots from the front row so enthusiastically she could out-cheer the entire cheerleading squad and actually does, as they sit along the edge of the court with their legs crossed. The only sign of life about them is the limp shake of their pom-poms.

"Oh God," Ches says, holding her stomach painfully. "Secondhand embarrassment is real."

I cringe and nearly shout, *Go, Johnny!*, but I have a feeling that would make things worse.

He clears his throat. "Anyway, the thing we're all here for . . . prom court! We'll start with nominees for junior prom king. When I call your name, please come down to the floor. And now . . . in no particular order . . . Gavin Hoang." He breaks for applause and then lists two more vaguely familiar names.

"Does it make you feel way old not to really know who these people are?" I ask.

Matt shrugs. "We're not old. They're irrelevant."

Ches nods in agreement. "I support that sentiment."

"And now," Johnny continues, "for our junior prom queen nominees . . . Lauren Silvers . . ." A thunder of applause as one of the cheerleaders hops to her feet and skips to the center of the court. "Tessa Parker," he calls, and the girl who I recognize as the junior class president stands and takes a dramatic bow before walking down the bleachers. "And lastly, with a huge show of support—and because apparently the rules don't specify you have to be a junior to be junior prom queen . . . Colleen Bristow!"

The gymnasium explodes with applause as Austin Snyder leans over and kisses Colleen on the cheek before she walks sheepishly toward the rest of the nominees.

My jaw drops so far it might as well be unhinged. "What! Colleen's a sophomore!"

Matt shrugs. "Popularity knows no grade, I guess."

The once mousy, constantly rumpled Colleen Bristow is nominated for prom queen. Forget the fact that she wasn't even in school half of last semester because she was busy trying to literally burn the world down. And now here she is, blushing and waving to her adoring fans. Solely based on the level of applause, she's a shoo-in for the crown. So much, in fact, that they might as well just hand it over now.

"Well," Ches says as the applause begins to quiet. "That was a surprise."

"I'm not surprised," Matt says. "Nothing feels better than seeing the underdog take the lead. Former loser who ran away nominated for prom queen. It practically writes itself."

"I don't feel good about this," I tell them both.

"What is she going to do?" Matt asks. "Torch the entire prom?"

"I wouldn't put it past her," Ches says.

After Johnny announces the senior nominees (which include Gretchen Sandoval, to the surprise of no one), the final bell of the day rings.

As we shuffle down the bleachers, I flash Johnny a quick smile and a thumbs-up.

"You can't be nice to him," Matt says. "Unless you're asking him to prom."

"We can just be friends," I argue.

"In the words of the great Faith Herbert," Ches says, "'that ship has sailed.'"

 **21**

By the time I get home from work, it's dark and someone is fumbling around in the kitchen.

"Hello?" I call as I flip on the lights.

Dakota rubs her eyes. "Wow. Was it really that dark in here?"

Even though I knew to expect her, it's still a surprise to find her here. Waiting for me. In my kitchen.

"What are you doing?" I ask, looking to the pile of tortillas and cheese on the counter.

"Making tacos for dinner . . . I thought we could eat together."

"Oh," I say. "Yeah, that would be nice. Any issues today with Miss Ella or anything?"

"Nope. Bumble started digging a hole into her yard, and I didn't know what to do, but the woman was out there within minutes and sufficiently scared Bumble away."

Bumble trots down the stairs at the sound of her name and pushes between my legs, like suddenly no one can see her there. "Awww, you just wanted to explore a little, didn't you, girl? It's okay, it's okay. Miss Ella is all bark and no bite." I think on that for a moment and then add, "Actually, sometimes she does bite."

Dakota slices through an avocado. "Dinner should be ready in fifteen. Maybe sooner. Light really does make a difference."

While I set the table, I tell her about my day and then, because I think Matt and Ches are totally done hearing about how suspicious I am of Colleen and because I know Dakota saw her powers firsthand, I say, "Colleen is back."

The knife in her hand clangs to the ground.

I rush to pick it up as she slowly turns to face me. "Back how?"

My arm brushes against hers when I reach to place the knife back on the counter, and a little undeniable shiver races through me. "Sorry. I should have led with a little more context."

She laughs nervously. "Uh, yeah."

"She just showed up at school a few weeks ago," I say. "The story is that she ran away, had some bad experiences, and came home a changed person. I didn't buy any of it, but when I confronted her, she acted like she had no idea what I was talking about. You should have seen her. When I mentioned fire shooting out of her hands, it was like I was talking to a corgi. She was all big eyes and big ears and teeny-tiny brain. It was really convincing. But . . . I mean, do you think that's even possible? That she really doesn't remember?"

Dakota turns back to her guacamole in progress with a shrug. "I don't know. . . . The people that Margaret was in with . . . they were into some real sci-fi shit. I wonder if there's some kind of way to deactivate a psiot."

I shudder at the thought, and yet I can't ignore the curiosity edging along the far corners of my brain. "You think they could do that?" I ask. "And who even is 'they'?"

She shifts to face me, one hip braced against the counter as she mixes all her ingredients in a bowl. "I don't know. That's the problem. It's a hell of a lot easier to hide from someone when you know who they are. Honestly, until Tweedledee and Tweedledum showed up, I thought the only things I needed to be scared of were Margaret and the paparazzi."

"But if you needed to run away from the people Margaret was working for, don't you think they would have . . . killed you already? When they had the chance?"

She places the bowl on the kitchen table, and I grab the rest of the food required to assemble our tacos. "Not if I'm bait," she says plainly. "If Margaret is a loose end for them, then so am I. Which is why I'm leaving first thing in the morning."

My jaw drops, and I can't even attempt to hide my shock. "Already?"

"Faith, we both knew anything more than a night was a gamble. I stayed when you said I could, because . . . because I couldn't leave you yet. I wasn't ready to say goodbye."

"And you're ready now?" I ask, my voice low and serious.

She huffs out a sigh, her eyes darting back and forth, like she might find the answer to all our problems just floating somewhere between us. "No. Of course not. Hell, I don't know if you even forgive me. That alone keeps me up at night."

My lips curl into a slight smile and I lean in closer to her. "Well, it doesn't seem like you've had much trouble sleeping since you've been here."

She rolls her eyes. "It kept me up at night—past tense. And yeah, I'm sleeping better here. Bumble has a yard, and I'm mostly sure that no one knows where I am . . . but I do wonder if you forgive me. I hate that I betrayed you, Faith. It's the biggest regret of my whole life. I've never lo-loved someone like I loved you, and I've also never hurt someone like I hurt you." The torment in her voice is written all over her pained expression.

My tongue feels too big in my mouth and it's impossible to form words. Loved. Dakota loved me. Maybe we weren't in love, but she loved me. I can't decide if there's a difference, but it doesn't matter. All my brain can see in bright neon letters is that word. *L-O-V-E*. But even then—even with the L word on the table—it's not enough for me to get over the havoc she wreaked in my life.

"If you leave, where will you go?" I finally ask.

She gives Bumble a few chunks of tomato. "I hadn't gotten that far yet."

I reach for a tortilla and begin to fill it with all my toppings of choice. "Then you're not leaving," I tell her. "You have no plan. And I don't forgive you, so you can't leave yet."

She looks down at her plate and smiles to herself. Her voice is quiet when she says, "Okay."

We eat dinner and talk about easy things like why restaurant ranch tastes so different from the kind you buy at the grocery store, and which of the animals currently up for adoption at All Paws on Deck are my favorite, and the video about an enclosed outdoor patio for cats I saw earlier that day. It's one of the most normal nights I've had in a very long time, save for the fact that I'm currently harboring a possibly dead/possibly criminal celebrity on the run from the law, the press, and a mystery villain so sinister neither of us even knows who or what they are.

As we're cleaning up, my phone buzzes with a text alert.

Matt: Slumber party at Faith's soon? Rowan's sister said she would buy me some booze if I ever wanted her to. What do you think? Do we want?

Ches: I've never been drunk before.

Matt: No duh. Who else would you ever have gotten drunk with if it wasn't with us?

Ches: I have friends.

Matt: Yeah. Two of them. Count 'em.

Ches: Faaaaaaith? Are you there? Should we do tonight or Saturday?

Matt: *INSERT AUDIBLE GASP* Or should we do both?

Ches: It could be like we're weekend roommates.

Matt: WEEKEND! ROOMMATES!

Ches: College freedom is so close I can taste it.

I told myself I would cross this bridge when I got here and well . . . I'm here. My fingers hover above the screen before I quickly type back.

Faith: Got caught up late at work, but I'll text back later.

Matt: boo

Ches: Weekend roommates, weekend roommates, weekend roommates!

"Everything okay?" Dakota asks as she passes the guacamole.

"Uh, just something I don't feel like dealing with right now."

She smiles. "Okay, then we won't."

I open my mouth to quickly explain that it's just Matt and Ches being extremely extra, but the doorbell startles both of us, and Bumble takes off to greet whoever is waiting there on the other side.

"Go wait at the top of the stairs," I whisper. "Do not move."

Once Dakota is well hidden, I swing open the door to find Miss Ella standing there in her housecoat and what she calls her "outside slippers," which are actually just Crocs.

She holds out a bag of clementines to me. "These have been rolling around my trunk for days. I kept meaning to bring them to you."

"Oh, thanks," I tell her. "My favorite."

I step backward into the house, pushing Bumble back with one hand. "You're gonna need to do something about that dog digging under the fence and into my flower beds," she tells me.

"Oh, I'm so sorry. I'll uh . . . figure something out."

She peers over my shoulder. "You got people over? You know, Lou might not be living at home, but you're still under her roof. I'd hate to tell her you—"

"Oh no," I tell her. "Just listening to . . . the radio!"

She nods, though I can see she's not convinced.

"Hey!" I step back out onto the porch and shut the door behind me. "How about I set up that DVR for you right now?"

"Right now?" she asks, her voice colored with shock, as if nothing appropriate happens past seven o'clock at night.

"I'm free!" I tell her. "And you know what a flake I can be." I made a fake grimacing face.

She waves a hand. "I've been saying so for years."

"Okay, I'll just come over right now and fix the TV for you," I say as loudly as I can so Dakota can hear me.

Miss Ella plugs her ears. "Quit your shoutin' or I'm gonna have to take you to get those ears looked at."

**22**

The three of us—me, Dakota, and Bumble—get into a little routine. The house stays quiet and dark until I get home, which isn't so bad on the days I don't visit Grandma Lou, since the sun sets later and later as we creep into spring.

Dakota cooks dinners. She does laundry. Sometimes even mine. She cleans. She sorts the mail. She makes sense of the piles of papers Grandma Lou left behind. She bathes Bumble, who chomps at the suds but is scared of the actual running water. Slowly and somehow all at once, we've morphed into a unit. It's a version of us that only ever existed in my wildest dreams. The only thing missing is a good-night kiss, but I don't think I could handle that. Heck, I'm really conflicted over the fact that I think about it every single night when Dakota smiles at me and that dimple flashes in her cheek.

Before I know it, a week has passed and it's Friday night. Dakota and I are sitting on the couch together. I managed to get out of hosting an adult-free sleepover with Ches and Matt last weekend by claiming I didn't feel well. They bought it. Barely. And I had to ham it up more than I really wanted to.

I hate that, after everything, I'm back where I started: keeping secrets from my best friends.

But I remind myself that it's temporary. And important. Really, super important.

"Thanks for getting that seed bread I like," Dakota says, pulling me out of my morose thoughts.

"No problem. Is there anything else you need? Like . . . not grocery stuff? Clothes or anything?"

She shrugs. "It's not like I'm going to be needing an outfit for prom or anything."

"I still can't believe Colleen was nominated for prom queen." It's only been a week, but it doesn't make any more sense today than it did at the pep rally.

"It's like something straight out of *Carrie*," she says. "Except I think the joke's going to be on everyone else."

"You think she could really be up to something?" I ask. My suspicions haven't gone anywhere, but it's hard to be suspicious when the suspect appears to be utterly normal. As in, the kind of person *without* superpowers.

"Who knows?" Dakota shakes her head and runs her hand through a tuft of hair. "If Margaret Toliver were writing this story, something big would happen at prom. But it wouldn't be what you expect. You might think you'd know and then *bam*, she'd do something spectacular."

Dakota smiles at some private memory, but it turns sad so swiftly I feel a little ache in my heart.

A breeze pushes through the open windows, ruffling the curtains we've been careful to keep drawn. The air is almost balmy as it brushes at our cheeks and bare toes. The quiet chittering of bugs and rumbling cars in the distance are just enough that the growing silence between us is a little less unbearable.

"Do you miss her?" My voice is soft, and for a moment, I worry she didn't hear me.

Then she sighs and does a thing with her head that's not quite a nod and not quite a shake. "I've spent a lot of time thinking about that. Margaret was the closest thing to a stable parent I had, and for a while, I really needed that. I needed her. She was really good to me, and even if she was doing it for nefarious reasons, it still helped me. For a little while, at least."

I love that Dakota uses words like *nefarious* in casual conversation. Like it's a word anyone might keep in their back pocket.

"Do you think she always knew it would end this way, though?" I ask. "Do you think she wanted to protect you and just couldn't figure out how?"

She scratches Bumble's belly until she rolls over, all four paws in the air. "I think that when Margaret found me, she had a little-sister-shaped hole in her heart that I fit right inside. I was a surrogate for someone she'd lost, but I do think she loved me in her own way. Then again, how much of the good we do for other people is for us and how much is truly for them?"

That's a question that makes me uneasy. Not that I have some huge superhero track record, but so many of my actions ultimately feel selfish. When I've saved someone or intervened in a dangerous situation, it's almost always because the thought of standing by and doing nothing makes me feel unbearably guilty. And that doesn't make me feel good exactly. More like . . . just not bad.

"Maybe it doesn't always matter," I say softly. "Maybe what really matters is that good was done and someone is better for it."

"I like that." Dakota shifts in her seat, her thigh brushing mine, and Bumble flops into her lap.

My tummy pitches and all I can think about are her lips and the day we sat in her car, snow falling all around us as we kissed for the first time. That moment is a lifetime away. We were two entirely different people. But now here we are again. Changed in many ways, and yet I still feel just as breathless and light-headed as I did that day.

"I should go to bed," she says.

I nod cluelessly for a moment, and then look around as I realize— "Oh, right, this is your bed. We're in bed together."

Well, that didn't come out how I meant for it to.

We briefly entertained the idea of moving her into Grandma Lou's room, but we made it as far as the door before we both wordlessly turned around. It just felt too weird. And I have to admit, it means a lot that it felt just as weird to Dakota as it did to me.

"You can stay and watch television," she says. "I'm just going to close my eyes."

I stand up. "I'll let you get some sleep without a TV blaring in the background."

Bumble whines as she realizes she can no longer use my leg as a snout pillow.

I give the dog a quick kiss on the forehead.

Dakota eyes her. "Lucky dog."

My cheeks flare with warmth and my brain short-circuits. "I like dogs."

Dakota laughs, tucking her feet up onto the sofa and dragging a blanket over them. "Good night, Faith."

The sound of her voice wishing me good night dances in my head until I drift asleep, and I feel so light that my body even begins to hover an inch off my bed. Like I'm buzzing with contentment. I think I might like the thought of her voice being the last thing I hear at night a little too much.

On Saturday afternoon, Mrs. Delgado drops off her tomato soup and fresh grilled cheese sandwiches, which makes me feel completely guilty. But it only lasts until Dakota and I pull apart the sandwiches and are rewarded by stretchy, cheesy goodness.

Sunday afternoon, Matt FaceTimes me from the Bean, with Ches and Rowan waving in the background. He deems me healthy enough for an excursion and threatens me with a home visit if I don't get my ass over there pronto.

I grudgingly agree, and even though it's only been two days since I've left the house, my eyes burn a little from the natural light.

Inside the Bean, the three of them are waiting for me with a frozen hot chocolate and a croissant. I can't complain, and suddenly it's hard to remember why I didn't want to leave the house. (As if it has something to do with the girl sleeping on my couch.)

"There she is!" Ches says as she pulls me down on the love seat beside her.

Matt shakes his head. "You have a whole adult-free house to yourself, and what do you do? You get the sniffles and go to bed early."

Rowan shakes his head. "Adult life comes at you fast. Before you know it, you'll be paying for car insurance and googling coupon codes."

"That sounds so depressing. I thought there was supposed to be some kind of cushion between high school graduation and full-blown adulthood," Matt says.

Ches snorts. "Yeah, I wouldn't worry, Matt. You're a mama's boy. Your cushion is so thick it's a swanky hotel pillow-top mattress."

Matt shrugs. "I am a very light sleeper."

"There's no shame in parental goodwill," Rowan says, resting his chin on Matt's shoulder. "Plus, you're an only child. I'm the youngest. By the time my parents got to me, it was like, 'Here's an old lunch box and twenty bucks. Good luck out there, kid!'"

Matt smiles at him. "You and your lunch box are very cute."

We spend the afternoon gathered around this little table, putting together a puzzle only to discover it's missing at least fifteen pieces. It's the first time we've all hung out with Rowan, and I'm surprised at how natural it all feels. Like Rowan was always a missing piece of our friendship puzzle.

We decide there's no real point in searching for the missing pieces, and I head up to the front for more fancy, frothy drinks for the four of us. The girl behind the counter looks at me expectantly while I peruse the menu.

"I know for sure I'll take two chai lattes, a caramel Frappuccino, and . . . what's your favorite iced tea?"

She sighs. "I guess, like, a fruity one."

The other barista spins in circles behind her, prepping drinks as she steams milk with one hand and closes the door to the ice maker with her foot. "The guava," she says with confidence. "It's got flavor without being too sweet."

A smooth peal of laughter drifts to my ear and my jaw drops. That voice. I know that voice. I lift my gaze and there, just on the other side of the counter, sits Colleen Bristow. And right beside her is the last person I expect to see here: Benji Aldrich.

I duck down instinctively. If they can't see me, then I can't see them, right?

Except everyone else can see the weirdo playing hit the deck in the middle of a coffee shop.

"So, the guava then?" the girl behind the register asks, waiting for me to use my mouth to make words.

"Are you okay?" the drink-prepping master barista asks.

And then I hear Benji's voice. It travels, in fact, as he walks over to the bulletin board on the wall only a few feet away. My heart hammers in my chest as he skims the board, then tears a tab off a flyer before heading down the hallway toward the restrooms.

Once he's out of sight, I stand a little straighter. I don't even know why I'm hiding, but something about seeing the two of them together feels off.

"I'm sorry. What did you say?" I ask.

The barista's patience is impressive. "I said, are you okay?"

"Sorry, yeah, just spaced out for a sec. Let's go with the guava. I trust the professionals."

Colleen sits with her back to the rest of the coffee shop, head tipped toward the phone in her hand, as she waits for Benji's return. A thick dread settles in my lungs. In fandom, Colleen and Benji would be considered a rarepair. Two people who never appear in the same scenes together because there's absolutely no reason for them to. But here they are. Existing together. And my mind is racing with suspicious thoughts. Mostly that between the two of them, they know both my biggest secrets and what makes me most vulnerable.

I hover behind the bar with all the sugar, cream, and lids and tilt my head down when Benji reappears. At that moment, the drink-making barista expertly carries all four cups over and places them on the counter for me. "Two chais, a caramel Frap, and a guava on ice coming up for Fa—"

"Thank you," I sing as I attempt to mimic her smooth barista moves and pick up all four drinks at once, but I'm wobbly at best.

"You need help with that?" she asks. Her name tag has only an upside-down smiley face, which is a little bit adorable.

"I think I've got it," I say, sounding like someone who absolutely does not got it.

I move at the pace of a snail across the coffeehouse, weaving through people and furniture as I attempt to stay out of Benji's and Colleen's line of sight.

Ches hops up to meet me. "I'm sorry," she says, "but did

I just witness little Faith Herbert flirting with that barista?"

"Uh, excuse me?" Matt chimes in, reaching for his latte. "Did I just hear something about you and a cute barista?"

"It wasn't like that," I say quickly.

"Well then, please explain what exactly it was like," Matt says as I sit back down.

And then I almost tell them how Benji and Colleen are sitting right over there—*together*—and how I have a very awful, dreadful feeling about anything the two of them could be discussing . . . but then my gaze lands on Rowan— who I like. I swear! But I don't know Rowan. Spilling my outlandish theories about Colleen and now Benji . . . Oh, and by the way, I can fly. I'm definitely not ready for that. And I don't think Rowan is either.

"Okay," I say. "It was sort of like that."

Matt shrieks and Rowan ducks his head in embarrassment. "My little baby Faith making rebound moves."

"Rebound, huh?" Rowan asks. "Oh, from . . . ?"

"Prom's coming up," I quickly say before anyone can acknowledge his blessedly unvocalized query. "I just . . . I don't want to fly solo."

"You won't fly solo," Ches says knowingly. "You never fly solo. Besides, I don't even have a date or a prospect of a date. We'll fly duo!"

"Make that trio," Matt adds. "Though I am definitely in the 'has a date but they're officially too cool for school' column."

Rowan shrugs, leaning back with a satisfied expression on his face. "As long as you wear a name tag that says 'Taken.'"

I roll my eyes. "I'm not sure that counts. And don't even act like you won't be able to land a date with a snap of your fingers, Ches. Honestly, I feel like you've always got at least three people crushing on you at any given time."

"What can I say?" Ches asks. "I have highly desirable energy."

We spend a while longer there, Ches elbowing me in the side every time the upside-down-smiley-face barista passes us or buses a table. We both go to the bathroom and return, and by the time I scan the seating area again, Benji and Colleen are gone.

Rowan and Matt, however, are involved in a light daytime make-out session, which I am both charmed and grossed out by. Ches and I break out in a mad fit of giggles at the sight of them, and Rowan grins.

A sigh sings through my chest. They're so cute it hurts.

Matt stands, pulling Rowan up with him. "Ladies, I think that's our cue."

Ches lets out a low whistle as the two of them leave, coiled tightly together like two cats so inseparable you can't tell where one begins and the other ends.

After Ches and I finish our drinks, I hover at the bulletin board for a moment before finding exactly what Benji was looking at. There's really only one option. A flyer featuring a giant blue llama singing into a microphone, with golden rays flaring out behind. The text reads: *Blue Llama Open Mic Night*. Below it, a few tabs with the website and social media handle remain. It's not even a little bit nefarious-looking, but now that Benji is a known associate of Colleen, if he's interested, I'm interested.

I tear off one of the info tabs and stuff it into my pocket before running to catch up with Ches.

 **23**

When I get home, I walk in to find a completely silent house. All the blinds are shut, the curtains drawn, and Dakota is dancing around with her eyes closed while Bumble weaves in and out of her legs.

Dakota has her earbuds in, and I have no idea what she's listening to, but it doesn't matter. I watch for a moment, letting myself imagine what it might feel like to come home and find this every single day.

Bumble gives me away, of course. She darts over and Dakota opens her eyes, gasping in surprise. Her tawny cheeks flush a rosy pink.

"Don't mind me," I tell her as I lock the door behind me. "What were you listening to?"

She holds an earbud out for me, so I maneuver past Bumble and take it. Taylor Swift's "Blank Space" blares on the other end.

"A classic!" I say, letting my head bob to the beat.

She giggles, but I can only half hear her.

"What?" I ask.

She presses a finger to my lips.

"Oh!" I laugh—quietly, I hope.

She hooks her pinky with my index finger, and soon the two of us are swaying to Taylor Swift, and it's already the kind of memory I can feel myself clinging to. A kind of joy I haven't felt in a long time swells in my chest as my feet begin to hover an inch or two off the ground. Not only that, but Dakota is right there with me.

She looks around a little frantically and then down at her feet as they graze the ground. "Are you—are we—"

I grip her hand tighter and grin. "Yeah."

The next morning, I text Ches as I pull up to Matt's house: I'm here.

Ches: Thank goddess. Matt is about to explode. Have you heard from Rowan? The plan is still on, right?

Faith: The plan is a go.

Moments later Ches walks out the front door, and a grumpy Matt isn't far behind.

"Good morning, sunshine," I say as he slumps down in the passenger seat.

"Sunshine might be a stretch," Ches says.

"Stop treating me like I'm in a mood," Matt says.

"But you are in a mood," Ches tells him.

Matt angrily buckles his seat belt, practically stabbing the buckle into place. "I just don't understand how keys disappear. They don't have legs! They don't have a mind of their own!"

"They'll show up," I tell him. "And I have Grandma Lou's car now, so it's no big deal."

"We could've just flown to school," Ches teases.

"Yeah, maybe I should request a landing pad in the student parking lot." I turn out of Matt's neighborhood and try to drive casually enough that he won't notice I'm going the long way.

"Don't any of your X-Men friends have, like, metal-detecting superpowers?" Matt asks.

I laugh. "Um, sadly, there's no local support group for fellow psiots, and there's definitely no online registry of powers."

"Which way are we taking?" Matt asks as he 100 percent notices that I'm driving the long way.

"I need to get gas," I tell him.

He peers over my shoulder. "You have a quarter tank left and school is three miles from my house."

"Uh . . ." He does have a point.

"You know what a control freak our sweet little Faith is," Ches chimes in.

"This is just going to take so much longer," he grumbles.

In the back seat behind me, Ches gives me big eyes and a very subtle shake of her head, then texts furiously.

Great. I need to stall, and Matt is already grumpy about it.

I stop at a light just as it turns yellow to buy us a little more time.

"You totally could have made that," Matt complains.

"Safety first, Matthew James Delgado."

He gasps. "Oh my God. Speaking of my full name, my mom saw the tattoo and flipped out. I panicked and told her it was henna and that it would fade in a few weeks."

"Uh, what happens when it doesn't fade?" asks Ches. She catches my eye in the rearview mirror and gives me a discreet thumbs-up after checking her phone once more.

The light turns green, and I head toward the railroad bridge instead of turning toward the gas station.

Simultaneously, Matt's phone rings. "Rowan? He's never up before ten." He answers on speakerphone. "Is everything okay? You hate mornings."

"I really do," Rowan says. "Look up."

"Huh?" Matt says.

And then I stop right there in the middle of the road with the Hamilton Street railroad bridge just a few yards ahead of us. Someone behind me honks as a massive white sheet unfurls from the bridge.

"Well?" Rowan asks.

The sun couldn't have been in a more perfect position.

It blazes in the sky behind us, illuminating the sheet that in huge black letters reads: *PROM?*

Matt shrieks and jumps out of the car.

Ches and I unroll our windows to listen in as the car behind me passes by, the driver flashing us the finger.

"They're having a moment!" Ches screams.

"You want to go to prom?" Matt yells up to Rowan. "With me?"

"Well, I don't want to go with anyone else," Rowan shouts.

Matt holds his hands to his chest, and I think there was never and will never be a more perfect Romeo and Juliet moment in all of Glenwood history. "But . . . but you're done with high school. I didn't think you'd want to go back for prom . . . again."

"You have to go to your prom," Rowan says, the sheet waving awkwardly up into his face. "And there's no way I'm letting you go with someone else. Plus, my prom sucked. I want a redo."

"You do?" asks Matt.

"They're so damn cute it's unfair," Ches says.

"I know. Totally unfair," I agree, my voice dreamy.

"So?" Rowan asks. "What do you say?"

"Oh my God, yes! Of course!" Matt looks around for a way to get up to where Rowan is. "I just want to kiss you, you doofus."

Rowan laughs and runs around the side of the bridge, where he has to carefully step down the gravel hill. "I didn't really think this through," he says as he loses his footing and slides down the rest of the way.

Matt runs to meet him and helps him to his feet, and Rowan sweeps the sheet over their shoulders, creating a promposal cocoon as their lips collide.

Yearning stirs in my chest, and I find myself wishing for a moment like this. Something so simple it's complex.

24

According to the Blue Llama Studio's latest Instagram post, tonight they're hosting a new-artist open mic night in their parking lot, and I decide it's the perfect time to sleuth around.

"Remind me again why we can't take your car?" Dakota asks as we stand in the backyard.

"It's simple," I say. "Miss Ella sits in her front room watching the news until ten o'clock at night. If she sees me leave this late on a Monday night, I'm going to have questions to answer, and the only thing scarier than Margaret's mystery boss is a litany of questions from Miss Ella. She already thinks something's up. She swears she saw someone in my garage yesterday, and now she's got the neighborhood watch patrolling our street three times as much as normal."

"I didn't know neighborhood watches were a real thing."

"They are a very real thing. A weapon in the wrong

hands. And Miss Ella knows exactly how to use it." I hold my hand out. "I promise this will be safe."

"So, you're just going to drag me along?" she asks. "Through the air?"

"Yes," I say. "But no. Or at least it won't feel like that."

"How do you know what it feels like? You're the one who can fly." She considers my hand and then takes it quickly, like she might change her mind if she doesn't act fast. "What does Ches say it feels like?"

I clear my throat, trying to get my brain to jump over the mental hurdle of Dakota's hand in mine. "Well, I haven't exactly tried this with . . . anyone else."

She drops my hand like it's the Infinity Gauntlet or something. "Did you just say you've never done this before?" She turns to walk back inside. "This is a bad idea. I can't believe it took the thought of plummeting to my second untimely death to realize that."

"No, no, no. Wait! Dakota. Wait," I beg. "Even you admitted something was fishy with Colleen and Benji. It doesn't make any sense that they would know each other, and I wish you could see Colleen at school. It's like she has everyone there under some kind of spell." When I told Dakota where I was going tonight, she demanded to come with me. I just forgot to include how exactly we would be getting there.

She turns back to me. Behind her, Bumble watches from the back door, waiting for us to either play with her or come inside for a cuddle. "Just please don't drop me."

"I've carried plenty of things in my force field," I say. "And I've had a lot of time to practice. I'm so much better at all this than I was even a month ago. It'll be just like it was in the kitchen the other night. Only easier, honestly. It takes way more control to hover like that than it does to really fly."

"Are you sure?" she asks. "Are you sure you can carry me?"

I nod. "I'm positive. If I thought there was any chance that I'd drop you, I would never, ever do this. I swear. Do you trust me?"

She steps forward and takes my hand, a vein in her temple twitching. "I trust you."

I pull her a little closer and slowly rise from the ground.

Dakota doesn't take her eyes off mine. She opens her mouth to say something, but the only thing that comes out is a soft gasp as her feet float an inch, then two, above the grass. At first, it's no different from our little dance session; then, suddenly, it's so much more.

The ground drops away and the houses slip past our peripheral vision, then it's all air and sky and that fluttering feeling in my tummy.

"I'm flying," she whispers, disbelieving. "How is it possible that I'm flying?"

"This is nothing," I tell her with a devilish grin. "Wanna see what it really means to fly?"

She nods and immediately lets out a squeal of delight as we accelerate, driving up into clouds painted in twilight, lilac and gold and cotton-candy pink. I take us higher and faster, letting the wind rip the laughter from our lips as we soar into a sky of our very own.

Dakota's eyes are wide as she takes in the smallness of the world beneath us. "It looks like we're in a plane," she yells. "But—but we're not."

"It's wild," I say, pulling her along for a little side roll. I wasn't about to take my first willing passenger without showing off.

Dakota shrieks like she's on the downhill of the biggest roller coaster of her life.

"How are you not addicted to this?" she asks. "I would fly everywhere. Think of all the places you could see, Faith!"

For a moment, I'm overwhelmed by a feeling of possibility. It's the same thing I felt when I dove off that building to save Peter's life and flew for the first time. I can *fly*. And once upon a time that made the whole world feel so much closer. It's a feeling I left behind when I realized that my future was here. With Grandma Lou.

But here it is again. Surging through Dakota and into me. My life doesn't have to be defined by one thing. A stubborn restlessness burrows down inside me. There's a whole world out there for me to explore. A world full of people like Dakota and Matt and Ches and Grandma Lou. People who might need someone who can watch over them. Someone who can see evil coming.

"Wait. Hang on a second," Dakota says as she digs into her backpack.

We stand on a dark street lined with dilapidated buildings and every single window shattered. Definitely not Glenwood's finest, but also a good place for us to land out of sight.

Dakota fishes out the long pink wig I used for my Rose Quartz cosplay from *Steven Universe* a few years ago. She tugs it over her hair, and I can't help myself from straightening it as best as I can, lining up the part and smoothing out the mermaid waves.

"You look good in pink," I tell her. She wears her usual black jeans and leather jacket, and even though the outfit is very Dakota, the hair transforms her entirely. "I barely recognize you."

"I'll take that as a compliment." She zips up her backpack, the sound of it unusually loud on the quiet street. "How do girls with long hair do it? I feel like I'm wearing a cape of sweat."

"That's pretty much how we do it. Sweat until our hair is a cape. Made of sweat."

In the parking lot of Blue Llama Studio, their new-artist open mic turns out to also be a weed farmers' market. The air is thick with the vaguely sweet smoke, and I lose count of the number of hemp T-shirts that go by.

"I didn't realize the Midwest went this hard for weed," Dakota says.

"Is it really that surprising?" I ask. "You ran an entire underground designer drug ring in this town for months."

She considers that for a moment. "No, I guess it's not surprising after all."

We circulate through the crowd of suburban hippies and hipsters, slowly making our way toward the stage at the far end.

"I didn't know Glenwood had this level of weird in it," Dakota says as we walk past someone taking aura photos at a little table sandwiched between a vegan bakery booth and a Church of Satan information booth, where a bored girl sits, twirling gum around her index finger and wearing a shirt that reads, Ask Me About My Lord and Savior, Satan.

"I feel a little bit bad about not inviting Ches. This is exactly her scene," I say.

"She strikes me more as a witchy free spirit than a devout member of the Church of Satan," Dakota says.

"You're right." That doesn't stop me from swiping a pamphlet off the table. "But I better take one just in case."

The girl smiles at us. "Let me know if you have any questions," she says, her voice sounding a little fried.

The crowd thickens the closer we get to the stage, and

Dakota takes my hand. I try not to read into it, but I'm definitely reading into it.

"Excuse me," I say cheerfully, nudging us closer to the official sign-up table near the stage. "Excuse us. Sorry, sorry! Thank you."

A tall white guy with a long, thin beard twisted into a braid stands behind the table, drumming his pen against a clipboard and bobbing his head along to the trio of screaming guys onstage.

"Hey!" I shout over the music.

"Hey, ladies." He nods to us. "Sign-ups are closed for the night, but I can put you on a waiting list in case someone, like, backs out or gets too drunk to perform."

I lean in over the table. "Um, actually, we were looking for someone." I hold a hand up a few inches above my head. "A guy about this tall. Curly blond hair. His name is Benji."

He examines us lazily, his gaze lingering on Dakota for a moment too long. Instinctively, I take her hand again. I don't want him to recognize her or think that either of us is in the market for . . . him.

"Uh, I'm not like a lost and found for people, but you could check inside the studio, I guess. Stew should be in there," he finally says. "Just tell them the Brockster sent you."

"Cool," Dakota says. "I really love when people refer to themselves in the third person."

"Third person?" he asks, still shouting over the music. "Like, y'all are looking for a third person to join you?"

We shake our heads aggressively, unable to hide our expressions of disgust.

"Um, no thank you!" I call as Dakota yanks me away, moving as fast and as far from the Brockster as we can get.

"Woof," Dakota says, gagging on the word. "That guy was gross." She shakes her head and rolls her shoulders back, like she might just be able to rid herself of that interaction. "What are you even hoping to find here?" she asks.

"I don't know. I thought if Benji was here, maybe Colleen would be too, and I could figure out what they're up to together." I shrug. "Come on. Let's find Stew."

She follows me back through the crowd as the screaming trio wraps up their song and the MC for the night, a tall, slender East Asian girl in platformed thigh-high boots, retakes the stage.

"That was Three Unwise Men," she says. "Now let's give it up for . . . Benji?" She checks her paper. "Just Benji?"

And sure enough, Benji gives her two thumbs-up from the side of the stage. He's wearing a white T-shirt and faded jeans, his blond curls artfully disheveled.

"That's him," I tell Dakota.

"The kid with the guitar?" she asks.

I nod as Benji perches on the edge of a stool, cradling an acoustic guitar.

"You don't think he's a psiot, do you?" Dakota asks.

"I guess he could be. I guess anyone could be."

He pulls the mic closer. "Uh, this is a slowed-down cover of, um, Kelly Clarkson's 'Since U Been Gone.'"

"I don't know," I mumble softly. I listen, a little hypnotized, as he plays the opening chords, the crowd still rumbling with conversation and distracted energy. *What secrets are you keeping, Benji?*

And then he hits the chorus, and I find myself singing along, and I'm not the only one.

Dakota watches me, a sad smile on her face, and I think she knows. I think she knows that for me, this total Kelly Clarkson blast from the past is about her. I fell so hard, so fast for Dakota, and I don't know if she realizes what a gaping hole she left in my life.

As Benji plays the last few chords, Dakota tugs at my fingers with a gasp. "I see Colleen. She just went inside the studio!"

That snaps me out of my haze. "What? You saw her? Let's go."

Benji stands and takes a quick bow, his charming smile absolutely sparkling as this crowd of oddballs whoops and hollers for him.

We weave through the audience until the sea of bodies thins. Dakota and I duck inside the studio. My whole body is tense and ready for whatever is waiting there on the other side of the door, but all we find is a white girl with thick-rimmed black glasses and a short lavender bob sitting at the receptionist desk.

Behind her, in an office chair, a Black guy in jeans, suspenders, and a bow tie sits with his hand hovering over a mouse, his eyes locked to the huge curved computer screen on the desk.

"Stew?" I ask him.

"I'm Stew," the girl says. "That's Jensen."

"Oh." I turn to her, surprised. "I just thought . . ."

"Stephanie Ewing," she says. "Stew for short."

I nod. "Right. Well, I'm . . . Louisa." It's not a total lie if it's my grandma's name, right? "And this is . . ."

"Ashley," Dakota says.

"We were actually just looking for our friend who came in here to find the bathroom. Long brown hair. Shorter than us."

Stew sits up a little straighter and rolls her shoulders back, and I can tell that people might underestimate her, but this woman is all business. "We're the only people in here."

Jensen shakes his head. "And we don't have any public bathrooms."

Dakota reaches into her bag and slaps five twenty-dollar bills on the desk. "Have you seen our friend now?" she asks.

My jaw drops along with Stew's and Jensen's. This was not part of the plan.

"Are you guys, like, drug dealers?" Stew asks.

I have to stop myself from laughing. She's closer than she knows.

From outside, the crowd roars, and Jensen stands up to look between the blinds and investigate. "Uh, Stew . . ."

"Fire!" someone screams from outside. "Fire!"

 **25**

"Oh shit!" Dakota says, sweeping the money away.

Stew runs over to the door, fidgeting with the doorknob for a moment too long.

"Stew!" Jensen yells frantically. "Not the time for butterfingers, my friend."

"That isn't helpful." She finally gets it and rips the door open. All four of us fall out of the building like dominoes.

Stew darts into the crowd. "Brock!" she screams. "Somebody call 911!"

I smell the smoke instantly. Sharp and acrid in the back of my throat. So familiar that for an instant I forget to breathe. I can't tell where it's coming from. There's a haze in the air. It could be coming from anywhere.

"We gotta get out of here," Dakota says, tugging on my wrist.

Jensen doubles back. "Still looking for your friend?"

Dakota yanks her backpack around and hands him a stack of cash. "Where'd she go?"

Behind him the Church of Satan girl walks way too calmly to her car on the other side of the street, while others sit on the curb to split a joint, and some, the more sensible of the crowd, flee entirely.

Jensen shoves the stack of twenties into his front pocket. "Some girl came in through the lobby just before you came in, but she cut straight past us to the alleyway. We tried to ask her what the hell she was doing, but she wouldn't even look at us. I think it was the girl you're after. Pretty, brown hair pulled back, on the short side."

"That's it?" I ask.

He shrugs with a coy smile as he backpedals toward the sidewalk. "I didn't say I had a lot of information."

I realize I should have seen this coming. I didn't. But I definitely should have.

"Thanks," I mutter.

Dakota takes my hand again with renewed determination. "Come on. We need to get out of here."

I look around once more, reluctant to leave if there's something I can do to help, but wherever the fire is, it's not actually close enough to create real panic. Just a moderate amount of chaos.

Dakota and I jog down the street in the opposite direction of the sirens. Neither of us wants to get caught up in official police business, but Dakota really *can't*. Only when the crowds have thinned and the sirens are firmly in our wake does she rip off her wig and stuff it in her backpack. "Ready for takeoff?" Her eyes betray her nerves, and I realize just how alarming this has been for her.

I nod and take her hand, shooting off the ground without warning. This time, she doesn't make a sound, but her hands cinch around mine like a vise as we rise high above any source of light to take cover in the velvety darkness of the night sky.

When I'm sure we're high enough that we won't risk being seen, I circle back toward Blue Llama Studio. "Thank goodness," I say with a sigh. The source of the fire is an old auto body shop behind the studio, and although I'm too high up to say for sure, the damage looks mild. Superficial, even.

We glide over the efforts of the Glenwood Fire Department, watching silently as the flames die beneath streams of water. It could have been an accident, but how many accidental fires can one person really witness in a lifetime? Much less a single school year.

Then, in the distance, angry red flames shoot up against the night sky.

"Did you see that?" I ask Dakota over the howling wind.

"Did I see wha—"

"Right there!" I point to another burst of flame in the exact same spot.

Without giving it a second thought, I push forward and swoop down to coast along the rooflines. It's trickier to fly like this, especially with another person in tow, but it's better than diving down in plain sight.

A third flame appears. It slashes bright orange against the black sky and vanishes again just as quickly, leaving a sharp, smoky scent behind. But nothing appears to be on fire. And that makes my skin prickle with cold sweat.

"Faith, where are we going?" Dakota asks warily.

I pull her closer and set us down carefully on top of a building. "I need you to wait for me here," I say as gently as I can.

Flames appear again, blazing for several seconds before they go out. It's as if they're being fired at a specific target. As if they are attacking something.

Or someone.

Dakota shakes her head and yanks me back. "Faith, if that's who I think it is, we should just keep on going."

"You know I can't do that," I say. "Stay here. Promise me you will stay here."

She looks around frantically. "We're on the roof of a four-story building. You're not exactly giving me a choice about that!"

"I'm sorry," I say, and I mean it. "But I have to look. If it is her . . ."

"Then what?" Dakota demands. "She's dangerous, Faith.

And I mean this in the most supportive way possible, but she's stronger than you are. You fly and you're amazing and wonderful, but you can't shoot fire from your fingertips or lightning from your eyeballs."

She's not wrong. I've spent plenty of hours thinking about how not wrong she is, but the fact still remains: I have powers that other people don't, and how I use them matters.

"What if someone's down there, Dakota?"

"I—" She stops. Another burst of flame draws her gaze, and her eyes fix on the spot, shoulders slumping in defeat. "I hate that I can't help you with this," she murmurs.

"You help me by staying here," I explain. "Do. Not. Move. Promise me you will not leave." I swear I'm having some real déjà vu here. "You have to promise me."

And she is too. "Okay," she finally says. "I promise." She steps forward and gives me the slightest brush of a kiss on the cheek. "Fly high. Fly fast."

The feel of her lips on my skin sends a flurry of butterflies fluttering through my stomach and into my lungs, but I take a deep breath and swallow it all down as I take a running leap off the ledge of the building and fly straight toward another explosion of flames.

I spot the source immediately. Standing in the alleyway below me is Colleen. She wears all black, and her hair is smoothed back into a severe bun. Flames sparkle in her light brown eyes, and her mouth is fixed in a hard line. She's not afraid or cowering, not half out of her mind or bewildered by anger. She stalks forward with confidence, eyes trained on her goal. This is no longer a girl overwhelmed by the power possessing her, and yet, there's no way this is the same girl I've passed in the hallways at school lately. This is a version of Colleen who understands exactly what she's capable of.

I slow my approach and lower myself behind her as quietly as possible, careful to keep myself several feet from the ground. From here, I can see what she sees, a silhouette diving behind a dumpster as she closes in, and I realize exactly what's happening: she's hunting someone.

Colleen opens her hands and flames shoot from her palms, burning a hole in one side of the dumpster. Her victim doubles back, and I catch sight of their face in the slashes of firelight flickering through the alley.

It's a miracle that I don't gasp out loud when my substitute journalism teacher looks straight at me as I hover six feet from the ground.

Flames erupt in the corner of my eye, and this time, they're aimed at me. I duck just in time, dropping down into the alley. "Liam! Go!" I shout, crouching down low.

Liam's eyes dart from me to Colleen, chin quivering with silent fear, body utterly, frustratingly frozen in place.

"Go!" I scream again as Colleen lets more fire rip in my direction.

I shoot upward. Warmth licks at my toes, and I'm

reasonably sure the soles of my shoes get a little melty. I arc around and hover so that I'm between Colleen and Liam. And yes, I know it's not the greatest plan, but it's all I've got at the moment. That and my stellar wit.

"Colleen, stop," I say.

"I don't want to hurt you, Faith." Colleen's voice is just as transformed as the rest of her. Measured and sure, with no hint of the shy girl she was, or even the popular girl she's become. "This is between me and him."

"Go!" I yell again over my shoulder.

Something clatters to the ground as Liam makes a run for it.

I spy a cluster of trash cans on one side of the alley, and in an instant I flex my force field, letting it expand outward so quickly it flings across the alleyway into Colleen. She flies back, momentarily lost in a sea of trash.

"Faith—what—" Liam stutters in complete confusion.

I turn to face him for just a second. It's all I can afford while Colleen recovers. "Do you want to live or die?" I ask sharply.

"I . . . live," he answers.

"Great. Questions later. Running now."

For a second, I actually think he's going to ask me another question. Then his eyes land on Colleen and he sprints in the opposite direction.

"That was the wrong move." Colleen's voice slinks

through the dark alley, and this time I'm pretty sure I hear a hint of the madness I remember from the old mill. "But you're always getting mixed up in things you shouldn't, aren't you?"

I flick a wrist in the direction of the smoldering dumpster, letting my force field scoop around it like a lacrosse stick.

"I never wanted to hurt you, Colleen," I say. "But I can't let you just come back here and terrorize this town and everyone in it."

Lifting something this heavy isn't the sort of thing I get to practice regularly, and every muscle in my body strains against its massive weight as I attempt to lift it without drawing Colleen's attention.

"You have no idea," Colleen says, voice quivering. "You don't have a clue what you're doing."

She raises her hands, and I swear I see the heat building in the cradle of her fingers.

"I'm sorry, okay!" I shake my head and raise the dumpster as high as I can. "I'm sorry all this happened to you. I'm sorry I didn't see you at the Harbinger Foundation." Last summer when I was at the Harbinger Foundation being activated against my will, I was so caught up in what was happening to me and what felt like a huge mistake that I barely even noticed any of the other kids who had been conned into going there—including Colleen. "I'm sorry you've had so many shitty people in your life," I continue. "But you can't take it out on Glenwood. I won't let you. So enough already with all your creepy little fires and whatever you have planned for prom. Leave. Now, you can walk out of this alley or we can see what happens when I drop this hunk of metal on top of you."

"You think I care about prom?!" She releases a feral laugh as flames shoot from her hands, arcing over my shoulder. I turn back to see Liam Hollis dodging just in time.

"I'm sorry," he yells. "I couldn't just leave you!"

Silently, I curse toxic masculinity for dragging this sweet, stupid man back to help me. If he gets both of us killed, I will do all that cursing and more out loud, I swear.

Colleen screams again, only this time, it's not just a scream. It's an attack.

Glass shatters in the buildings around us and my ears ring painfully. I don't even think before flinging the dumpster straight at Colleen. A guttural scream tears through my lungs as the huge hunk of metal crushes Colleen against the wall. Crumbling bricks and dust rain down around me, and when they settle, the alley is completely silent.

"Colleen?" I call in a tiny voice.

I fly over to where Colleen's body should be flattened against the wall, and even though I don't regret stopping her, I really hope I haven't killed her. But between the dumpster and the wall is just crumbling brick.

"Colleen?" I ask again, this time urgently. But again, she doesn't answer.

"Faith?" Dakota's voice calls from afar.

I want to let her know I'm okay, but I can't leave yet. I head to the end of the alley and look both ways. Thankfully, the street is empty save for Liam "Sweet but Stupid" Hollis, slumped against his Dodge Charger. He moans, head rocking back and forth just enough that I know he's okay.

"Is that thing gone?" he asks, raising a hand to his head. "What was that even? Who just carries a giant blowtorch around?"

I almost smile. That is definitely not what I thought he was going to take away from this moment, but I'm glad to see his brain is going with the possible explanations rather than the impossible. Like a flying fat girl hurling dumpsters through the air.

"Are you hurt?" I ask. "Are you okay?"

He looks a little shaken but nods. "I've, uh, I've been through worse," he mutters, but I'm not convinced he believes it.

"Faith?" Dakota's voice is louder now.

"Mr. Hollis . . . Liam, I mean, I've gotta go, but are you okay to drive home?"

He nods. "My car . . . it's just around the corner."

"It's right behind you," I say gently. "You're sure you can get yourself home?"

He turns around and stares at the car he's been leaning against with no small amount of confusion. "I'm sure. But we should—we need to—what was that jumping stuff you were doing back there? You were like—a spider or something."

"Uhhh, lots of years doing the long jump on the track-and-field team. Maybe we can talk about this some other time?" I ask. "Like, when we're not in a dark alleyway."

"Right," he says. "We'll do that. Man, you must have quite a few schools interested in you."

I nod and simultaneously hope he forgets this entire conversation by the time I see him in class. "Big decisions for sure."

He climbs into his car and starts the ignition, and I watch until he's actually driving away. If I were him, I might just keep driving until Glenwood was only a speck in my rearview mirror.

Once he's out of sight and the coast is clear, I push away from the ground and glide back to where I left Dakota. She stands on the very edge of the building, arms tightly crossed against her chest, her expression stiff with worry.

"You didn't come," she says breathlessly, rushing to my side. "You didn't come when I called you."

I hold her hands, clutching them in mine. "I came as soon as I could."

"I called your name, and you didn't answer," she continues. "You have to answer me, Faith. Please."

I can still feel the nausea I felt that day I realized Dakota wasn't going to walk out of that burning building. When I realized there was nothing I could do to help her. I normally forgive so quickly, but her concern is also a little validating.

"It's not such a great feeling, is it?" I ask.

Her mouth opens and closes, eyes widening with distant horror and shame. And I immediately feel guilty for bringing it up. For putting the spotlight on this old wound between us instead of letting it continue to heal in peace.

"I'm sorry," she says softly. Helplessly. Like she has nothing left to offer me.

I frown. More at myself than at her. "Me too," I say.

Her gaze darts away and back, and she nods as though she's just come to a decision. Then she asks, "Do you want to tell me what happened back there?"

I weave my fingers through hers, resting my forehead in the crook of her shoulder with a little sigh.

"I do," I say.

26

The next day, Liam waltzes into first period as the final bell rings, looking like nothing in the world is wrong. I don't know what I expected after a fire-shooting psiot very nearly ended him, but chipper with a fresh cup of coffee and bright eyes isn't it.

"Good morning, fellow humans," he says as he smoothly takes off his leather jacket and drapes it over the back of his chair.

"Good morning," a few students mumble back to him.

"Looking rather dapper today, Liam," Johnny says in a voice that makes me want to gag.

"As are you, Johnny," Liam says with a nod.

"Seconded," Rebecca says, her cheeks rosy as she smiles at Johnny, who doesn't even notice her.

"Let's get to work, everyone. Daylight's wasting and all that. Johnny, you have the helm. Uh, Faith." Liam pauses, and for the first time this morning, I see a hint of what went down last night. "Could I see you in the hallway for a moment?"

Johnny watches me over his shoulder. The jealousy radiating off him at the thought of me getting special Liam Hollis treatment is palpable.

I have to stop myself from rolling my eyes as I rise from my desk. If only he knew.

Last night I was so wiped out that when we got home, I fell asleep in my clothes with the lights on. I slept right through my alarm, and if it weren't for Bumble nudging my face so diligently this morning, I'd probably still be asleep now. I didn't have a thought to spare for what I might say to my journalism teacher this morning as I rushed out the door and into Matt's car. Or what would happen if Colleen dared to show her face again at school today.

Liam closes the door behind us, giving us all the privacy the long, empty hallway can offer. I really wish I'd had time to think of plausible explanations for any of the things he's about to ask me. My "I'm good at jumping" excuse is so flimsy and easy to discredit that even Dakota couldn't believe he bought it.

At least, he bought it last night. Now, with a full night of sleep and coffee in his system, I expect he has a list of difficult-to-answer questions, like *What exactly are you?* or *How do you defy the laws of gravity, Faith?*

Instead he says, "I've . . . um . . . decided not to report what happened last night to the police, and I'd appreciate if you didn't tell people about . . . it."

I'm too stunned to respond, which is great, because he just keeps going.

"That person was clearly demented, and having to be rescued by your own student is, well, sort of embarrassing."

"Oh," I say. "Right."

"Not because you're a girl!" He shakes his head. "I'm a feminist, but I also have a certain reputation to uphold. You get it."

"Sure." I blink for a moment, trying to piece together what he's just said. Any other person would be badgering me with questions about what I saw, or what I did, not deflecting like this. None of this fits, and that makes me wonder . . . "What were you doing out there last night, Liam?"

"Me? Oh, I was just, you know, out."

Maybe it's that I was too exhausted to think clearly last night, but Liam wasn't even here last year. He has absolutely no connection to Colleen that I'm aware of. So why was she attacking *him* of all people?

"Okay, how did you end up in a dark alleyway? Facing off with a . . . demented person with a blowtorch?"

For a split second, his eyes widen, but he recovers quickly, smiling and shrugging in that smooth way of his. "How do I ever find myself in precarious situations? Following a lead.

But I'm afraid that's as much as I can say at the moment."

Damn. The journalism cover is a good one. In fact, I'm going to tuck it into my back pocket for a rainy day.

"Sure, well, maybe you should take more care with those leads," I say. "They seem dangerous."

"Will do. So, we're good then? We're keeping this between us?"

I can't imagine a better outcome, but I also don't really understand how this was so easy. "Yep. Between us."

"Great." He smiles. "By the way, did you know that person? Didn't I hear you call them Collin or something?"

I stiffen but manage to shake my head. "I definitely didn't call them Collin. . . . You must've misheard in the heat of the moment."

"Ha! I get it. The heat of the moment."

I laugh loudly, and sure, it's a little fake, but not completely. "I love a good pun."

Sidestepping him, I walk back into the classroom and smile widely in the face of a confused Johnny.

"Were you two . . . laughing?" he asks.

"Oh yeah," I say. "Turns out Liam has excellent taste in humor."

Liam smiles easily as he sits down at his desk. "Now, what news awaits us today, class?"

I hardly hear what goes on in the rest of class. I'm too relieved that Liam was more concerned with his reputation than mine. It's a strange kind of miracle, but I'll take it. By the time the bell rings, I'm ready to deal with whatever comes next. Which is probably Colleen. I don't know how she escaped my expertly thrown dumpster, but she did, which means she could be anywhere.

But I don't see her. I search for any sign of her during lunch and every passing period, but she's simply not here.

Maybe—just maybe—she took the hint and left Glenwood altogether.

When I get to Cedar Hills that night after work, Miss Ella is in the recliner while Grandma Lou sits up in bed.

"Well, you're all cozy," I say to Grandma Lou.

But when she looks at me, there's a blankness in her eyes I don't quite recognize.

On her other side, Miss Ella shakes her head discretely and says, "Lou, Faith is here to see you. Your granddaughter. Isn't that lovely?"

My gut twists into a knot. "Hey, Grandma Lou," I say softly. "Hey, it's me."

Her chin quivers as she looks from me to Miss Ella. She looks so lost, but she says, "Hello, Faith."

"Is it okay if I pull up a chair and watch TV with you?" I ask, trying desperately to hold on to something that feels normal, that feels like *us*.

She looks to Ella for confirmation, and I realize it's

because in this moment, I'm a complete stranger to her. Something inside me begins to crumble.

"I'd like that," Grandma Lou says when Ella gives her an encouraging nod.

I put my bag down just inside the door and pull one of the kitchen chairs over so that I'm between Miss Ella and Grandma Lou.

The three of us sit there quietly, and even though I've never been a religious person, I begin to pray. I pray that Grandma Lou will suddenly come to her senses, as though all her brain needs is to smooth out a little wrinkle. I pray that she'll fall asleep for a few minutes and wake up herself and that Miss Ella will tell me it's all no big deal and that she'll be fine tomorrow.

I lay my hand on the side of the bed, palm up, as an offering in the hope that maybe some sort of muscle memory will kick in and she'll take it.

After what seems like hours but is only a few moments at most, Grandma Lou's fingers lightly drag along my palm, and I close my hand around hers. Her skin is cool against mine, and I feel the slightest breeze of relief moving from my chest through the tension coiled in my shoulders.

I try so hard not to, but one tear falls and then another. I quickly wipe them away with the sleeve of my sweatshirt before Grandma Lou can notice. On my other side, Miss Ella gently touches my back.

We sit there, watching some game show where contestants basically play a giant game of Plinko. My tears slowly subside, and eventually Grandma Lou's grip loosens as she drifts to sleep.

I wait a few moments to make sure she's definitely asleep. "What happened?" I ask softly.

Ella shrugs, shaking her head. "Nothing happened," she says. "I showed up and she wasn't sure who I was or why I was here. I mentioned being her neighbor and that seemed to spark some kind of memory, but she just kept saying she wanted to lie down."

"Did you call her nurse?" I ask.

"She came and brought her meds by earlier, but Faith, there's nothing much her nurse can do other than make sure she's safe and comfortable."

Miss Ella stands and pulls a turquoise windbreaker over her head. "I oughta get home," she says. "Lord knows what that damn dog of yours did to my fence line today."

"I'll fill it in this weekend," I tell her.

"Yeah, yeah, yeah." She walks over to the door and stands there for a moment, looking at me and Grandma Lou. "Don't you stay up here all night. School in the morning. She'll wake up a new woman. Don't you worry."

"Thanks, Miss Ella." It's not like her to lie or sugarcoat anything, so I'm not sure if her optimism is genuine or for the sake of our own sanity.

I stay at Cedar Hills longer than I should. Not because

I'm waiting for Grandma Lou to wake up, but just because I'm not ready to let go of her hand.

When I finally leave, the hallway is entirely dark except for a sliver of light coming from Augustus's door. I creep down the corridor, so I don't disturb him, but suddenly someone swings the door open and violently slams it shut behind them.

"Benji?" I ask.

He glances over his shoulder and grins. "Faith, what are you doing here so late?"

I hike a thumb over my shoulder. "Visiting. Like always. Why are you slamming doors?"

"What?" he asks. "Oh, this one won't shut at all unless you slam it. I keep meaning to put in a maintenance order."

"Oh?" I ask as I lean past him and hit the down arrow for the elevators. "Seems like maybe you should do that instead of startling half the hall with the noise."

He shrugs, unbothered by the accusation.

I think about letting him know that I saw him with Colleen or that I watched him perform at the Blue Llama Studio open mic night, but I don't. I'm not sure how to say either of those things without sounding like a creeper.

The elevator dings as the doors slide open. Benji catches the door and motions for me to step inside ahead of him, so I do. I move to one side, so he can join me, but he shakes his head.

"Going up," he says. "But I'll see you around."

"Sure," I say. "See ya."

On the way home, I'm barely aware of each turn and stop. I'm on autopilot, because now that I'm thinking about it, I realize how odd it was that Benji was in Augustus's room at all. It's late. Too late for the usual checkups and pill distributions. If Benji and Colleen really are working together, then maybe this is all connected to Colleen's seemingly random attack on Liam. Maybe Benji is there to threaten Liam's father. And maybe that is why Liam decided not to pursue any legal action.

The whole theory unfurls so completely in my mind that I nearly turn around to find Benji and confront him. But I don't, because when I pull up to my house and see that it's pitch-black, I remember that I've left Dakota and Bumble in the dark for way too long already.

"Hello?" I call as I open the door. "I'm sorry I'm so late."

Bumble trots to meet me, her wet nose nudging one hand as my other hand struggles to find the light switch. "Dakota?"

"Faith, we have a problem," she says, her voice even, yet full of warning.

I flip the lights on and sitting there in the living room, tied to Grandma Lou's recliner with a familiar sneer on her face, is Margaret Toliver.

 **27**

I am not a vengeful person, but I have spent the last few months dreaming of what it would be like to give Margaret Toliver a taste of her own medicine. Tying her to a chair is a really perfect start.

"You didn't think to stuff her mouth with something?" I ask.

Dakota shakes her head as she side-eyes Margaret. "She wasn't screaming or anything, and all the dish towels are dirty."

"I do appreciate that consideration," Margaret says.

"No," I tell her. "You don't get to talk." I turn to Dakota. "Could I speak with you, please? Privately?"

"Could we maybe turn the television on?" Margaret asks.

I give her the most withering look I can manage. Then I march over to the coffee table and turn the television on to something I know will make Margaret's ears bleed: the

Christian TV station that is always asking for donations in exchange for things like bottles of sand from Jerusalem.

She rolls her eyes and throws her head back against the recliner.

I turn the volume up all the way before pulling Dakota into the kitchen doorway just enough that I can keep one eye on Margaret.

"What exactly is happening here?" I ask in a hushed voice. "And how long has Margaret been inside my house?!"

Dakota shakes her head. "It all just happened! Around three or four, Bumble started losing it, but I couldn't see anything outside or anywhere in the house. Then she started barking at the garage door and I found Margaret slithering through the same window I used to sneak in—"

"I'm making a mental note right now to brick that window over."

"Yeah, it does seem to attract strays," Dakota answers with a smile.

"Did she try to hurt you? What does she want? Why is she here?" I have so many questions. These aren't even the most important. Just the most immediate.

Dakota squeezes my hands as though this isn't cause for high alert. "She says she just needs a place to hide."

"Well, that's not our problem," I scoff.

She gives me a desperate look that makes something inside my chest ache. "Faith, I've been running for months. I know my life will never be what it was again. I'll have to live with the mistakes I've made. But if we can just find out who she was working for . . . maybe I won't always have to be on the run. Maybe I can settle down somewhere and disappear without the fear that someone could come crashing through my door at any moment on a mission to kill me."

I want that for Dakota. I do. I just don't know that she can get that from the person who betrayed her in the first place.

"How do we know she'll give us any information? Or that what she says will be true?"

"I don't know, but we don't have very many options." She pauses, her eyes holding so tightly to mine. "Please, Faith," she pleads. "I need to at least try."

And that's exactly the point. I nod. "Okay. But we're going to have to find some way to hide her." I smile. "And she's not going to like it."

"Did it ever occur to you that I sought you out?" Margaret asks as Dakota and I carry her down the stairs and into the basement, where we transfer her to a kitchen chair.

"I don't know if you remember that one time you tried to have me killed," I say nonchalantly. "So, excuse me if I don't trust you enough to give you free range in my house."

The basement of Grandma Lou's house is half-finished, with a small laundry area and some storage, while the other half is dark with dirt floors. It's pretty much uncharted territory for me, which when I think about it too much, really freaks me out. There's basically an entire section of the house that I never see. That makes it perfect for the likes of Margaret Toliver.

"Are you just going to leave me tied up down here?" she asks.

"Actually, I was thinking we could untie you since you'll be locked in down here. There's a toilet." I point over to the tiny toilet that Grandpa Fred randomly installed down here using the water line from the washing machine. "And here's a cot."

I grab the metal frame on top of a pile of old junk sent down here to die a slow death and tug. It emerges in a cloud of dust.

"I think not," Margaret says, a note of actual fear vibrating in her tone. "That thing looks like it's been stuffed with dead birds. And that toilet might as well be a hole in the ground."

"Isn't that really what all toilets are?" Dakota asks.

Margaret begins to shake back and forth, rocking her chair wildly. "This is inhumane treatment."

"We don't have to untie you," I remind her.

She stops with a heavy sigh.

I step forward and begin to untie the truly sloppy knots that Dakota and I managed to tie. They wouldn't have held her long anyway, but she doesn't need to know that.

"We'll see you in the morning," I tell her. "And if you try anything funny, we'll make sure that the people looking for you find you."

Her complexion pales, and she's silent as we walk back up the stairs.

After I shut the door, I twist the lock and turn to Dakota excitedly. "I've never kept anyone prisoner before. How'd I do?"

She pats my arm. "Like you were an old pro."

Bumble follows us into the living room. We both flop down on the couch and I immediately turn the volume way down.

"We need ground rules," I say.

Dakota nods, swiping the TV control from my hand and changing the channel to something less evangelical.

"We only go down there together. So, morning and night. When I get home tomorrow, we'll try to get some information out of her."

"What if the people looking for her come here?"

I shake my head and shrug. "I don't know, but you better believe I'm giving her up before I let them hurt either of us."

We both sit there for a few moments, lost in our own thoughts, before Dakota flops her head to the side and says, "What the hell are we doing?"

"Winging it."

 **28**

It turns out "winging it" is pretty complicated when it comes to holding an adult woman hostage. Dakota and I quickly realize that we need to watch Margaret around the clock, because neither of us is exactly comfortable with her in the house. I don't get much sleep, and by morning, I'm dragging and so is she.

I offer to stay home from school, but Dakota insists she'll be fine. Besides, nothing is more suspicious than a kid who lives alone calling in sick to school. Miss Ella would be over here in a heartbeat, followed shortly by Matt and Ches, then Matt's mom. Which would be decidedly worse than going to school a little tired.

By the time lunch rolls around, I fully intend to tell Ches and Matt everything. Dakota, the alleyway run-in with Colleen, holding Margaret prisoner.

It's not a big deal, I tell myself. I'm not keeping anything from them. We've all just been busy, and it's not like I had anything significant to go on until recently, anyway. They probably won't even care. Compared to last semester, my life is almost normal now . . . right?

As I leave the lunch line, I spot Matt and Ches waving me over. It's a relief to see them. If I tell them, maybe they can help. I begin to nod in their direction, but my jaw drops when I see who is sitting at the table directly behind them.

Colleen. Colleen "I don't know what you're talking about" Bristow. Oh, heck no. This has officially gone too far, and I'm too tired to be subtle. She doesn't get to terrorize my town by night and play innocent by day.

"I have something to take care of," I tell Matt and Ches, dropping my tray on the table with a clatter.

I circle around to where Colleen is sitting next to Austin Snyder. I know she sees me approaching, and it's really annoying that all she does is give me that mousy little smile that she's used to hoodwink the rest of the school. I really wish I had another dumpster to drop on her head.

I tap on her shoulder with my best *may I speak to the manager* face.

She turns, her eyes wide and dreamy. "Faith?" She says my name like she's lost in a forest and I'm the last person she expected to see.

"Hi, Colleen," I say gently, but through gritted teeth. "Could I maybe talk to you for a sec?"

"I'm sort of eating lunch right—"

"It's important," I say.

She stands, and I hook my arm through hers like we're the closest of friends. Like she hasn't tried to burn me alive more than once.

"Faith, you seem upset. Where are you taking me?" she asks frantically.

We walk right out one of the side exits of the cafeteria and into an alcove. There's no one out here but us, which is exactly what I was hoping for.

She yanks her arm free. "Stop it! What is wrong with you?"

I take a step closer, backing her against the wall with no escape. "I told you to leave."

"What are you talking about?" she asks.

"Stop pretending, Colleen. I told you to leave. The other night in the alleyway. You know. When you were trying to burn Liam Hollis alive? And what about the fire next to Blue Llama? That's what I'm talking about."

"I think you might need help," Colleen says. "Maybe I should go get the school counselor or—"

"I'm not the only one who saw you," I say. It's not entirely true, but she doesn't know that.

She wraps her arms around her middle and shakes her head, committing hard to the innocent act. "I really don't know what you're talking about, Faith."

"Why are you doing this?" I ask, my frustration mounting to the point that it feels out of control. "I saw you, and I know you saw me." I grip her arms and my voice drops an octave as I say, "I know who you are, Colleen, and I won't let you hurt anyone."

"Colleen?"

Instantly, I let her go. We both turn to see Austin Snyder watching us, his expression a little uncertain and a little angry. The latter of which is directed entirely at me.

"What's going on here?" he asks.

"Austin, would you mind telling Faith where we were on Monday night?" Colleen's voice quivers a little.

"Uh, okay. Sure. We were at that hot dog place downtown," Austin says without missing a beat. "And I told you not to order the quinoa salad, but you did it anyway."

"And then I got sick," Colleen adds, her eyes steady on mine.

"Yeah," he says with a groan. "We're never eating there again."

Colleen sidesteps to stand beside Austin. "Sorry I couldn't be of more help, Faith."

Austin defensively slings an arm over her shoulder as he guides her back into the cafeteria.

Once they're both gone, I lean back against the wall and rake my hands through my hair, wishing I could just pull it out at the roots. I know I'm missing something, and I know it's right in front of my face. I just can't see it yet.

Matt and Ches wander out to find me.

"Uh, do we even want to know what that was about?" Ches asks.

"Just perfectly normal teenage things," I tell them, suddenly feeling too unsettled to try to explain everything to them now.

"Do we need to beat her up?" Matt asks. "Like, metaphorically. I don't think I'd actually do well in a fight."

Ches pulls Matt along and the two of them circle me in a hug. "We're not, like, fancy superheroes or anything," Ches says. "But we're here for you."

Just being in physical contact with them recharges me a little. It doesn't answer any questions or fix any problems, but it's a good reminder that I'm not alone, even when I don't know how to tell them everything.

I call in sick to All Paws on Deck, which I hate to do, especially because I'm not sick, but after my run-in with Colleen, I need answers. And the only place to get any right now is waiting at home in my basement.

When I walk in the door, I am shocked to find Margaret sitting on the couch beside Dakota, sharing a bowl of popcorn while the two of them watch soap operas on mute with the closed-captioning on.

"Uh, Dakota?" I ask.

Dakota jumps to her feet with a gasp. "I—I thought you were working after school today."

"I was. I called in sick."

"Oh no!" she says, instantly worried. "Are you okay?"

"I lied," I blurt. "I'm not sick. I just was eager to deal with our . . . situation."

"Deal with your situation?" Margaret asks as she cranes her neck back. "Were you planning on killing me and burying me in that sad excuse for a garden in the backyard?"

"No," I say as I cross my arms over my chest and sit down in the recliner. "If I was going to kill you, I'd never dispose of your body in the backyard. Especially not while there's a dog living here."

Bumble saunters over and places her snout in my lap, so I massage the spots behind her ears.

"I thought we had a plan," I say to Dakota. "One where Margaret stays in the basement like the worm she is?"

Dakota sighs. "We did. Then the worm decided to bang two cast-iron pans together until I let her out. We compromised with the zip ties."

I take a closer look at Margaret and see that in spite of enjoying my sofa and my popcorn, her hands and feet are very securely zip-tied together.

"I still require a shower," Margaret announces. "And we need to discuss my dietary needs. I'm both gluten-free and a pescatarian, so perhaps you have some wild-caught salmon on hand or—"

"Maybe—just maybe—we can talk about those things after you give us some information," I say.

Margaret flinches ever so slightly and stares intently at

the blank wall above the television. "Then you can just take me back downstairs. I don't have anything to tell you."

I look to Dakota. If anyone's the Margaret Whisperer, it's her.

She takes a deep breath and nods before placing a hand on Margaret's knee. "Marge. You see this?" She points to the fading gash beneath her eye. Over the past weeks, it's faded into a long, dark scab. "Remi and Carl tracked me down. They beat the shit out of me before they would believe I didn't know where you were."

A shadow falls across Margaret's face, and even though she's pretending not to, I can see she cares about Dakota. She cares that Dakota was hurt.

"Who do they work for?" Dakota asks.

"They worked for me. Or so I thought," Margaret scoffs.

"Okay, let's try this. The person you worked for—what did they want with A+ and Honor Roll? We know the drugs were designed to identify psiots, but why did they want to? What was their plan?"

"Would you believe me if I told you I thought he wanted to make the world a better place?" She shakes her head with a humorless smirk. "Think about it. You're one of the smartest, richest people in the world. What would you want with a bunch of kids full of hormones and superpowers they can barely wield?"

Every show I've ever seen and every comic I've ever read

points to one answer. An answer so absurd I'm almost embarrassed to say it out loud, but my whole world has turned into some far-fetched fantasy at this point.

"An army," I finally say.

"That's a bingo," Margaret says with a dark laugh.

"Who is it?" I ask. "It can't be Toyo Harada."

It's been months since I've thought about the man behind the Harbinger Foundation, the sketchy site where I was originally activated. But Toyo Harada had no interest in identifying psiots prior to activation. He didn't care enough to figure it out, even though the activation process itself either reveals a superhuman power or kills the person. I'm still not sure what kind of body count Harada is responsible for. And after all that, I almost felt like a drug like A+, which had the potential to identify psiots before going through the activation, could be a good thing.

But the drug tore through Glenwood, turning first animals and then people into living science experiments. The results were very nearly devastating.

"Trust me when I say you don't know him," Margaret says. "And no, it isn't Harada."

"What do they want with you then?" Dakota asks.

Margaret is quiet for a moment. "Nothing. That's the problem. The same is true for you. We're loose threads, my dear. Nothing more. Once his people find me and kill me, they'll do the same to you."

"And so you thought it was a good idea to lead him right back here?" I ask, anger surging through me.

With an eye roll, Margaret turns to face me. "I thought you might be connected with more superhero types who could actually help me, but it seems like I have grossly over-estimated you. Much to my disappointment, trust me."

"I know people," I snap back. "They're just . . . doing things. In other places that are not . . . here."

"Right," she says. "Well, if it's all the same to you, I'll take my dinner downstairs in my dungeon."

"Wait," I say, as if she can go anywhere without us. "What do you say we trade you a shower for your ex-boss's name?"

"A bath," she says shrewdly. "With a bath bomb. Followed by a steaming-hot shower. And I want a gluten-free cookie after dinner."

"Whatever. Fine," I tell her. "But we wait outside the bathroom for you and check in every ten minutes. No sharp objects, including razors."

"Lucky for you I've had laser hair removal," she says.

I motion for her to keep talking, and Dakota's eyes widen as we both wait for a name.

Margaret clears her throat, and I can see that she's enjoying this a little too much. "He goes by lots of names, but I first knew him as . . . Dr. Silk."

 **29**

I don't know why I thought having a name would make a difference. I spent all night googling and scouring the internet for anyone named Dr. Silk. The only thing I came up with was an eighteen-and-over adult entertainment site with a paywall.

I was so sure that having a name would give us some sort of direction, or at least a way to better protect Dakota. But the only thing I have to show for all my research efforts is a really gross browser history that I can't delete fast enough.

Margaret, however, did thoroughly enjoy her bath.

The next day I work late at All Paws on Deck and swing by Cedar Hills on my way home. Grandma Lou had a long day of water aerobics and mahjong, so by the time I get there, she can barely keep her eyes open for the second half of her favorite movie, *National Treasure.*

I get home so late that Dakota is already asleep on the

couch. Margaret is safely ensconced downstairs, content to keep to herself and stay quiet for the time being. We decided that at least while she's benefiting from this awkward-as-hell arrangement, we don't need to keep a rigid watch on her.

Bumble follows me into the kitchen, and I give her a few treats before going up to my room. She trots along at my heel, probably under the assumption that there are more treats where those came from.

"Where are you going?" I ask her. "What about Dakota? You're not going to leave her on the couch all by herself, are you?"

But she just continues on behind me down the hallway until we're at my bedroom door. "All right, all right. You can keep me company for a little while."

I kick off my shoes and pull on my favorite *Star Wars* fleece pajama bottoms and a Twin Cities Comic-Con T-shirt before jumping into bed and pulling the covers up to my chin.

Bumble paws at the pillow beside me until it's just fluffy enough for her and plops down, twisting her body into a dog-shaped croissant.

I set up my laptop and cue up some good old comfort television, which would normally be *The Grove*, but I don't think I'd ever get over Dakota catching me binge-watching her old show. I know I should hate the show now, but I can't bring myself to write it off entirely. I settle for *Seinfeld*. I'll be honest: I don't entirely get the humor, but Grandma Lou loved it, and it always reminds me of her.

The laugh track picks up as George and Elaine stand in line for soup, complaining about Jerry's new girlfriend.

"Bumble?" Dakota's voice softly calls from the other end of the hallway.

I glance over, but Bumble doesn't budge. Her head is full of doggy dreams.

"In here," I whisper, even though the only person who could hear us is literally underground right now.

Dakota stands in the dark doorway, wearing boxer shorts and a white tank top. She folds her arms over her chest as a shiver rolls through her. "Oh, I'm sorry," she says. "I didn't realize she wandered. I didn't even hear you come in."

"It's no big deal," I tell her. "If I'm being honest, I lured her with treats."

"Who can resist treats?" She steps toward the bed and pats Bumble on her bum. "Come on, B. Let's leave Faith alone so she can get some sleep."

"Oh, no, she's fine."

Dakota tilts her head to the side as she watches Bumble roll over onto her belly and let out a half snore, half whimper. "You watching anything good?" she asks.

I shake my head. "Just *Seinfeld*. I don't even like it, but Grandma Lou always did."

"I know it's supposed to be like the gospel of network

television, but I've only ever seen the soup episode."

I turn the laptop so she can see. "That's the one I'm watching! Do you . . . want to join me?"

"Here?" she asks. "In your bedroom?"

"Not if that's weird to you," I quickly say. "I guess we could go back down to the living room."

"No, no," she says. "And leave this warm bed behind? It's not weird for me unless it's weird for you."

I shake my head and pull back the blankets. "Get in. It's cold."

She darts around the other side of the bed and pushes Bumble down to the foot so she can squeeze in with us.

"This dog thinks every bed is a dog bed," she says with a snort.

"Aren't they, though?"

We sit there watching my laptop with Bumble sprawled out near our feet. Dakota's toes brush against my leg and I let out a stifled shriek. "Your toes are freezing," I say.

"I'm sorry," she moans. "But all I need is just a little—" She slides her feet along my calves. "A little bit of body heat!" She moans again as her feet begin to warm.

"You monster!" I say jokingly.

She sighs, flopping back against the headboard. "That's better."

"I feel really used right now."

"My toes thank you."

"How was it today?" I ask, obviously referring to Margaret.

She sighs. "That woman gave me even more mommy issues than I already had. But it was fine. No new information. But . . . I don't think this Dr. Silk guy is done. Whatever he was doing is still happening. Why else would he be after her? And me?"

"Do you think he's here?" I ask. "In Glenwood?"

She thinks for a minute. "This guy was the reason the show started moving around to different locations, so he chose Glenwood for a reason. I just don't know if his reason was good enough for him to stay. Then again, it's kind of a smart move to stick around, if you think about it. No one would expect him to stay after you foiled his A+ plan."

That certainly makes a lot of sense, but it's unnerving to think that he's been in Glenwood this whole time.

We finish the *Seinfeld* soup episode and it runs right into the next. As we sit there with the glow of the laptop illuminating my room, it's easy to wonder if there's a version of me and Dakota in some other reality where she's just a girl and I'm just a girl and we're planning our mundane futures and worrying about prom and what we'll wear and how many tickets we'll get to graduation and—

"You're thinking," she says.

"Huh?" I turn to her, still half in my head.

She gives me that almost smile I fell so hard for. "You

don't have to live in that brain all by yourself."

My knee brushes her thigh, and I suck in a sharp breath. Even the smallest touch between us is enough to make my heart flutter in the way it used to.

"Don't you ever wonder what it might have been like?" I ask. "If we'd just met like two regular teenagers?"

Instead of answering me, she asks, "What would we be doing right now?"

A small laugh bubbles up in my throat. "This," I say simply. "Watching old TV shows. Talking about college or prom."

"Prom," she says, a hint of marvel in her voice. "Do you know how many prom or school dance scenes I've filmed? And I've never even been to a single real one."

"Well, Glenwood is probably not the one to start with. It's in a gymnasium and the theme is On Cloud Nine."

"Wait. Proms actually have themes? That's not just a TV thing?"

"Apparently not," I say.

"So, are you going?" she asks, her voice aggressively casual.

"I guess so. I mean, yes. Of course. Matt and Ches would kill me if I didn't, but I just haven't given it much thought."

I watch as her fingers trace the geometric pattern on my sheets. She nods but doesn't say anything.

"When I was a kid," I say, "prom was this huge thing in

my head. Like this magical night where I'd be this impossibly cool version of myself, but it's kind of weird to get to all these high school landmarks and realize that I'm still just . . . me."

"Just you?" she asks. "Just Faith Herbert? The absolute human wonder. Smart, charming, and she can fly. I'm going to go out on a limb and say that childhood Faith would think eighteen-year-old Faith is pretty badass."

"Maybe," I concede. "If you were going to your high school prom, what would you wear?"

"Well, I don't wear dresses . . . unless it's for a role. And on the red carpet I always felt most comfortable in suits." She smirks. "Marge always called them steal-your-girlfriend suits."

"Do you have a lot of experience with stealing girlfriends?"

She traces a trail across the blankets and closer to me until her fingertips drag along my thigh and into my lap. I hold my breath as her index finger lightly dances up my hand and begins to draw the lines of my tattoo.

"You didn't tell me you got a tattoo," she says faintly. "You got your wings."

"It was Ches and Matt's idea. We got matching ones over spring break." My words come out breathier than I expect them to.

She runs the pad of her thumb along the outline over

and over again, like she's checking to see if it's temporary. "May I?" she asks.

I nod even though I don't know what exactly I'm saying yes to.

Wrapping her fingers around my wrist, she pulls my arm closer to her as she studies the lines and shadows permanently seeped into my skin. Without any warning, she leans down and presses her lips to my skin, and I didn't think someone kissing my arm could send my whole body into a frenzy, but everything feels like it's moving too quickly and not fast enough, and I'm nothing but a pile of contradictions as the heat of her mouth makes me shiver.

Instead of pulling away, she burrows her nose into the soft skin of my arm, and something urgent and desperate builds inside me.

"I'm—I'm sorry," she says suddenly as she gently places my arm back in my lap. "I just don't think you realize how maddening it is to exist in this house with you and not to touch you or be near you at all times."

I stare at her, my mouth hanging open, waiting for words to materialize.

"I should go to bed," she says finally, turning to go.

This time it's me who reaches for her. I grab her wrist. "Don't. Just stay here. Bumble is passed out. And—and your feet are already warm. Stay. We can just . . . sleep. We can just be near each other. Besides, when's the last time you slept in a bed?"

She sits there for a moment, staring out the moonlit window. "I didn't, like, come up here to try and—"

"Put the moves on me?"

Light cascades off her silhouette as she looks over her shoulder and laughs. "Sometimes I think there's a sixty-year-old woman living in your body."

"If there is, she's very disappointed with my inconsistent bedtimes. Come on." I lean forward to shut my laptop, startling Bumble just enough for her to bury her snout in her paws but not fully wake up.

As I slide the laptop below the bed, Dakota shimmies back under the covers and sighs with relief. Pulling the blankets up to cover my shoulders, I roll over and find her there just inches from me. Our heads rest so close together our noses nearly touch.

"Good night, Dakota Ash," I whisper.

"Good night, Faith Herbert," she whispers back, her voice already heavy with sleep.

 **30**

"This," Matt says, waving one hand at the peach ball gown I am currently wearing, "is not fulfilling the vision I had for you."

Ches rolls her eyes. "Faith, what do *you* think?"

I turn to look in the floor-to-ceiling mirror outside my fitting room. The dress is strapless, which of course, I did not come prepared for, so the light blue straps of my bra are on full display, and I have to admit that I don't have full confidence in this dress's ability to stand up to a strapless situation.

"It's . . . peach," I say. "I like the little sparkly bits." And I do. The bodice is lined with what I can only describe as crushed crystals. It's purposely imperfect, which is something I can get behind, but the rest of it is a little . . . much.

The sales associate hovers near the entrance to the fitting rooms, and after thirteen dresses, I can see that her patience is running thin and that she has plenty of unexpressed opinions—a state of being that my dear Matthew has no experience with.

I step down from the platform, so that I can speak a little more candidly with the two of them. They both perch on a huge chair shaped like a red high heel. Matt, of course, has had his outfit picked out for months—a black kilt with hematite metallic thread woven through it and an oversize suit jacket with the sleeves perfectly rolled. He did, however, need to shop for the perfect knee-high socks and was appalled to find that Ches and I were just thinking of wearing things we already owned. The minute he found out, he planned this trip, and first thing Sunday morning we drove out to the Mall of America.

We've spent six hours now being paraded around each store that matched our aesthetic (in Ches's case) or carried our size (in my case). Ches eventually found the perfect crushed-velvet gown that's a little bit Victorian and a little bit boho, which means there's just me, and I've tried on enough dresses to break even the strongest of shopping spirits.

"Are you sure there's not anything in the back?" Matt asks. "Maybe some gem waiting to be discovered?"

The sales associate's lips twitch as she forces a smile. "Let me see what I can find."

Ches and I give him our best dagger stares.

"What?" He shrugs defensively. "You never know until you ask."

While we wait, I check the price tag under my armpit

and try my best to choke back my audible shock. "Matt! I can't afford this dress. Or anything in this whole store even."

He checks the tag and says, "We can split it. I mean, we could if this was the one, but it's obviously not."

"I'm sure I have something at home," I say. "And even if I don't know that for sure, I know you have something I could borrow, Matt."

I look to Ches for backup. The one thing we've always bonded over is the fact that when it comes to money and spending it, neither of us can keep up with Matt. But this time she's not so committed to echoing my concerns.

"It's okay to get a new dress, Faith," she says gently. "It's going to be one of the last big things we do together . . . at least in high school. And I know these dresses are expensive, but it's okay to let the people who love you help."

I feel slightly betrayed. When did Ches turn into a therapist? "Well, I guess it doesn't matter if we don't find a dress," I say diplomatically.

Behind us, the sales associate clears her throat. "We had one new dress in our incoming inventory. I went ahead and put it in your fitting room."

"Thank you," I say, doing my best to express *I'm sorry my well-meaning best friend is so demanding* with my eyes alone.

"Sure," she replies flatly.

Ches unzips me and I head back into the fitting room for

what I promise myself is the last dress I'm trying on . . . for today at least.

I free myself of the piles of tulle and hang it back on the hanger as best I can, which it turns out is actually a very difficult thing to do with a strapless dress.

Standing there in my blue bra and Minnie Mouse underwear, I peel the plastic garment bag off the dress, which is unlike any plus-size formal wear I've ever seen. It's a two-piece coordinating set, which I vaguely remember Matt saying is very chic right now. The color is a vibrant blue that reminds me of Zephyr, the alter ego I'd claimed before the warehouse fire that changed it all. A name that's pretty much hung in my closet, collecting dust along with the T-shirt I hand-stitched a *Z* onto.

It's the kind of blue that isn't too serious or regal, but stands out in a playful way. The top is slightly cropped with a halter neckline, and running past the sweetheart shape of the bodice is a sheer jewel-encrusted mesh that cuts high around the neck. The skirt is long with a slit up the side, the jewels and mesh carrying through.

I didn't care about finding the perfect prom dress, because I didn't know it existed, but as I slide this on and it settles against my torso and waist, as my thigh peeks through the slit and the skirt just barely dusts the floor, I know . . . wearing anything else will feel like mourning clothes.

But then . . . it's just a dress. It's not *that* important, Faith,

I tell myself. Just some fabric and rhinestones. That's it. I'll have fun no matter what I wear. I'll be with my best friends having the time of our lives at the most ridiculously themed prom ever.

"Faith?" Matt calls through the door. "Do you need help in there? If you don't like it, you don't have to come out, but at least let me see it so I can rule it—"

I open the door.

"Oh," he says, his hand flying to his chest. "Oh, Faith."

"Is it bad?" Ches asks from behind him, but then she opens the door a little wider to see for herself. "We're buying it," she says definitively.

"Ches—wait—no. I don't even know how much . . ." I struggle to find the tag. It's not under the arm. I reach around to the back, searching with my fingertips.

"It doesn't matter," Ches says. "We'll pool our resources. I don't care. That's the one, Faith."

"Ma'am?" Matt says over his shoulder. "Could we get this one wrapped up for us? Thanks."

"Gladly," the sales associate responds dryly.

I try protesting a few more times, but it's pretty half-hearted. It feels so good to wear this dress and be loved by my friends. I can't find it in me to feel anything but incredibly, wonderfully happy.

Once they help me unzip, I give myself one last look in the mirror. "Perfect," I whisper.

As we're waiting in line to check out, I peruse the accessories. It's mostly sparkling costume jewelry that I might consider if my dress weren't already sparkly on its own.

On the back side of the necklaces is a display of hair clips with letters on them. I reach for the *F*, the whole thing outlined in rhinestones.

"Next," the associate calls from behind the counter.

"Come on, Faith," Ches says. "We're up."

I bend down to return the *F* to its original place, and just as I'm about to walk away, I see one single *Z* hanging out all by itself at the very bottom.

"I'll take this too," I say as I slide it off the hook and walk up to the register.

 **31**

When I get home from the mall, Dakota is asleep on the couch so deeply that not even Bumble wakes her as she greets me.

After hanging my garment bag up, I lean over the back of the couch and pull her blanket up, and her fists curl around the fabric like a cat stretching its claws. I wonder how awkward it would be if I told her to sleep in my bed again tonight. *Hey, Dakota, me, you, my bed? Same place? Same time?*

With Dakota looking sufficiently snuggled up, I head downstairs and find Margaret in the basement smoking a cigarette out of one of the narrow, high windows.

"Don't worry," she says. "I've been quiet, but I was going to explode without some fresh air."

"I'm pretty sure the whole cigarette part negates the fresh air." I sit down at Grandpa Fred's workbench. "But it's fine as long as Miss Ella doesn't see the smoke and call 911."

"That woman is a tyrant," she says. "And I've only heard her yelling over the fence for the past few days." She puffs out a ring of smoke, something I didn't realize you could actually do and had always assumed was some sort of movie magic. Despite being on the run from some pretty hardcore bad guy types and her life being in very real danger, Margaret Toliver is still painfully cool.

I'm struck by how much I still like her and how incredible it is to me that she's here, in my home. I've heard people say not to meet your heroes, but what about being taken prisoner by your hero one month only to take *them* prisoner the next?

I glance around at the pile of Herbert family treasures keeping Margaret company down here. Between my parents and Grandpa Fred, the basement has pretty much become the final resting place for a lot of things neither myself nor Grandma Lou wanted to part with or needed regularly enough to keep aboveground. Everything is coated in a healthy layer of dust, except for a few boxes, though, which have been wiped clean and stacked into neat little piles.

"Have you been going through my stuff?" I ask, feeling a little violated. But then again, I did set her loose down here.

She shrugs. "Underground entertainment options are limited, and you clearly aren't that concerned with it, judging by the layers of sediment. A lot of them are old family photos you should probably have a look at." She stubs her cigarette out on the windowsill and slides it back into the carton. "I'm rationing myself," she explains. "Gotta save the rest for later."

She takes a few long strides over to a stack of photo albums and flips to a page she's clearly looked at before. "Are these your parents?" she asks.

I join her, turning the album to face me. And there they are. My mom with her blond curls and Dad with his over-grown brown hair that always seemed to have a mind of its own no matter how hard he tried to tame it. "This must have been before I was born. They took me everywhere with them. Especially cons." Mom and Dad dressed up at least once or twice at every convention, but this must have been a down day for them, because Dad's wearing a Ninja Turtles T-shirt, and Mom's T-shirt simply reads, Slayer, as they both pose on the convention floor.

Margaret leans down, squinting at the photo. "That looks like Dragon Con in Atlanta. God, I used to love the con circuit."

"They did too," I said. "I remember Mom saying she heard you speak at Planet Comicon in Kansas City. You were her hero."

She makes a *hmph* noise. "Well, I'm sure she'd just love to know I very nearly killed her daughter. What a hero I turned out to be."

I laugh, even though I feel a little bit bad for her. "You said it. Not me."

"I'm sorry," Margaret says, her words so soft I barely hear them. "That was a . . . uh, shitty thing to do."

"I know you did all this because of your sister," I say, quite familiar with the story by now. Margaret's sister was one of Harada's failed activations, which happens more often than I can stomach. The problem with activating a psiot is that you either live and you have superpowers—or you die. It's not a survivable procedure, and Margaret's sister was one of the many unlucky ones. "But what did Dr. Silk promise you?" I ask her. "Surely this was about more than proving a point."

She sighs and studies the floor for a moment. "He said he could bring her back."

"W-what? That's not possible. You can't just bring people back to life."

"Faith, come now. You walked into an underground bunker and came out with the ability to fly. Surely you know now that there are no limits to what humans can accomplish. Only what they are willing to sacrifice."

"So Dr. Silk . . . he has your sister's body somewhere?"

She nods. "Morgan's body was preserved, if that's what you're asking."

"Would she . . . would she agree with all of this?"

She perches on a stack of boxes. "My sister would probably hate me for the rest of her life when she realized what I've done, but I wouldn't care. She'd be alive." She opens an old album to a photo of me at my Spider-Man–themed fourth birthday party, my parents hovering behind me as I blow out the candles. "Isn't there someone you'd risk it all for, Faith?"

"Of course," I say. "Grandma Lou. Matt. Ches. And . . . Dakota, I think."

She glances up from the album. "Oh, you've already put plenty on the line for Dakota. No question about that."

Heat rushes from my chest to my cheeks.

"We're more alike than you know, Faith. Me and you . . . we've got a fierce kind of love. The kind of love that can move mountains just as easily as it can crumble them."

There was a time in my life when I would have probably fainted at the sound of Margaret Toliver comparing us to each other, but now it just scares me. Margaret might give the appearance of having perfect confidence and conviction, but I can see the cracks in her armor and all the evidence of her failures. All the ways her love has choked out everything of value in her life and left a ghost town in its path.

"You were a cute kid," she says, pointing to a photo of me sitting on Dad's knee one Easter. I can't be more than three or four years old. My hair was in full ringlets and I wore a lavender overall dress, with a melting chocolate bunny clutched in one hand and a fistful of jelly beans in the other.

"I used to get the Easter bunny and the tooth fairy confused," I tell her. "So I was always telling the kids at school that the tooth fairy visited me on Easter."

She lets out a grunt of laughter and continues to page

through my childhood memories. Soon, the photos of my parents stop sometime around when I was seven, and it's just awkward pictures of me standing by myself or sometimes with Grandma Lou. School award ceremonies. Plays. Band concerts. A few photos of Matt and Ches at our house for my first birthday without Mom and Dad.

Now I remember why I don't seek these out.

I think Margaret realizes it, too, because she casually closes the album and turns her attention to a stack of old magazines that she cannot possibly be interested in.

The doorbell rings, and Margaret freezes in place before turning back to me, concern wrinkling her brows.

"It's probably just a delivery," I say, even though it's after seven o'clock on a Sunday.

A knocking follows and that's enough to get me running straight past her and up the stairs. Visions of flaming doll-houses and dumpsters flash through my mind as I take the stairs two at a time.

Somehow, Dakota is still passed out on the couch. I consider waking her, but I've already decided that whoever's on the other side of that door isn't coming any closer than the front porch.

I open the door to find Matt standing there with a small bag containing my hair clip from the mall dangling from his finger. I recognize the logo on it immediately and berate myself.

"Oh!" I reach out, careful to keep the door as closed as possible. Which also means I'm acting as awkward as possible. "Sorry, I didn't realize I left this."

"I've been texting you for, like, twenty minutes." Matt is wearing his suspicious face. Brow furrowed, eyes narrowed. "I was just going to give it to you later, but then I had time to kill waiting for Rowan to get off work, so—" He tries to peer over my shoulders. "What are you hiding, Faith? Is somebody in there?" he asks, taking a step closer.

"What? No. Who would be in here?"

"I don't know, Faith," he says, his tone turning playful. "Who would be?"

Behind me, Dakota lets out a long, loud, throaty snore.

I cough into my elbow in an attempt to cover the sound.

"What was that?" Before I can stop him, he pushes forward through the door and past me. "Oh. My. God," he gasps.

I spin, ready to explain.

But Matt isn't looking at Dakota.

Margaret is there leaning against the kitchen doorframe as though she lives here. Which I guess she kind of does.

She yawns. "Hello, youth."

"What are you doing?!" I snap at her.

An entire host of emotions dances behind Matt's cocoa-brown eyes. Shock, betrayal, and even a little bit of excitement.

Dakota sits up and groggily asks, "Was I snoring?"

"Yes," I say with a sigh.

She rubs her eyes. "Matt?"

But he doesn't answer her. He's busy texting furiously.

"What are you doing?" I ask. "Matt?"

"Calling in the cavalry," he says. "I'm staging an intervention."

 **32**

Ches's brother drops her off a mere fifteen minutes later, and I have a feeling it's because Matt decided he couldn't leave. Like I'm a flight risk or might somehow make Margaret and Dakota disappear if he gave me even a few moments alone.

I hate this. I hate that after revealing so much to Matt and Ches, I kept something so major from them. Again. Judging by the way Matt has kept his arms crossed for a solid fifteen minutes, he also hates this.

"I'm sorry," I say to Matt for the millionth time.

Matt holds up a hand and shakes his head. "Not yet."

Ches walks in at that moment. Right through the front door, which I forgot to lock, because I'm super great at hiding fugitives.

"Holy shit," she says, gaze jumping from Dakota to me. "Holy shit."

"You didn't warn her?" I ask Matt, sounding a little more outraged than I deserve to be.

"I don't know who's reading my text messages!" he says. "Doesn't, like, NASA spy on us regular citizens?"

"The NSA," Margaret says dryly from the kitchen, where she's making a cup of coffee. I guess our prisoner isn't such a prisoner anymore.

Ches's eyes widen at the sound. She marches toward the kitchen for a better look then turns back to me. "Have I already said holy shit? Because *holy shit*."

Margaret emerges from the kitchen with a steaming mug in her hands and looks right at Dakota. "You know what this means."

Dakota reluctantly nods, her hands gathered in her lap.

"Wait. What does this mean?" I ask, my voice shaky and frenetic.

"It means that we've officially overstayed our welcome."

"Welcome is kind of a strong word, don't you think?" I say, trying to lighten the mood, but I can't stop what's coming.

Margaret sighs and says, "We'll leave first thing in the morning."

I turn to Dakota, suddenly frantic. "You're not really taking this seriously, are you? You can't leave. Especially not with her!"

"Are you saying this didn't *just* happen?" Matt asks. "As in, this has been an ongoing situation that Ches and I didn't know anything about?"

To Matt, I say, "I promise you, I will explain everything.

In a minute." And then to Dakota, I add, "Explain to me why you think leaving with her is a good move?"

"I'm sorry, but is that the woman who kidnapped me? Just hanging out all chill in my best friend's house?" Ches asks.

Matt walks into the kitchen and digs into the cabinet for a glass.

Dakota turns to me with an apology in her eyes. "Faith, I should've left weeks ago. I just . . . I wanted to think we could make it work."

"We can," I say quietly. "We are."

"Yeah, I'm going to let you four play this delicious little drama out," Margaret announces, retreating up the stairs. "I'll just go help myself to a bath."

"Here, drink this," Matt says, handing Ches a cup of water as she concentrates on her breathing.

"It's not fair to you," Dakota says gently. "Every minute we stay here puts you in more danger."

"Do you want me to go up there and start reading mean tweets to her about herself and her show?" Matt asks Ches, soothing her hair back.

"No, I want to know why Faith has been sheltering the people who nearly destroyed my life." Ches's voice is hard and cold. There's so much anger there and most of it is directed at me.

The four of us are having two completely different

conversations, and I'm trying to track all of it. I'm going to check on Ches, but I also need to find a way to make Dakota stay. There has to be something I can do. Something I can say to convince her that she's safer here with me than she'll ever be on the run with Margaret.

"There's danger here whether you're with me or not," I say. "I'd rather you stay. I'd rather you *both* stay than leave me here alone."

"You want them to stay longer?" Matt demands.

"You think you're alone?" Ches asks, anger transforming into hurt.

Dakota stands and walks over to the bag that she's lived out of since she got here and begins to fill it with her stack of clean laundry.

My brain goes into a flat panic. I cannot let her leave. No matter what else is happening right now, I cannot let Dakota walk out of my life for a second time.

Ches steps up to my shoulder. "Faith, whatever you've been dealing with—"

"We have to talk about this later," I say, abruptly interrupting her.

Matt's jaw drops and Ches cocks her head, taken aback.

"This is later," Matt says. "You lied to us. Again. Now is the time to talk about it."

"Faith," Ches says, her voice full of hurt. "We can help you. You promised you would let us help you."

"I know, I just—Right now, what I need is time to sort things out here," I say. "With Dakota and Margaret. I promise. Later, we'll—"

Matt stands and grabs Ches's hand. "Message received. Loud and clear."

Ches stands and follows him out the front door, watching me over her shoulder for a moment before turning away. The look in her eyes pains me.

Matt's engine revs outside, and Dakota says, "You didn't have to ask them to leave."

I'm just barely holding on right now. It takes everything in me to control my tears when I say, "I can't handle you leaving and them spinning out at the same time."

She frowns. "I was always going to have to leave, Faith. You know that."

I want to deny it. I want to tell her that our future has to have something good in it for once. But the truth is, I did know.

I just didn't want to admit it.

We eat a dinner of leftovers and Dakota sits in the kitchen with Margaret for a long time after. The two of them quietly discuss their plans over cups of coffee. They decide it's better if I don't know all the details, so I spend most of the night lying on the couch with Bumble, thinking about how this silly sofa will never be the same again. It will forever and always be Dakota's bed.

Later that night, I lie in bed, staring out the window, trying not to panic over how I'm going to exist in this house all by myself and considering how I can smoothly invite Dakota to sleep in my bed again tonight. I've just decided there's no way to do it without seeming creepy or desperate when I hear the sound of the hallway floorboards creaking.

I scoot up, blankets falling to my lap, and find Dakota there with Bumble at her side.

"We thought you might be missing some icicle toes and paws tonight," she says.

Without an invitation, Bumble bounds forward and onto me before settling at the foot of the bed.

I nod. "I knew something felt off."

She comes around the other side and slides in beside me. "Is this okay?"

"Yes." I lie back down and pull the covers over our heads, using my cell phone to illuminate us.

"I forgot to ask," she whispers. "How was prom dress shopping?"

"Was that really today?" I ask, unable to fathom the events of the last twenty-four hours. The highs and lows of it all.

She nods glumly. "I was sort of looking forward to seeing you off to your prom."

"We almost made it," I say. "Less than a week to go."

"I guess I won't get to see you in your dress."

"I could try it on for you," I offer, despite how warm and

cozy this bed is at the moment.

She wraps her fingers around my wrist, and my pulse quickens beneath her touch. "No," she says. "I don't want you to get up. Just close your eyes and tell me about it."

I smile awkwardly, feeling a little self-conscious. "Um, okay. If—if you really want."

Her voice is low as she says, "I really want."

I close my eyes and conjure up the memory from earlier today as I studied my reflection in the mirror. "It's blue."

I can hear the smirk in her voice. "I'm starting to think blue might be your signature color."

"Like the sky," I say. "And it's two pieces and it's . . . it's glittery . . . but not too glittery. Just enough to catch the light. And I bought a hair clip with an initial on it. But not an *F* for Faith. It's a *Z*."

"The letter *Z*?" she asks. "Why?"

"It's . . . you're going to laugh."

"I won't," she promises. "Really."

"*Z* for Zephyr."

"Zephyr?"

"It means gentle breeze," I explain as I squint and peek through my closed lids, but everything is too blurry. "And was the name of the Greek god of the west wind. I know I'm not a superhero or anything, but I just . . . if I ever were and if I had a secret identity . . . it would be Zephyr."

She gasps softly. "The *Z* on your shirt. That day at the

warehouse. You had a Z on your shirt, and I just—"

I fully open my eyes then, something inside me lighting up. "You remember?"

She laughs quietly and rolls her eyes. "Are you kidding? Of course I remember. That day is burned into my skull— no pun intended. It's not every day your ex-girlfriend shows up in a cape with the letter Z stitched to her chest, flying through the air."

"Your ex-*girlfriend*?" I ask.

"I . . . uh, yeah. Is that . . . is that what it was to you?"

And even though I know it's ridiculous, there are fireworks exploding in my chest. "No one's ever called me their girlfriend," I say. "Well, I guess, technically you called me your ex-girlfriend, but no one's called me that either."

"That's what you were to me," she says simply.

"This is . . . weird," I say. "I'm giddy that I was someone's girlfriend, but also you're leaving tomorrow. Or today actually. In just a few hours. And it's not like you're going to college or something. You're disappearing, and hopefully, you'll do a really good job of it so that no one ever finds you. Including me."

"Including you." Her voice is thick with sorrow. "Sometimes . . . I start to miss all the moments we won't have. Arguing over silly things like what movie we're going to see or going on little weekend adventures, but . . . Faith, my life has never been normal. And I don't think yours will ever be either. So maybe the only thing we can do is just feel every moment as deeply as we can."

"Is that all we are? A moment?" I ask, my voice quivering slightly.

"Sometimes the brightest moments are the briefest." She leans closer to me, cradling my cheek in her hand.

I let her pull me to her, our lips meeting. Finally. Finally. Finally. The moment my mind, body, and heart have danced around for weeks now.

"Is this okay?" she mumbles against my lips.

I nod, wrapping my arm around her waist until our bodies are touching completely from head to toe. Her lips part against mine, and the memory of every kiss we've shared is simmering inside me. She hooks her leg over mine, and my toes curl as our bodies are suddenly even closer. I fall into this moment fully. Our brief, bright moment. I feel it as deeply as I can, because when the sun crawls across the horizon, she'll be gone, gone, gone.

33

"And it's got mesh up top," I explain to Grandma Lou during an after-school visit as she squints at the picture of my prom dress on my phone. I'd quickly snapped it before I left the fitting room. Matt insisted on taking it so I'd have it for reference if I needed it. Looking at it now is a reminder that he's not talking to me, but I try to focus on Grandma Lou.

She grins in a way that tells me she is definitely humoring me. "Well, I don't know much about dressy dresses, but I think this is stunning. Real wow factor, if you ask me."

"Maybe I could come up here before prom so you can see me off," I tell her. "Or maybe you could come home for the day."

She nods as she strokes the stuffed cat in her lap. He's black and white, with a collar that reads *Timothy*. When I got here, the orderly checking in on her explained that it was a gift from George. The cat itself is a very lifelike robot, and it even purrs beneath her touch. I remember reading about lifelike robotic animals for dementia patients as a therapy tool to combat anxiety.

"Maybe," she says. "We'll see."

I wish I could jump back in time and ask Grandma Lou from five years ago for advice. Would coming home confuse her? Make her upset? Am I not visiting enough? Too much? Nothing makes me feel so much like the kid I am than having to think about these big questions on my own.

"Did I tell you I brought a dog home from the rescue?" I ask. "She dug under Miss Ella's fence."

She snorts with laughter. "You might need to put that dog into protective custody."

Her door slowly eases open and Benji appears, pushing a cart of snacks and various beverages, and I realize I've barely seen him since that night at Blue Llama. "Snack trolley," he says. "Any takers?"

Grandma Lou stands to peruse his offerings. The woman loves a prepackaged snack cake.

He reaches for the robot cat and holds it to his chest like he believes it's real just as much as Grandma Lou seems to. "How's Timothy doing?" he asks. "Oh! We've got an official name tag on him now, I see."

"That was very nice of your grandfather," I whisper.

"I'm honestly surprised he didn't buy her a whole colony of robotic kittens," he answers. "He spends more time up here with her than he does at home."

Grandma Lou deserves that. She deserves to be doted on. "That somehow makes me feel better and guilty at the same time."

He nudges me with his elbow. "Don't beat yourself up, Faith. You can't be everywhere at once."

I'm not sure why, but something about the way he says it feels vaguely threatening. Like he knows more about me than he's saying. I still don't know what he and Colleen are up to with Liam. But between flat-out attacking him on the street and keeping a close watch on his dad right here in Cedar Hills, I just know it can't be good. I feel it in my bones.

"Yeah, it's not like I'm a superhero or something," I say. Testing.

But he merely grins. "Exactly. You have to take care of yourself so you can keep taking care of her. And beating yourself up about it won't help either of you."

It's a nice thought, but this isn't really getting me anywhere. I decide to take a more direct approach.

"I didn't get a chance to tell you, but you were great last week at Blue Llama Studio," I say.

He blushes. Fast and all the way up along his ears. It's adorable and not a reaction I think he could fake.

"You were there?" He has momentarily lost his usual calm demeanor, eyes wide, voice a little tight. It only lasts a split second before he clears his throat and throws on an expression of vague disinterest. "Yeah, well, I like to hit up their open mic night every so often. That night was wild though."

"Did you see the fire?" Or maybe help the person who caused it, I add silently.

He shakes his head, blond curls bobbing as he pushes his cart toward the door. "Only the smoke. I'm just glad it wasn't the actual studio. That was really lucky."

There's no guile about him right now. No double meaning to his words. And I'm starting to wonder if maybe I'm way off base about him. Maybe he isn't working with Colleen. Maybe he's just a guy who likes to get coffee with girls and sing at open mic nights and takes his job seriously.

"Next time, could you bring me a cherry Coke and a Butterfinger?" Grandma Lou asks.

Benji smiles with that lazy charm. "I'll send your request up the line."

Grandma Lou rolls her eyes as she plops down in her chair. "They're always trying to pump us full of all this granola health-and-wellness nonsense," she whispers conspiratorially. "Well, never mind it. Would you like to take a walk with an old lady?"

I smile. "I'd love to."

On our way to the elevator, I peer into Liam's father's room, but the recliner he normally occupies is empty.

"Have you met Augustus?" I ask, gesturing to the open door.

"Oh," she says, "his sons are so charming."

"He only has . . ." My voice trails off. It's not worth correcting her.

We stop off at the cafeteria and get some soup and salads. Employees and residents alike wave to Grandma Lou at every turn. Sometimes her eyes light up with recognition, and other times she simply nods politely. After we eat, we walk around the interior courtyard, which is full of fountains and gardens and greenhouses.

"It sounds like George has been spending a lot of time with you," I say. "Rekindling that old flame?"

She smiles and shakes her head bashfully. "We read," she says. "He'll come most evenings, and we'll have dinner and sometimes I'll read to him or he'll read to me. I don't think his mother appreciates me keeping him out at all hours."

"George's mom passed away, remember?" I gently remind her.

"Oh." She nods. "Right. Yes. Well, I do suppose it's nice to spend the evenings with him when he's done taking over the world for the day."

We sit down on a stone bench in front of a bush of blooming white roses.

"Grandma Lou, what kind of business does George do? Besides Cedar Hills."

She tilts her head to the side and holds her chin in her hand. "Well, there's all the real estate. But his son—Benji's dad—has really taken over a lot of that, from what I can tell.

I know he and his family are invested in pharmaceuticals as well."

That strikes a very specific chord. One that's a little too familiar. I'm suddenly very alert. "What kind of pharmaceuticals? Do you know?"

"Oh, I don't know," she says with a wave of her hand. "I don't really know drug words. I think he's working on supplements or prescription vitamins. Things that are supposed to improve your memory or enhance the power of your mind. Stuff like that."

My mouth goes dry. A moment ago, the idea that George Aldrich was connected to A+ and Dr. Silk himself might have made me laugh. But now, it seems almost too obvious.

"Hello, Dolores!" Grandma Lou calls to an employee, who waves from the other side of the courtyard.

I don't want to push her, but I wonder if George has ever slipped up around her and said something that he didn't mean to.

"Does he do his research here in Glenwood? Is it approved by the FDA and everything?"

She shakes her head and stands. "I don't know anything else about that, Faith." Irritation escalates in her voice. "Why are you asking so many questions? Is it asking too much that we just enjoy our time together?"

And she's right. I shouldn't be dragging her into this. This is the last thing Grandma Lou needs, and I can't ignore the guilt settling in the pit of my stomach at the thought of doing anything that would take George away from her.

I stand alongside her and take her hand. "Sorry. I was just curious. What do you want to do tonight?" I ask. "I'm yours all night."

"Oh, come on now. Surely you've got plans with friends."

"Actually," I say, "I don't. Not even a little bit."

I stay late enough that Grandma Lou shoos me out the door, because she's expecting George, and who am I to stand in the way of elder love? Even if it's between my grandmother and someone who might be in league with a supervillain.

But the thought of going home is dreadful. For the first time in weeks, I'll return to an empty house. No Bumble. No Dakota. Heck, I even miss Margaret's sardonic presence. Just a little bit.

But I can't very well tell Grandma Lou any of that, so I hug her goodbye and close her door behind me.

I wait too long for the elevator and finally give up and walk back down the corridor to the stairs. So, of course, just as I open the stairwell door, the elevator dings and opens. I turn, ready to race back to catch the elevator, and freeze.

Standing there, her eyes locked on mine, is Colleen.

For a second, all we do is stare at each other. Her eyes dart to Augustus's open door and back to me and I know, I just know that she was here to threaten him or Liam or both.

Or maybe just to burn it all down.

Well, not on my watch.

I push off from the ground and jet down the corridor to catch up with her, but she lunges forward and hits a button, closing the doors right in my face.

As I spin around, I slam right into a human-shaped wall.

"Whoa," Benji says as he trips backward. "You really walk with determination, don't you? Where's the fire?"

"Sorry, I just have to go," I say as I try to dodge him, but he bobs over to block me.

"No, really. Are you okay?" he asks.

If he wasn't standing between me and the pursuit of a Very Dangerous Psiot, I might take the time to be more gentle. Instead, I say, "This isn't a joke, Benji. You need to move."

"Is everything okay?" he repeats sincerely.

"I—it's none of your business," I say as I push him with such force that he crashes to the ground.

"What's your damage?" he calls after me as I slam the door to the stairwell shut behind me.

There's no time to do this the usual way. Colleen has to be halfway to the lobby by now, so I dive over the edge of the railing and swoop down headfirst like a hawk after its prey. In seconds, I'm on the floor again. Breathlessly, I tear through the door and am met with perky waiting room music and a very confused receptionist.

My eyes dart over every corner of the room, but she's not here. Yet.

"Miss, can I help you?" the receptionist asks, her plump mauve lips in a confused frown.

I slap a grin on my face and give her two thumbs-up. "Just trying to work in some cardio."

She chuckles. "More common than you think."

I turn to the elevator, hands curling into fists at my sides as the display steadily ticks down the floors from 3, 2, L.

I wait. Preparing myself for anything from a baffling conversation to a full-blown firefight. But the doors don't open.

After several long seconds, I hit the button myself, but again, the doors don't open.

"It does this sometimes," the receptionist calls.

"Does what?" I ask.

"Every so often, it says that the car is here, but it actually isn't," she explains. "I think it's some sort of glitch because the maintenance guys say everything's working like it should. Just be patient and they'll open up."

A few seconds later, I hear the elevator car approaching, but even before the doors open, I know it will be empty. Just like I know that Cedar Hills has enough money to fix a faulty elevator. Just like I know that there's something here I'm not supposed to see.

But Colleen has.

34

The house is so quiet. There is evidence of absence every-where. From the lack of a pillow on the sofa to the silence coming up from the basement. I even get choked up when I vacuum the last of the dog-hair dust balls from the living room carpet.

I decide to sleep with Grandma Lou's television on down the hallway. Even then, I can barely keep my eyes closed. I almost call Matt and Ches multiple times, but knowing I'll have to jump through hoops of apologies and explanations before we can get to anything else makes marinating in my own angst for a little while longer much more appealing.

So, that's what I do.

On Tuesday morning, I wait on the front porch for twenty minutes, just in case Matt and Ches decide to forgive me out of the blue and pick me up for school. But no such luck.

When I see them in the hallway at school, Matt takes Ches's hand and pulls her tight to him and away from me like he's scared I might give them rabies.

After work that night, I head over to Cedar Hills. The moment I get off the elevator, I can hear Grandma Lou laughing. It's the sweetest sound.

I knock softly on the cracked door before letting myself in so I don't startle her.

But she's not slumped back in her recliner, watching television. Instead, she's bright and alert as she and George sit there at her kitchen table. Both of them are laughing so hard that there's barely any oxygen left in the room.

Dread crawls up my spine. He makes her so happy, and if he's involved with the kind of people I think he is . . . this isn't going to end well.

Grandma Lou wipes away tears and presses her hand to her chest as she catches her breath.

"Am I interrupting something?" I ask when they still haven't noticed me.

Grandma Lou swivels her head around to see me standing there. "Oh goodness, Faith, what are you doing here?"

I shrug. "Just thought I'd swing by, I guess. What's so funny?"

Grandma Lou turns back to George and he just shakes his head, the two of them rolling with laughter. For the first time since I met George that day in our kitchen, I feel resentful toward him. Is it . . . jealousy?

"Oh dear," Grandma Lou finally says. "Just a sordid memory from my past that my granddaughter should never, ever hear about."

George holds his hands to his stomach. "And you just stood there like no one would notice . . ." He looks to me. "Faith, your grandmother was a wild woman."

"Was she now?" I hover a few feet away. There are only two chairs at the table, so my options are to awkwardly perch on the bed or sit in the recliner on the other side of the room. "Well, I just wanted to check on you after work."

"Oh, let me leave you two to catch up," George says as he begins to stand.

Disappointment passes over Grandma Lou's face, and everything I might feel about George, from suspicion to irritation, vanishes.

I shake my head. "No, no," I say, backpedaling out of the room. "I've been going nonstop since this morning and I still have an econ test to study for."

"Well, I suppose you better get to it then. Call me later tonight?" Grandma Lou asks.

I nod with a too-bright smile and quickly walk back to the elevators. I wait for too long and finally give up and decide to take the stairs.

On Wednesday, I have to stop off at home before work, because I forgot my uniform. I run in quickly to change into my scrubs, and just as I'm stepping out the front door, the doorbell rings.

A startled woman with shoulder-length brown hair and a boy no older than thirteen, who looks like he might make a run for it at any moment, stand there on the steps.

"Sorry," I say. "I was just walking out the door."

The woman, her composure regained, says, "Oh, this will only take a moment, won't it, Brody?"

He rolls his shoulders back, moving just outside of her grasp as he looks down at the steps and mutters something.

His mother holds a hand to the back of his neck. "Let's try that again."

"I'm sorry," he finally says.

My attention bounces from him to her and back again. I shake my head. "I think you might be at the wrong house. I don't really understand what's going on here."

Brody sighs and steps back down onto the walkway. "There. I did it. Can we go?"

His mother takes a deep breath, like she's attempting to center herself. "I'm Viv. That is my son, Brody. Because there was a time in my life when I decided it would be fun to birth another human and attempt to keep them alive and let them devour entire actual pieces of my soul in exchange for them turning into a little shit as soon as they hit puberty."

This woman seems to be unbalanced, but if I had a thirteen-year-old child and they treated me like Brody is treating her, I might be just as batty. "I'm . . . sorry?" I say.

She inhales again, exhaling through her nose. "One day, when you have a kid of your own—if you have a kid of your own—I hope that they don't turn into the neighborhood pyromaniac, sending both of you on an apology tour of the entire town."

I shake my head. Whatever she's getting at still isn't quite clicking.

She throws her arms up in defeat. "My kid's been setting shit on fire all over town, and I'm pretty sure he lit his little sister's dollhouse on fire on your sidewalk."

"Thank you for telling me," I say to him. "But why?"

He shrugs. "I said I was sorry, okay?"

"Anyway," Viv says, "we'll let you get going. If you incurred any sort of damage, please let us know. Brody would be happy to work off the cost. We're one street over on Juniper, in the green house."

She turns and walks briskly past her son, who looks to me and shrugs again before jogging to keep up.

"Brody," I call quietly.

He turns and rolls his eyes as he doubles back.

"I don't want to get you in trouble," I tell him. "But the fires you started . . . were they just little things in the neighborhood?"

"What do you mean?" But the way he bristles tells me he knows exactly what I mean.

"Does the dumpster behind All Paws on Deck ring a bell?"

"Brody," his mother calls without turning around.

He glances over his shoulder. "I don't know what you're talking about, lady."

I dig my fists into my hips and scoff, "I'm not a lady. I'm barely even eighteen."

He shrugs again and runs off to catch up with his mom.

As they turn the corner, I get back into the car and sit there with my hand on the keys in the ignition. If Brody, the neighborhood menace and fire enthusiast, is the one behind all the little fires, then I was wrong. Colleen wasn't sending me messages or threats. This has only ever been about Liam. But why? What does Liam, or his father for that matter, have to do with what happened to Colleen? I can't find any connections between them.

One thing's for certain: Viv is right. Brody really is a little *S-H-I-T*.

That night, I visit Grandma Lou after dinner. It's a bit of a flyby, but any time is better than none. She gently excuses me just before 8 p.m., and I'm pretty sure it's because she expects George to show up any moment.

I leave, pulling her door shut behind me, and pause. At the end of the hallway, the light from Augustus's room stretches into the corridor. Standing there with their backs to me are George and Benji. Neither of them appear to be happy as they trade hushed whispers.

I duck back so I'm hovering in the alcove of Grandma

Lou's room, completely out of sight.

"I'm not comfortable with this," I hear one of them say. Benji, I think.

"Resolve it." This voice is harder, more sinister. It has to be George. I wish I knew what they were talking about.

I get as close to the corner as I dare, straining to hear whatever comes next when my phone releases a stream of extremely loud chirps as someone texts me not once, not twice, but three times in a row.

Great.

"Good night, Grandma Lou," I call as though I'm just now walking into the hallway. I pull out my phone like everything is normal before looking up. "Oh, hello," I say, feigning surprise. "I keep running into you."

Benji grins, but it's more like a grimace.

"Faith," George says warmly. "It's so good to see you. How is Lou today?"

I nod. "Good. She told me all about your visits. It means a lot to her. And to me, too," I add. "You two have a good night."

I step into the elevator and am a little surprised when Benji follows me with his cart in tow. He turns and gives George a stony look.

"I'm going down." There's a challenge in his tone I definitely do not understand.

George does, though. He holds Benji's gaze, smiling

serenely as the doors close between us.

"Big plans tonight?" I ask like that wasn't an obviously loaded exchange I just witnessed.

"Nothing too maniacal," he says with a humorless smirk.

A thick silence settles between us. I don't know where to look so I look at everything. The ceiling, Benji's cart, the strange panel on the wall I've never noticed before with a keyhole and a second series of unlabeled buttons.

I'm relieved when we arrive at the ground floor and the doors open. I'm three steps into the lobby when I realize he isn't behind me.

I turn to find him still inside the elevator. He looks transformed from just a moment ago. Light spills over his hair, casting his eyes in shadow, and the veneer of politeness he adopted at the sight of me is gone. Replaced by a nearly electric tension I can feel from here.

Maybe I wasn't wrong about Benji.

"Are you coming?" I ask, uncertain.

He jams a key into the strange panel inside the door and hits one of the unlabeled buttons. "Going down," he says.

The doors shut and I immediately hit the elevator call button.

Every suspicious thought I've had about Benji comes racing back. Only this time, I'm convinced they're all true. He's up to something. He's working with Colleen and if I want any answers at all, I need to know where he's going.

Abandoning the elevator, I circle the empty lobby. It's eerily quiet with just creepy/relaxing spa music playing in the background. Then, a doorway marked *Official Personnel Only* swings open, and I quickly duck behind it as a woman in scrubs with her headphones in walks out and heads for the exit. She passes barely a foot from me without noticing a thing. I manage to grab the door just before it shuts, and sneak right into the stairwell.

Looking up, flights of stairs wind around and around leading all the way up to Grandma Lou's floor. I see the same thing when I look down. Flights and flights of stairs leading to who knows where. But this has to be where Colleen disappeared to the other night.

I take a deep breath, and dive down the dim stairwell, taking the stairs two at a time. I'm not sure how many floors I've descended when I finally discover another door. It's unmarked and unlocked and I open it to find a dark corridor equipped with motion sensor lights. If only I had the power of invisibility instead of flight.

Well, I'm all in now.

I fly-run down the hallway, letting my feet touch the ground occasionally for the sake of any security cameras.

Finally, I turn down a hallway that is entirely lit, which tells me someone has already been this way. And recently. I follow the lights down the next hallway, which leads me down another staircase and several flights of stairs. I'm careful not to make any noise and don't even let my feet touch the floor now. Cameras be damned.

I nearly give up and turn back, feeling certain I've gone down some fruitless rabbit hole and might actually be lost. But just before I descend one more flight of stairs, I see him.

Benji has come to a stop on the landing beneath me. He stands in front of a door, hunched over in front of a keypad. He raises a card and taps it against the reader, then angrily shuffles it to the back of a rather impressive stack of keycards and tries another with the same results. He keeps trying. Card after card, his frustration growing until he's practically growling at the door, like he might try to tear it open.

I hover, watching him from above, my body hidden by the bend in the stairs.

Eventually, he throws the cards on the ground in a fit of anger and it's like 52-card pickup, but not even a little bit funny. He pounds his fist against the door. And then again and again. Until he steps back, and I can see a dent in the metal.

"Dammit," he mutters.

He turns and begins to pick up the cards. And that's my cue.

I fly back up the stairwell as quickly and quietly as I can, then retrace my steps through the labyrinthine complex. I hardly breathe again until I'm safe in the lobby once more.

As I get to my car and drive home, a thick uneasiness

settles inside me. I keep expecting someone to stop me. Someone to tell me security needs to have a word with me. Or that I match the description of some girl flying through the hallways on the security tape, but when I drive past the last gate, the guard is snoozing inside his little hut and I'm home free. For now.

Whatever's going on at Cedar Hills—whatever George and Benji are up to—it's linked to Colleen and Margaret and A+. I know it in my gut. I wish Peter were here. I wish there was someone I could call to confirm my intuition. All I have is myself, but maybe it doesn't have to be that way.

 **35**

"Shouldn't this be the yearbook staff's job?" asks Rebecca on Friday morning as she steadies the ladder Johnny is currently climbing to hang the prom photo backdrop.

"Well, maybe if half the yearbook staff weren't banned from prom for selling premium yearbook placement to students, then we wouldn't have to help them out," Johnny says from above.

"They got banned for selling ad space?" I ask.

"It wasn't ad space," he clarifies. "It was all the superlatives. Most likely to succeed. Most likely to join the cast of *SNL*. Most likely to go viral. Half the yearbook staff were selling spots on the black market."

"Our school has a black market?" asks Rebecca, her eyes wide with wonder. "What else have I been missing out on?"

"Apparently," Johnny says as he pulls the backdrop taut and uses a huge clamp to secure it to the PVC pipe. "Is this straight?"

"Looking good," Liam calls from his perch in the bleachers.

"It would look better if you helped us," Rebecca says under her breath.

"I wouldn't want to take away your sense of accomplishment," he says without looking up.

"How can he hear me?" she whispers.

"Echo, echo, echo, echo," Liam says softly, his voice reaching us.

Rebecca sighs. "Is there no respect for privacy?" As Johnny steps down the ladder, she says, "Were you able to find a coral bow tie?"

He swallows and nods.

"Coral, huh?" I tease.

His cheeks redden.

Rebecca crosses her arms, waiting for him to explain, but he doesn't. "To match my dress," she says matter-of-factly before marching off to retrieve more decorations.

"She asked me to prom," Johnny says without meeting my gaze.

"That's great," I tell him, and I mean it, but I also am trying not to sound like an overeager kindergarten teacher. "You'll have a great time together."

He jams his fists in his pockets. "You going with Matt and Ches?"

I nod. "And Matt's boyfriend, Rowan, and whoever Ches

is planning on bringing." I pause because suddenly I'm not sure if any of that is true. "Well, actually, I was supposed to. I guess we're not really talking right now."

He shakes his head. "Don't do that."

"Don't do what?"

"Don't be all weird with your best friends right before prom. You'll regret it forever."

I roll my eyes and lie through my teeth. "My friends don't care about prom."

"You mean to tell me Matthew 'I Have an Outfit for Every Occasion' Delgado doesn't care about prom?" He gives me a look.

My shoulders droop as I sigh. I hate this. I hate that I was so secretive and that I didn't just immediately apologize to them both. As the end of the school year creeps nearer and nearer, I can feel time disappearing, and soon they'll both be busy with college and new friends and love lives and we'll have lost this precious time we still have together.

"I know things have been hard," he tells me. "I wish . . . I wish Dakota hadn't broken your heart. And I heard that your grandma moved to Cedar Hills . . . but don't you deserve one good night?"

He's being so kind to me that it hurts, and I can barely look him in the eye. "I'm glad you're going with Rebecca," I tell him.

"I didn't realize it was going to be a matching tie and

dress situation," he whispers.

I grin. "Don't pretend like you don't love it. I haven't forgotten about your show choir days."

I cut out of last period a few minutes early so I can beat Matt and Ches to Matt's Jeep and catch them before they leave. My plan is to corner them in a public place. Surely they'll take pity on me in front of an audience of our peers. And if that doesn't work . . . well, my backup plan is still cooking.

"Well, well, well," Matt says as he sees me waiting there. "I'm guessing your houseguests departed and you suddenly need us again."

Okay, that's fair.

Ches crosses her arms over her chest and suddenly finds the parking lot gravel extremely interesting.

"That's not it," I tell them. "I mean, it sort of is. But . . . I can't stand the thought of us not being together for these last few weeks of high school, and I'm not letting either of you go anywhere until I know we're okay. So, let's do this. I messed up and I'm sorry, and I'm here to listen and make it right."

"I don't know why you feel like you can't trust us, Faith," Ches says softly.

I take a step closer to her and lean my head against her shoulder. "I know it feels like I don't trust you, but that's not it. I promise it's not it. It's just—have you ever felt like things were so out of control that you didn't even know where to start? You didn't even know how to take the first step to let people in? That's how it felt. Dakota showed up and then Margaret, and I was so focused on keeping them safe, that I just locked down completely."

"It's okay. But if we're going to be your wings," Ches says, pointing to the tattoo on my forearm, "you have to trust us to fly."

Matt pulls us both in for a hug. "Honestly, our prom outfits are too good not to take a group picture, so I forgive you . . . and I know I'm not always the easiest to talk to and I need to learn to be a better listener."

"It's okay." I don't want to let them go. But as we pull back, I say, "Actually, if you're in the mood for listening, I have . . . a lot of things to catch you up on."

The three of us pile into Matt's Jeep, and it takes me about ten minutes to catch them up on everything. They listen with bated breath as I unspool every loose thread. Benji. George. Whatever's in the basement of Cedar Hills. Margaret's mysterious ex-boss, Dr. Silk. Colleen's return. The little fires all over town that may or may not be at the hands of Colleen. But the thing that shocks them both is the alleyway duel between Colleen and Liam.

"So you're telling me the supercute substitute teacher thinks you're just really good at pole vault?" asks Matt.

"Actually, if I recall correctly, I think I said long jump."

"And he also thinks Colleen was some sort of maniac

with a blowtorch?" Ches asks.

"It was dark," I counter, though I don't know why I'm defending him.

Matt's thick brows furrow into one. "And why exactly was the substitute journalism teacher in a dark alleyway in the middle of the night?"

I shrug. "How should I know? He's a grown man. Maybe he was at a bar or visiting friends or just—I don't know. The point is I saw Colleen openly attacking someone, and then she just pretended like nothing happened."

Matt stares out the windshield for a moment. "You'd think she'd slip up at some point. Especially with you pressing her so much."

"It's almost like her memory is being reset every night," Ches says. "Oooooh, do you think that's possible?"

"I don't know," I tell them. "But if I've learned anything this year, it's that secrets never stay that way."

Ches snaps her fingers in agreement.

"Whatever happens," Matt says, "we're here for you, Faith."

Ches nods. "Yeah. Consider us your sidekicks. For life."

On Saturday afternoon, I pack a bag full of makeup, hair products, shoes, and a strapless bra.

Matt had plans for me and Ches to get ready with him at his house, but I wanted to make sure Grandma Lou could see me off to prom. So the plan is that they'll meet me at Cedar Hills for pictures with Rowan and we'll all go together from there.

As I strut into the lobby of Cedar Hills, one of the women sitting out front in a rocking chair motions to the dry-cleaning bag slung over my shoulder and says, "What a beautiful dress!"

"Thank you," I call over my shoulder.

As the elevator doors open, I half expect to find Colleen there waiting for me, but of course it's empty.

Upstairs, Grandma Lou is towel-drying her hair after water aerobics. "You know," she says, "I used to make fun of all those old biddies at the Y jumping around in the water, but it's a real workout."

"Maybe I'll have to come and join you one day," I tell her as I hide my garment bag behind my back. "I've got my dress. Do you want to see it now or all at once?"

"Well," she says with a laugh, "it's possible that if you show me now, I'll forget by the time you're done, but I guess I'll wait to see you all at once in the whole getup."

She smiles as I hang the bag in the closet. "No peeking then." She's having a good day today, and I feel luckier than a hobbit.

I've never been good at doing hair or makeup, but I managed to dig an old curling iron out from under my sink, and Matt designed a makeup look for me, including explicit instructions that he promises will make the whole process easier than paint by numbers.

Grandma Lou brews a fresh pot of coffee and I sit down at her bathroom vanity with my curling iron. I've only done this a handful of times, so I burn myself a couple of times— first on the iron itself and then on my hair, which is hot to the touch.

"Here, here," Grandma Lou says as she stands from her chair with a groan. "Let me help."

I pull the iron back before she can grab it, because I don't want her to burn herself and because— "When exactly in your life have you ever used a curling iron?" I ask her.

"Excuse you," she says, "but do you think your father's cosplay wigs styled themselves before he met your mother?"

Still feeling weary, I hand the curling iron over. "Be careful not to touch the barrel."

She stands behind me and wraps the ends of my hair around the iron section by section. "Did you really help Dad with his wigs?" I ask.

Her lips curl into a smirk. "No, but you believed me, didn't you?"

Despite being totally gotten, I laugh. "Grandma Lou?"

"Yes, dear."

"What if I had a really cool opportunity after high school that took me away from Glenwood?"

"Well," she says, "I'd miss you terribly, but you know

what my answer would be. Go places and see things while you can, baby."

I nod. Her response doesn't ease the tightness I feel in my chest every time I think of leaving her.

"Don't go wiggling around on me too much," she says as she lays a curl flat against my back.

My voice is soft when I ask, "What if I leave and come back and you forget me?" I can't help but think of Liam's dad down the hall and what it was like when Liam came home to find him in his current state.

"What if you stay right here and go to community college, which is a fine thing, and I forget you just the same?" Her eyes lock with mine in the reflection of the mirror. "Faith, I can feel things slipping. I can. I won't lie to you about that, but it doesn't feel as aggressive as I feared it would. Besides, we would talk every day, and the thing about leaving is that you can always come back."

When Peter invited me to join him and other psiots after high school, I put his offer away in my mental junk drawer, but with graduation just weeks away, I can't help but wonder what comes next. I might never solve the mystery of Colleen or find out what or who exactly Dakota is running from, and I don't think I can let my whole life revolve around finding some sort of resolution to all of this, because the hard truth is: there might not be one. I've felt myself spinning out of control for months now. I have to find a way to move on, and a change of scenery might be just the cure.

After a few moments, Grandma Lou sets the curling iron down on her dressing table. "It ain't so bad," she declares as she pats my shoulders.

I turn my head from side to side, admiring the way the curled ends of my hair lie just so. "It's perfect," I tell her.

It takes me longer than expected to do my makeup, but despite Matt's instructions, it still feels like too much. There are steps for things like baking and setting and contouring that overwhelm me. So, I stick to what I know and put on some foundation with my fingers before adding mascara, blush, and lip gloss. It might not be Matt's vision, but I look like a shinier version of myself rather than someone else entirely, and I like that quite a bit, actually.

I use Grandma Lou's bathroom to change into my dress, and after buckling my shoes— strappy silver heels—I reach for the finishing touch. My Z hair clip. Careful not to mess up Grandma Lou's work, I slide the Z into my hair and get it right on the first try.

Looking in the full-length mirror on the back of the bathroom door, I can say that I've never felt so beautiful and yet at home in my body at the same time. There's an immediate twinge in my chest. It's the same one I feel every time I reach a big milestone. It's a quiet heartbreak as I wish Mom and Dad were here to see me. But I'm so glad Grandma Lou is.

I take a deep breath and step out into her room, where

she's waiting for me. She claps her hands together as I do a little twirl I can't resist.

"Well? What do you think?"

"Oh, Faith! You're a dream!" With her knuckle she dabs her eyes. "We need a picture!"

She steps out into the hallway and returns seconds later with Benji.

"Faith," he says, grinning at me devilishly. "You look great."

"Thanks," I say, unable to stop the warmth rushing to my cheeks. I remind myself that Benji is suspicious AF and I should not be blushing when he is quite possibly involved in something nefarious. "Uh, sorry about knocking you over the other day."

He shakes his head. "It's cool."

"Thanks. Let's get this picture."

I reach for my phone and I see a text from Ches waiting for me.

Ches: Car troubles! Long story. Okay if we meet you at prom?

Feeling a bit deflated, I write back with a quick Of course, before handing the phone over to Benji. "Make it good," I tell him.

Grandma Lou and I follow Benji's directions and pose a few different ways before he passes the phone back to me. "Those good?"

I swipe through them quickly.

"Just ravishing," Grandma Lou says as she looks over my shoulder.

Benji excuses himself while I pack up my stuff.

"Oh, just leave all that stuff here," Grandma Lou says, plopping down in her chair. "You head on to prom and come tell me all about it tomorrow."

"Okay, okay," I say as I'm willingly shooed out the door with nothing but my tiny matching clutch Matt instructed me to buy.

I smile to myself and close the door behind me. It might not have been the getting-ready-for-prom montage you're promised in the movies, but Grandma Lou did my hair, we got a couple of great pictures, and I feel perfect.

When I walk out into the hallway, I see Benji's cart sitting unattended. On it is a gold key card—one that I'm pretty sure I would have seen the other night when he shuffled his stack faster than a Vegas poker dealer.

I hear his voice from inside a resident's room, and make the split-second decision to swipe the card from his cart and shove it in my clutch with my keys and ID.

"Faith?" Benji's voice calls.

I smooth down the front of my top before spinning around. "Yes?"

"Just . . . have fun. I skipped my prom this year." He shakes his head. "I already regret it."

I open my mouth. An invitation for him to join me is on the tip of my tongue, because despite how certain I am that something with Benji is very off, I can't help but find him charming in a persistent sort of way. "Thanks," I finally say before swallowing my guilt and stepping through the open elevator doors.

The moment the elevator begins to drop and I'm certain I won't be running into Benji, I pull the card out to examine it. It's heavier than a credit card and made of actual metal. I can't help but wonder if this is it. If this is the key Benji was searching for that night.

I guess there's only one way to find out, and seeing as Matt, Ches, and Rowan are already running late, it wouldn't hurt to do some snooping. Just a little bit.

Down in the lobby, I'm as discreet as possible as I try the key card on the *Official Personnel Only* door. The deadbolt unlocks with a buzz and I'm in.

Because these shoes weren't made for walking and because I have no time to waste, I slowly float down the center of the stairwell, being certain to check for any employees I might accidentally stun with my levitating trick.

I make it to the door leading to the corridor with the motion-activated lights. This time it's entirely dark, and I have to rely on my memory to retrace my steps to the second stairwell, which I finally stumble upon after accidentally walking into a laundry room and storage facility.

I fly down this stairwell a little more carelessly with the key card gripped tight in my hand.

There could be anything on the other side of this door and I don't know that I'm prepared to handle what's waiting for me, but I didn't come this far to—

"Faith! Wait!"

I look up to find Benji barreling down the steps behind me, a look of panic on his face.

"Don't!" he yells.

Without a moment's hesitation, I hold the card to the door and step inside.

 **36**

The door shuts heavily behind me, and inside everything feels immediately quieter. Like I'm in some kind of nuclear bunker.

I've never experienced darkness and silence this deep. An eerie calm settles over me as I realize the only sense I can process is the sound of my rapid breath.

I startle with a gasp when, seconds later, I hear something slam against the outside of the door.

Benji.

But I'm definitely not about to lock myself inside a mysterious underground vault with him.

I pull the phone from my clutch and use it as a flashlight. It takes me a moment to find a panel of switches, and when I do, I hit them one by one. The lights above hang down on long metal cords and slowly begin to buzz to life from left to right, illuminating the scene.

To the left there are huge, hulking bookshelves encased

in glass, with books inside that have to be as old as . . . well, printing itself. The shelves create their own sorts of walls with what appears to be a laboratory inside of them. It's a small room inside of a huge unfinished underground bunker with a ceiling that is too high and dark for me to see and stacks of randomly placed cinder blocks. At the center of the lab are three metal gurneys—one of which supports a body covered by a sheet.

A chill races up my spine and I cover my mouth with my hand as I absorb what it is that I'm seeing, but before I can even process the creepy library/lab/morgue, the rest of the lights begin to flicker on, and I can see that the far wall of the bunker is lined with . . . incubators. People in various stages of growth, suspended in some sort of clear fluid as though they're embryos. Each one is more developed than the previous. It's like seeing the human life cycle in a science book, but in real life.

And then, the most shocking, disturbing thing of all. In clusters at the center of the bunker are people in hospital gowns, standing with their shoulders drooping down as though they're hypnotized. Completely, perfectly still.

I hold my breath, waiting for one of them to look up and see me, but there is no movement among them. It's as if they're made of stone. I do a swift count and there are at least forty of them. Forty bodies that might not be living or dead.

I may not know who Dr. Silk is, but I think I might have found his army.

Everything inside of me is telling me to go. Just leave. To walk right out of here and enjoy my prom like a normal teenager. But something else is pushing me to move closer and learn as much as I can.

I walk until I'm inches from a person—a body. Her shoulders are slumped and her bright red hair is smoothed back into a low, utilitarian ponytail. With skin this pale, she's more than white. In fact, I'm certain she's never even seen the sun before.

I can't help myself, I reach forward and take her hand, hoping that I might find some proof of life. I think of Gretchen Sandoval in that corn maze last fall, completely nonresponsive, and Colleen lying in that hospital bed. Maybe if I'd done something more, I could have saved her from what she became. Maybe there was something in her still worth saving.

But this feels different, too. With the incubators and the almost virginal skin. There are no scars or marks or proof of some previous life.

I rub a finger over the redhead's wrist, searching for a pulse and—

Faster than I can inhale, the woman's arm shoots up and grips my throat tightly, her grasp tightening with alarming strength. Immediately my breath grows shallow and labored.

I struggle to push off from the ground and fly free of her grip, but she's as strong as steel.

"Can't . . . breathe . . . ," I manage to say, but it doesn't matter. Her head is still bowed down.

I slap and punch at her arm as my vision begins to cloud.

"Heel," an authoritarian voice commands.

And then suddenly, she lets go and I fall to the floor in a puddle of fabric, my chest heaving.

"Neat trick, isn't it?" the voice asks. "I like to think of it as a built-in security system. An improvement, really."

With my hand on my throat, I stumble to my feet, in search of the voice, but I can't see beyond the lights.

"Marco," the voice says playfully.

I trip forward, squinting against the glare. My throat burns and I can already feel a bruise forming on my neck.

"Now you say Polo," the voice says.

My heart pounds in my chest. Whoever this is, he's toying with me. I am trapped and alone with a villain and his strange, creepy army. But how can I get out of here if I can't even see where he is?

"Faith," another voice gasps. Familiar and unrecognizable at once. "Run."

Without a second thought, I push off, levitating a few feet from the ground on instinct.

"Tsk, tsk, tsk. You lied, Faith," the first voice drawls. "You weren't on the track team."

"Liam," I say just as he steps forward into the light. He looks so much like he always does—jeans, leather jacket, flawless hair—but there's a danger to him now. A harder edge that feels sharp enough to cut. He smiles, one hand hooked behind him where he drags Benji by the collar like a rag doll.

"I have to say, I wasn't expecting to see you here tonight." His eyes drip down my body. "But that is quite a stunning dress. I found this trust fund baby banging on the door outside."

Shock and terror roll through me in waves. It's the same type of feeling I had that night when my parents and I were in that car accident. The moment our car spun out of control. "Who—What is this?" I ask. While my brain screams, *Is Liam Hollis really Dr. Silk?*

"The result of hard work and dedication," Liam answers with a grin.

"Let him go," I say, pointing to Benji.

"Oh," Liam says with a dramatic pout. "Surely you don't mean that. Surely you don't think all this could exist right here without the Aldrich family knowing all along."

Benji is pulling at the collar of his shirt. "Don't. Listen," he rasps as his face begins to turn a sickly shade of bluish gray.

"Let. Him. Go!" I growl as I bear down on Liam. I fly at him with my whole body weight, knocking him to the floor like a dive-bombing bird on a mission. He slams into a cement pillar, and I'm both amazed and surprised by my own strength.

Benji skitters off and breaks into a fit of choking coughs as Liam loses his grip on him.

Liam looks up at me with rage burning in his eyes. The charming, relatable man I've come to know in the last few weeks is nowhere to be found.

"What is this place?" I ask.

"We're building an army, Faith. And that requires a lair. Welcome to the lair," he says as he stands up.

"And you?" I ask. "Are you a psiot?"

He grins and curls his muscles before kissing each bicep. "Nah, I just work out." He points to the clusters of unmoving people in the room. "Those. Now those are psiots. And someday soon, they'll destroy Toyo Harada and everything he's created."

I shake my head. I'm not exactly a fan of Harada, but I'm also not a fan of psiots being turned into mindless soldiers who answer to commands like well-trained dogs.

He saunters over to a cluster and picks up one of the psiots' arms. He's a Black boy just older than me with a peachy birthmark on his neck. Liam holds the boy's arm up before bending his index finger so far back that it snaps with a stomach-churning sound.

"What is wrong with you?" I scream.

"Mend," he commands into the black watch on his wrist.

My expression shifts from horrified to confused as the finger snaps back into a normal position and the boy's arm drops back to his side, as though nothing has happened.

Next, Liam turns to the white, blond girl beside the boy. She is petite, with generous curves in her hips and thighs.

He touches a hand to the top of her head and says, "Shift." Her board-straight hair begins to curl at the ends as it turns lavender until every strand is a purple corkscrew curl.

"We can use their powers on demand." Liam turns back to me. "Think of the good we could do, Faith. Our science is on the cusp of resolving so much that plagues us. Like dementia."

"Don't listen to him, Faith," Benji warns as he charges Liam from behind and smashes a cinder block across the side of his head.

I gasp as my feet touch down on the ground beside Liam, who is out cold, a trail of blood streaming down the side of his head. "Did you just kill him?"

"I don't know," Benji says frantically. "But he's obviously some kind of evil dude."

"And you're not?" I ask. "Your whole family owns this place. How do I know that they're not somehow behind all this?"

"You have to trust me," he yells as he runs over to the lab, throwing cabinets open.

"What are you looking for?" I ask.

"Rope. Cords. Anything we can use to tie that guy up."

I don't know if I should trust Benji yet, but tying Liam up is something we can both agree on, so I run over to a wall of cabinets and fling them open. The only things I can find are coils of cables. "Try this," I tell Benji.

"Perfect."

I help roll Liam over on his side, which is harder than I expected and not the kind of thing I hoped to be doing in my prom dress.

"This guy is ripped," Benji says with a grunt.

"I never noticed." I watch him wrap the cables around Liam's wrists and then around his ankles in a hog tie, like I've only ever seen in thrillers involving kidnappings and car trunks.

"You know this guy?" he asks.

"This guy is my substitute journalism teacher," I tell him.

"Whoa."

"Yeah. Your turn. What the hell is your family up to?"

He yanks on one of the cables with a grunt and Liam moans. "This is all my dad's fault. He's been trying to edge my granddad out of the business since he had his little memory lapse. He briefly took over, and when my granddad was feeling better, he agreed to slowly pass things over to my dad. But then I started noticing some weird stuff being moved in and out of the facility."

"Like human incubators?" I ask.

"I wouldn't call them humans," he says.

"So what are they?"

He shakes his head. "I don't know and I don't want to know. I just want them and whoever is running this thing out of here."

"What about Liam's dad?" I ask, thinking of the lonely old man just a few doors down from Grandma Lou.

"I don't know," he says. "We get people in here all the time who are supposed guardians for the elderly when a prospective resident doesn't have any family. They're sick vampires leeching off people in the late stages of their lives. My guess is that Liam used that guy as an in."

"So you think your dad is behind all this?" I ask.

"I think my dad wanted to make a quick buck and knew about this unused space under the facility."

"What is all this even for?" I ask.

"Grandpa planned to lease this space down here for some kind of doomsday prep planning. People love that shit."

I sit back on my haunches as he finishes his work on Liam's restraints. "Where'd you learn how to tie knots like that?" I ask.

He shrugs. "Boy Scout dropout." He helps me to my feet. "What the hell do we do now?" he asks.

I pull my phone out and begin snapping pictures. This'll get Peter's attention. "I've got a friend," I tell him. "He'll be able to help us."

"So you can fly, huh?"

I laugh a little. I doubt the track and field excuse is going to work this time. "Yeah, does that weird you out?"

"Pretty girl who can fly is way less disturbing than human zombies with death grips."

I do my best to hold my lips in a straight line without grinning. "I guess we should just wait here until I hear from my friend."

"Why?" he asks. "Liam is . . . incapacitated and you're dressed for prom. What's the worst that could happen in a few hours?"

I can think of plenty of ways this could go south in a matter of minutes, but he's right. I'm wearing the dress of my dreams and there's no chance in *H-E*-double hockey sticks that I can figure out what exactly to do with all this by myself.

"I have an idea," I say.

After a minute of exploring, I find an empty incubator free of fluid.

The two of us drag Liam over and clumsily shove him inside.

Just before we shut the lid, I reach inside and yank the watch off his wrist. "Just in case," I explain as we pull the lid down and it clicks into place. "These things look like they can't be opened from the inside."

"Let's hope so," Benji says as he checks the time on his phone. "I think you'll still get in a few dances if you leave now."

 **37**

When I did my hair earlier this evening, I didn't expect to be flying to prom, so I'm pretty thankful I've had so many reasons to practice using my force field recently.

By the time I resurface from the creepiest underground lab I've been to in my life—and I've only been inside two—I send a message to Peter and fly as fast as I can to the high school.

When I land in the parking lot, my phone vibrates with three responses.

Peter: We're on it.

Peter: Don't go back alone.

Peter: Actually, just don't go back at all.

If getting him to respond to a text message was as easy as uncovering an underground lab full of an army of barely human psiots, I would have done that a long time ago. And who is *WE*?

Regardless, by the time I walk into prom, I'm feeling pretty pleased with myself despite my windblown hair. I've defused a potentially catastrophic situation and help is on the way. Help in the form of psiots! People like me! Maybe I'll finally get to meet other psiots who might return my calls or who might not try to torch me every time they see me. Is this the kind of relief people feel when they know what the heck they're doing after high school?

"Faith!" Matt says as he stands from the table off to the side of the dance floor where he, Rowan, and Ches are sitting. "You're here! And your hair looks so good!"

"Sorry, I got caught up with something!" I say loudly enough for Rowan to hear, and then when Ches and Matt crowd me in a hug, I add quietly, "'Something' being a secret underground lab with human beings in incubators."

Ches pulls back, her jaw slack in shocked silence.

"I'll tell you more later," I whisper, "but for now—prom!"

"Prom!" Matt agrees as he smooths my hair out. "I can see you skipped the contouring stick I gave you, but it doesn't matter, because you still look flawless."

"Thanks!" I beam with pride before taking a moment to look all around at the fluffy clouds and glowing stars hanging from the rafters of the gymnasium. "This place doesn't even look like a gym anymore." Despite the awful things I've seen as recently as tonight, I can still be amazed by some absolutely next-level party decor.

Rowan stands with a big smile on his face. "Now can we dance?"

Matt and Ches each grab one of my hands as Matt proclaims, "Now we can dance!"

The four of us charge the dance floor as we twirl and gyrate wildly to a mash-up of Cardi B and BTS.

On the other side of the dance floor, Johnny spins Rebecca in a circle as they laugh.

I wave to him and he gives me a little smile back. I'm going to have to figure out some kind of story to sell him on when Liam doesn't show up for school on Monday. I think in this case the truth might be harder to accept than a lie.

As the music turns slow, Rowan curls an arm around Matt's waist, pulling him in tight, and Ches and I share a look before she offers me her hand and we hold each other close as we sway to the music.

"So an underground lab, huh?" she asks. "Does this solve a mystery or uncover a whole new one?"

"I'm not sure," I tell her. "But I think it might answer some big questions."

Ches nods and her lips split into a grin as she notices something behind me.

I nearly ask her what is it just as someone taps my shoulder. "Wha—?"

I turn around to find Dakota. My Dakota Ash. She stands there in what I can only imagine is one of her steal-your-girlfriend suits. A perfectly tailored black suit with her shirt unbuttoned down to her sternum and crushed velvet loafers. Her hair is smoothed back and she looks . . . incredible. But more shocking than that— "You're h-here," I stutter. "In a room. Full of people."

"And you look superhot," Ches adds.

"Seconded," I say. "Obviously."

Dakota blushes. "Hi." She holds up a corsage with white roses and blue ribbons. "I got you this, um, for your wrist."

I hold my hand out for her. "I love it."

She carefully slides it over my hand, her tongue clenched between her teeth.

I help her by guiding my wrist, and once the corsage is perfectly in place, she doesn't let go of my hand.

"I think I need some punch," Ches announces, her eyebrows jumping up and down as she winks at the two of us.

"Dakota Ash," I say with a giggle bubbling in my voice, "will you dance with me?"

"I thought you'd never ask." She snakes an arm around me as we press our foreheads together.

"What are you doing here?" I whisper. "Someone could recognize you."

She sighs. "Margaret and I made it to the Canadian border, and I just decided I couldn't run anymore. If Dr. Silk or whoever they are wants me, there's no safer place to be than in the public eye."

"You can't be serious!" I say. "The press will grill you to no end."

She shrugs, and I can see how miserable just the thought of returning to a life under a microscope makes her. "It's better than looking over my shoulder for the rest of my life," she tells me. "Of course, if I had it my way, I'd buy a piece of property out in the middle of nowhere and like . . . I don't know, have a tulip farm with Bumble."

"A tulip farm?" I ask.

She shrugs with a starry-eyed smile. "It's an evolving dream, okay?"

I inch closer to her and kiss her tentatively, waiting for her to return the gesture, and when she does, it's like we're flying all over again. Except this time, we're in my school's gymnasium at my prom, surrounded with decorations ranging in cheesiness, but somehow this is just as magical and just as perfect. Finally, we're both basking in the moment neither of us ever thought we'd be lucky enough to share.

The next song comes on, and I'm glad for another slow one as I pull back from her just enough for the two of us to drown in each other's gaze.

"Is real prom better than TV prom?" I ask her.

"Well, for one, there's music, and for two, there's you."

I bite down on my lower lip as fireworks go off in my chest. Maybe—just maybe—Dakota and I can make this work, but we have so much ground to cover first. "There's no music at TV prom?"

She shakes her head. "They have to edit it in during postproduction, so we all just dance in silence. It's a little bit soul-sucking."

"Well, I hope this makes up for it."

"It definitely does."

"Where's Margaret?" I ask, hesitant to ask a hard question that could bring this whole moment crashing down to earth.

"Gone. We, um, dropped off Bumble in your backyard—I hope that's okay—and then she left town." There's a tone of sadness in her voice. "I guess you could say our philosophies on how best to stay alive were vastly different."

"I'm sorry," I tell her. "I know you two have a complicated relationship."

She nods before resting her head on my shoulder. "Did I miss anything exciting?"

"Well, actually . . ." It takes me about five minutes to unload the details of the last few days and then tonight as well. When I'm done, the song is over and she and I are just standing there in a crowd of everyone I've gone to school with for almost my whole life as they dance to some sort of peppy dance music, and it actually does feel like we're at a TV prom, because I can barely even register the music over the terror in her eyes as her gaze drifts beyond me.

308

"It's Dr. Silk," she says as she bites down on her lip so hard I'm scared it might bleed. "It has to be Dr. Silk. He was developing A+ and Honor Roll to identify psiots."

"But who is Dr. Silk?" I ask.

"Well, it sounds like it's your journalism teacher or whatever." She shakes her head. "Faith, I don't want to ruin your prom, but we gotta get out of here. Maybe I can get Margaret to come back and—"

"It's okay," I say confidently. "Liam isn't going anywhere for now and I've already called in for reinforcements."

The music begins to fade as Principal Peck's voice comes over the speakers. "It's that time of night, folks. Time for us to crown junior and senior prom court."

"We should talk—after this," Dakota says. "Come up with some kind of plan."

"Nominees," Principal Peck says, "please join me onstage."

Ches clears her throat. "Uh, Faith." She and Matt have wormed their way through the crowd to me, with a very confused Rowan just a few feet behind them.

"We've got a problem," Matt whispers in a singsong voice as he points over at the photo backdrop, where Dakota and I really ought to take a—

I gasp. "No. How could he—how is he—"

"Who is that?" Dakota asks, looking at the man in black slacks, a white button-up shirt, and a black leather jacket.

"That's the substitute journalism teacher," Ches says.

Dakota squints. "Uh, the same one who's supposed to be tied up in the underground bunker of Grandma Lou's assisted living community?"

"The one and only," I say softly.

I turn to Matt and Ches. "Remember how I said everything would be fine?"

They nod.

"Well, it's not. And I need your help."

"Finally," Ches says with a groan. "Say it one more time, please."

"I need your help," I plea urgently.

"What about me?" Dakota asks.

"I need everyone's help," I tell them, and the words on my tongue are a relief sweeter than finding out your favorite TV show is getting another season.

 **38**

Dakota keeps an eye on Liam while Matt and Ches search for the fire alarm in case we need to make everyone think prom is on fire before prom is actually on fire.

As I march out of the gymnasium into the dark hallway connecting it to the rest of the school, a shadowy figure freezes just a few yards away.

"Hello?" I call.

The figure doesn't move.

"Who's there?"

A small, controlled orb of fire sparks against the shadows, illuminating the hallway.

Colleen! I don't give her an inch. In one motion, I'm off the ground, ripping a panel of lockers from the wall with my force field. They hover between us as a threat.

"You don't want to mess with me tonight," I warn.

"Faith," she says as she pulls the orb closer. It lights

her face from below, throwing ghastly shadows against her pale skin. "Could you maybe wait a second before dropping another hunk of metal on top of me?"

"Well, maybe you wouldn't have hunks of metal dropped on top of you if you weren't trying to kill my teacher and what—now you're trying to torch the whole gym full of juniors and seniors?"

"That wasn't your teacher," she says, taking a slow step toward me.

I raise the lockers another inch.

"Not another step," I hiss.

She freezes. "Liam Hollis isn't your teacher," she repeats.

"I figured that part out, thanks," I say, relieved that she's finally dropping the act. "But if you have some beef with him, then why did you come back to school in the first place? And why do you keep *messing* with me?"

"I'm not back at school," she simply says. "I never was."

I shake my head furiously, the lockers wavering as my hold on them begins to slip. "Gaslighting is a patriarchy move. I see you every day. Let's not waste our time with more lies."

"You're not listening to me, Faith." She rolls her eyes. "No one ever did. But hear me now: That." She points toward the gymnasium. "Is. Not. Me."

"Prove it," I demand.

"Fine," she says through gritted teeth. "If I'm here, then who's being crowned junior prom queen right this moment?"

I slowly turn my head and look through the porthole window in the gymnasium door.

The lockers clatter to the ground as they fall out of my force field and my feet touch the ground. "But—but you don't have a twin . . ."

And before the words are even out of her mouth, I know the answer. Every science fiction book I've ever read couldn't prepare me for this moment.

"No," she says, "but I do have a clone."

"You have a what?" I shout into her face, because suddenly Colleen is standing right next to me and staring through the window in the other door. "I'm going to need you to download these deets to me ASAP."

She rubs her temple, already exasperated. "Well, after the fire, I was on my own for a few days. I didn't know where to go or who to trust. I could barely control my own body. Do you know how terrifying that is, Faith? You can fly! Your superpower is a cool circus trick. If you get mad, the worst you can do is, like, float away or something. If I even got a little annoyed, I could kill my whole family."

"I'm sorry," I tell her. "I didn't know how to help you."

She shakes her head. "You got thrown into the deep end along with me. It's not your fault." Her lips part with a sigh as her gaze drifts to Liam standing with a smug grin on his face as he sips a glass of punch. "Then I met Liam . . . well, his real name is Fitz. He took me in. Said his boss could help me. And Fitz helped for a while. He showed me how to control and manipulate my powers . . . but then one day, I found out that Fitz and his boss, Dr. Silk, weren't just helping me out of the goodness of their hearts."

"Is Liam—I mean, Fitz—a clone too?" I ask.

She nods. "There are three to four Fitz clones in rotation at any given time."

My eyes feel like they're about to pop out of my head. But then I remember what Grandma Lou said about seeing Augustus's sons—plural!

"Dr. Silk, Fitz, Margaret, A+, and the disappearances—it was all connected. They'd created a drug to identify psiots and planned to use us to build an army. But an army isn't an army if you can't control them. Just because they'd identified us didn't mean we would listen. So they started—"

"Keeping you as prisoners," I say breathlessly.

She nods. "I managed to escape, but not before they made that monstrosity." She motions to her clone dancing with Austin Snyder, a plastic crown affixed to her head.

"Peter said clones were disappearing, but he didn't know why."

"Well, that wasn't entirely true," she says. "But that wasn't the first time Peter was light on details."

"Wait. You know Peter?"

She nods impatiently. "He told you he'd send you help, didn't he?"

"You—you're help? You're the help Peter was sending?"

"Don't sound so disappointed," she tells me. "He had to leave town for a while to gather up his own army of psiots to fight—"

"Dr. Silk and his psiot clone army. I get all that. But what do Liam—I mean, Fitz—and your clone want with the school? And prom? What kind of evil genius cares about a random high school prom?"

"One who wants to drug every junior and senior with their new and improved drug and put a target on every potential psiot's back. That's why I'm here."

"Well, if it's the punch, we're already screwed," I say as I look back out into the gym. "That bowl's been drained more times than my neighborhood pool."

"The punch is too obvious. And, honestly, too well protected," Colleen says. "I mean, they're using those little testing strips in every glass."

She's right. When the student body demanded a traditional punch bowl, the school demanded a method for ensuring it couldn't be spiked. The solution was the testing strips that turn purple if there's anything other than high fructose corn syrup and red food coloring in every single glass. It can't be that.

But if it's not in the punch, then what? The only other things in this room are corny decorations, a photo station, and air. I guess it could be in the air, but how?

Liam walks over to Principal Peck, who stands near the huge bubble machine that promises to spit more bubbles than at a kindergarten birthday party. "Colleen, you don't think it could be the bubble machine, do you? Surely this drug isn't airborne."

"The bubble machine?" she asks. "I thought maybe the balloon drop."

I shake my head. "The environmental club protested a balloon drop."

She bites her lip, thinking for a moment. "We have to stop those bubbles."

"Would a fire alarm help?" I ask.

She holds her palms open, both red with heat. "Music to my ears."

I shoot off a text to Matt and Ches. "We should be in business in five . . . four . . . three . . . two . . ."

The emergency lights begin to flash as sirens blare, the sound of them growing closer.

"One," I say.

"Let's take down a couple of clones," Colleen hisses.

 **39**

The alarm sounds and the music stops and for a moment, everyone looks at each other, like this is some kind of joke. Surely someone was smoking in the bathroom or pulled the fire alarm by accident, but who would want to ruin prom for the sake of a prank?

In the far corner by the stage, Liam shoulders his way past a distracted Principal Peck and makes a beeline for the bubble machine.

"You take Liam," Colleen says.

"You've got knockoff Colleen?" I ask.

She nods as we push through the gymnasium doors and I scream at the top of my lungs, "FIRE!"

Dakota, Matt, and Ches join me, and soon the stampede of students in ball gowns and tuxedos begins.

But not soon enough. Bubbles float up from the far corner, cresting like a drug-laced wave and slowly descend down through the paper clouds and glittering stars. I have a second to imagine how these bubbles would have been absolutely dreamy to dance under with Dakota. But I'll count myself lucky that I was even here at all. That's more than I ever hoped or expected.

With the mass chaos, I roll the dice and dive upward, shooting off from the gymnasium floor and gliding over the top of the crowd, which is for the best, because it only takes me a moment to spot Liam. And for the second time tonight I'm diving down on him—or some version of him—like a murderous crow.

We both hit the ground in a somersault and when he tries to move, I let my force field unfurl like a wave, pinning him to the wall.

"Rowan!" Matt screams from behind me.

I spare a quick glance and find Matt throwing himself on top of Rowan's unmoving body. Matt looks up, panic and uncertainty in his eyes.

"Ches!" I yell.

She spins around and sees me before her gaze quickly settles on Matt.

"Get them both out of here. Now!" I shout.

If Rowan is passed out on the floor, it can only mean one of two things. 1. He's super sensitive to chaos and fainted, or 2. One of these bubbles got him, and he's a latent psiot.

I turn back around to find that Liam has disappeared,

just as a chorus of people on the other side of the building shriek. I really need to master this whole force field thing.

"There really is a fire!" someone yells.

Ches helps Matt pick up Rowan and the two shuffle out a side door. My muscles unclench a good 20 percent now that I know they're at least safe.

I run over to the bubble machine to try to turn it off before things get even more out of hand. The machine is a huge black hulking thing that looks like a cross between a speaker and an AC unit. I'm actually a little impressed that the prom committee even had the budget for this.

As I push it away from the wall, I discover the lever used to turn the machine on and off has been ripped off. I guess this means the school isn't getting its rental deposit back. There's only one way to shut this thing off now.

"Colleen!" I scream past the thinning crowd.

Both Colleens stand onstage, one in a singed baby-blue trumpet gown and the other in black jeans and a black T-shirt, as flames shoot from both of their palms, meeting in some sort of fiery death match in the middle.

"I could use some flames!"

They both turn at the sound of my voice, and the real Colleen quickly ducks behind the podium before shooting a ray of fire directly at the bubble machine. "Faith! Duck!" she calls, and I fly up into the rafters.

In the brief moment it takes for the real Colleen to send

the bubble machine up in flames, counterfeit Colleen has her surrounded in a ring of fire.

"Help is on the way," I call as I swoop down so low I can feel the heat of the fire on my cheeks.

With an arm outstretched, I pull her into my force field, out of the flames, and safely back on her feet.

"Thanks for the assist," she calls.

I turn back to the rest of the gym in search of Liam. And that's when I see her. Dakota lies as peacefully on the ground as she did in my bed just last week. Eyes closed, one hand stretched out beside her as though she was reaching for something, or someone, just before she fell. My heart skips into my throat.

It can't be. Surely if Dakota were a psiot, she would know already. Margaret would have found out somehow and handed her over to Dr. Silk. Maybe she was just knocked unconscious in all the chaos. Whatever it is, I have to get her out of here.

Unfortunately, I'm not the only one who's noticed Dakota.

With a smug grin on his face, Liam bends over and scoops her into his arms like a rag doll.

Bile rises in my throat at the sight of it, but not on my watch. There's no way that piece of scum is about to walk out of here with Dakota.

I descend to the gym floor, blocking his path.

"Put. Her. Down," a voice says in unison with mine.

Just as Liam turns his head, Margaret Toliver punches him in the jaw with a set of engraved brass knuckles that read *The Grove*.

I stumble forward and just barely catch Dakota as Liam hits the ground.

"Brass knuckles?" I ask. "Really?"

She shrugs. "They were a cast gift for the season Claire's dad got swept into a cage-fighting ring." She points to my shoe. "You think I could borrow that?"

"Sure," I tell her, kicking my left heel off.

A groggy Liam attempts to sit up, but she punches him once more and this time in his temple. "Nice try, Fitzy Boy."

I watch, both stunned and amazed, as she flips him on his side and proceeds to hit him on the back of his neck over and over again with the pointy end of my heel.

I scream in horror. "What—what are you doing? You can't just kill him?"

She shakes her head. "Trust me. Fitz is a cockroach. He never truly dies. And these things, Faith . . ." She shakes her head. "No matter how human they look, they aren't. Every clone is chipped so that they can be controlled or killed from a distance. At any moment. But if you're feeling barbaric, or simply have no other option, destroying the chip does the same job."

"They're chipped?" I ask. "Like dogs?"

She tilts her head up for a moment as she thinks about that. "Yes, actually."

After three more strikes, Liam's eyes fly open and his body jerks as though he's just been shocked. A small stream of blood leaks from his nose and he doesn't move again.

"Come on," she says. "Let's get out of here."

"I have to help Colleen," I say.

She nods as I pass Dakota to her. "Don't take her away before I can say goodbye. Please."

"Okay," she says solemnly. "Besides, she'll kill me if we leave without Bumble."

"Marge? Does this mean Dakota's a psiot?"

She nods again. "I can only assume."

"Did you know?" I ask.

She sighs before shaking her head. "No, but I always wondered."

"Will she wake up soon?" I ask.

"I don't know for sure, but I think so. Dr. Silk's work has only gotten more and more advanced."

"Who is he, though? How can he have all these people and clones running around doing his bidding and he never even shows his face?"

She grunts as she hikes Dakota up a little higher over her shoulder, the weight of her getting to be a bit much. "I wouldn't be surprised if you've met him before, Faith. Men like Dr. Silk have perfected the art of hiding in plain sight.

To them, we're all just disposable chess pieces."

Behind me, glass shatters. "Go," I tell Margaret. "Keep her safe!"

She nods intently. "I promise. And don't forget: the kill switch is in the base of the skull."

I turn just in time to see a blur of black shoot through one of the gymnasium windows. I stiffen, tracking the figure as they coast through the giant puffs of cotton clouds. That's when I see her. Hovering right there in front of me against a smoky backdrop of blackened clouds and melting stars is a girl in a black catsuit with knee-high boots. Not only does she look hot as hell, but she looks like . . . me.

 **40**

I did not have "battle an evil clone version of myself" on my senior year bingo card, and yet, here I am.

With the gym empty of students, I take a running leap off into the air to meet the fake Faith as she circles above me like a vulture.

"Oh, I've been waiting for this day," she says.

"Enjoy it while it lasts," I sneer.

She shakes her head. "I'm everything you are and everything you can't be. All those weak moments of indecision and feeling sorry for yourself? No more, so how about you do both of us a favor and come with me."

"So you can just farm my body and create more bogus versions of me? Not a chance," I say as I scoop up the ring light from the selfie booth behind her and yank it forward. The metal and plastic smashes against the back of her head, knocking her into a fluffy cotton cloud. She growls, struggling to stay upright, and I use the distraction to dart above her, joining real Colleen on the less fiery side of the gymnasium.

"How ya holding up, Faith?" Colleen calls to me.

"I'm okay considering the fact that there's a freaking clone of myself and she looks like she just walked off a high school production of *Grease*," I yell back. "Oh, and go for the back of the neck," I tell her. "That's their weak spot."

"Roger that!" she says as a stream of flames shoot from her hands and catch the train of her clone's dress on fire. "Talk about a fashion disaster."

My clone snarls as she untangles herself. How did this happen? How was this even possible? Colleen was taken in by Fitz and Dr. Silk for weeks before they were able to clone her. But as far as I know, I've never been close enough to Fitz for him to snatch any part of my DNA and I've never even met Dr. Silk. When could anyone have collected a DNA sample from me to create this atrocity? I guess Liam could have, at some point, found a strand of my hair on my desk or maybe an eyelash even—

That's it. Margaret's voice rings in my ears. *I wouldn't be surprised if you've met him before, Faith.*

It was weeks ago. Just as I was leaving Cedar Hills and Liam asked me to sit with his father, Augustus. Except he wasn't his father at all. I can still feel the touch of the old man's thumb on my cheek as he swept away my eyelash. He was there all along right under my nose and I—

A gust of wind hits me in the chest and I'm thrown back into the bleachers. My head lands with a smack against a sharp corner, and immediately warm blood begins to trickle down my hairline and onto my dress. Ugh. Come on. Really?

My vision begins to blur and I blink, over and over again, trying to regain my composure. Since I don't have a moment to spare, I get to my feet, relying on the adrenaline pumping through my veins to keep me upright. I was pissed off before, but now I'm really in a mood.

I lock eyes with other Faith's eyes. In a way it's incredible to see myself reflected back to me. She's like my shadow, and even though she isn't me, I feel a sense of pride at how badass she looks. Wow. I think I might need therapy after all this.

In a moment that almost makes me wonder if she can read my mind too, we each take a running leap, pushing away from the ground, to collide in midair. All around us, state championship flags and cardboard stars flicker with flames.

I grip her shoulders and push down with all my might as a feral growl rumbles in my chest. Both of us crash into the ground with such force that something cracks, and I think it might have been one of our bodies.

She gets to her feet first and flies toward me. She kicks out, catching me square in the chest just as I'm standing up. A cruel laugh bubbles out of her as I fall back so hard that I slide under the punch table, which is miraculously not yet on fire.

On the other side of the gym, a bloodcurdling scream slices through the sound of sirens approaching from outside, but my view is blocked by a wall of flames, and I can only hope that awful noise wasn't coming from the real Colleen.

My clone hovers over me a few feet in the air, and as she circles me, I can see that I'm not the only one bleeding. There's a gash in her neck, right at the base of her skull. If her chip is exposed, this might be my in.

"Have you ever been to a high school prom?" I ask her.

She tilts her head, immediately suspicious. "I'm three weeks old," she says. "What do you think?"

"Yeah, this is my first one too," I tell her. "Too bad we didn't get a photo."

Her nostrils flare as her frustration grows. "I'm bored. Are you done putting up a fight yet?"

"Almost," I say with a grunt as I launch from a crouch and pull her into my force field. I use every bit of energy inside me as I pull her down to land right in front of the punch bowl.

"You can't go to prom without visiting the punch bowl," I say through gritted teeth before using my gravitational pull to dunk her face-first into the ginormous bowl still smoking with dry ice.

Here's hoping these chips aren't liquid resistant.

She reaches back, her hands flying as she searches for me, hoping to grab my wrist or pull my hair, I'm sure. Her body flails as she tries to push off from the table. I hate the sight of this. For as much as I revel in the potential for good that my powers can manifest, this is something I can't imagine myself ever getting used to.

In this case, there's no other way, and I think that I'm starting to realize that my life as a psiot is going to mean learning how to reconcile the fact that sometimes you have to do horrible things to ensure even worse things don't happen.

But I can't think about that too much right now. I can't let myself get lost in the morality of this or what it means that I'm killing an actual clone of myself. If I don't destroy her, she'll take me with her, and there's no telling how that could end. So for now, it's Operation Drown the Clone in Prom Punch.

After a moment, a shock goes through her body the way it did through Liam, and she goes limp. I hold her under for a minute or two longer just to be sure. Grandma Lou always taught me to double-check my work.

Finally, I let go with a sigh and she slumps against the table before slithering down to the ground.

"Faith," Colleen calls. "I could use an emergency rescue."

I spin in a circle, and everywhere I look is flames. "Uh, right. On my way!"

I push off from the gymnasium floor in my tattered and bloodstained dress. I've got no shoes, and my whole body feels like it's been run over by a freight train full of internet trolls, but I'm alive and my clone is not.

The flames have reached the ceiling now, so I'm careful to dodge the heat as I look for Colleen. I find her at the very top of the bleachers with the body of her clone just a few feet away, her prom dress blackened and singed so that she looks like the prom queen from hell.

"How do I know you're the real Faith?" Colleen asks as my toes touch down on the bleachers.

"I'm pretty sure that other Faith wouldn't dodge a fiery basketball hoop to CareFlight you out of here," I say with a smirk.

"So I guess it's safe to say clone Faith is no more?"

"Death by prom punch bowl."

She nods, impressed. "Nice. Good catch on the robot chips in their necks, by the way."

"A friend tipped me off."

We both duck as a huge flaming star decoration comes crashing down into the bleachers below us, along with the metal beam it was hanging on.

"I think that's our cue," I tell her.

"Hang on just a sec," she says as she runs over to the clone of herself, yanks the tiara off her head, and puts it on her own. "She never deserved this thing anyway."

"Agreed." I take Colleen's hand and we fly through the flames and out a small hole in the roof. On one side of the gymnasium, there are fire trucks, TV crews, and throngs of students—some being loaded into ambulances and others clustered together. If your prom going up in flames isn't a bonding exercise, I don't know what is.

"What the heck do we do now?" I ask as our feet touch the ground on the back side of the gym.

She shrugs. "Turn that corner and pretend like we just escaped a fiery disaster."

"Wouldn't be the first time I did that this year."

"Let's do it," she says.

Ches and Matt sit on a curb with Rowan, his head in Matt's lap and his eyes wide, like he's trying to process what he's just seen.

A tidal wave of déjà vu washes over me as I search the crowd for Margaret and Dakota, but I don't see either of them anywhere nearby. Of course. She left again. I can't fully blame her. I know that spending prom with Dakota was a stolen moment neither of us expected, but—

"Faith!" Ches jumps to her feet and runs to me.

Her body collides into mine and she wraps me in the tightest hug as she begins to sob into my shoulder.

"I'm okay," I tell her as I return her embrace. "I'm okay. It's okay."

Beside me Colleen nods with a smile before giving me a little curtsy and peels off in the other direction. Maybe she's going home for the first time in months, or maybe she's going to track down Peter. I don't know.

Ches pulls back and wipes her eyes with the back of her

hands, causing her mascara to smear across her cheeks. "I don't think I can handle watching you stumble out of another burning building ever again."

"Excuse me," I say with a chuckle. "I was not stumbling."

She leads me back to Matt and Rowan.

"Hey." I give Rowan an encouraging, knowing smile. "You okay?"

He shrugs.

"We can talk," I tell him. "I can answer anything you want to know."

Matt slings an arm around him. "We're still processing," he says in a way that tells me Rowan still has no clue what's going on.

I turn to Ches. "Has anyone seen Dakota?"

Ches places a hand on my shoulder and opens her mouth to speak just as—

"Present," Dakota says as she props herself on her elbows from where she's been lying in the grass behind them. "Sorry . . . just a little light-headed."

Ches nudges me in the ribs, and that's all the hint I need.

I step over the curb, the grass tickling my bare feet, and lie down beside Dakota. All the tension in my body slowly begins to unfurl. "Ahh, yes, this is a much better view."

She looks at me, her smile a little dopey, before lying back down beside me. "Do I want to know what exactly it means that a few random people passed out in that gymnasium and I was one of them?"

"Let me ask you this: Have you ever considered a career as a psiot?"

Her hands fly up to her face, covering her eyes, as she shakes her head furiously. "I . . . let's talk about literally anything else. I can't even think about that right now."

"Okay, where'd Margaret run off to?" I ask.

"That is a question I can answer. She scattered as soon as the cameras showed up."

"You probably should have done the same."

She shrugs. "Turns out the best distraction for a missing TV star is the local high school's prom going up in flames."

"Thanks for coming back," I tell her.

She sits up and places a gentle kiss on my lips.

A spark ignites in my chest as her lips brush mine.

"I couldn't miss prom," she says.

We all stay there for a little while longer before Matt stands with Rowan in tow. He holds out a hand and pulls Ches up with him. "I'm going to get this guy home," he says, and then points to me and Dakota. "You two want a ride?"

I look to Dakota, who seems to be perking up. "Nah. I think we'll take the scenic route. I'll text you all later, though."

Ches blows me a kiss, and the three of them wander into the sea of cars and people and flashing lights.

"You up for a short flight?" I ask Dakota as I stand up.

"As long as we don't take any burning building detours." She takes my hand and I help her up.

We walk, our fingers woven, into the wooded area behind the cafeteria, the chaos of the still-burning gym and the news trucks at our backs.

Once we've found enough coverage, I shoot off into the warm night sky with Dakota by my side. My lungs burn with each fresh breath of air, and it reminds me how lucky I am to have survived tonight.

As we circle the school and head for home, where Bumble is waiting for us, I make a decision. No matter how scared I am to leave this town and Grandma Lou, I know what I need to do. I know what she would want me to do. It's time for me to join forces with other psiots. It's time for me to forge my own path.

I don't know what comes next, but I know that greater heights await.

# EPILOGUE

"I can't believe you're ditching us for the summer," Ches says, her glossy lips in a frowning pout.

"Look who's talking," I tell her as Matt drops the last of my stuff into the trunk of the car. "Let's not forget who ditched who last summer."

"We visited my grandma in Georgia," Matt reminds me. "You hardly missed anything. And besides, you wouldn't be some sort of superhero if we hadn't left you here to discover your powers." He rubs Ches's shoulder. "And it's not technically the whole summer. Just half."

"He's right," I say.

I'd waited until July 5, so the three of us could watch the fireworks together from my rooftop. Plus, they've spent the last month helping me clean Grandma Lou's house out to sell. The *For Sale* sign just went up in the yard this morning, and Miss Ella has agreed to keep an eye on the place until we find a buyer.

And me? I landed an internship out in LA working for a brand-new website that covers everything from celebrity gossip, funny quizzes, and viral internet content to actual, serious news. Conveniently, Peter and his band of misfits are also going to be in the area, so if all goes well, I'll be living two of my dreams at once: reporter by day and superhero by night.

"I saw Colleen yesterday," Matt says. "She took a part-time job at the Bean."

"That's great. It sounds like things are going better with her sister, too," I say.

When Colleen left prom that night, she decided to go to the one place she'd been avoiding for months: home. There was no way she could explain to her sister, who also happens to be her legal guardian, that the Colleen who had been living with her for months wasn't the real Colleen, so it's been a difficult adjustment and thankfully one her sister has pretty much written off as teenage angst rather than a clone swap situation. She's planning on finishing out high school here, and then who knows? Maybe she'll join up with us in LA, or maybe she'll go to college and have a family or become a doctor—or a firefighter, if she's feeling ironic.

Peter followed through on his promise. He used his own enemy against Dr. Silk and put in an anonymous call to Toyo Harada, who had Dr. Silk's lab cleaned out in hours, according to Benji. When I asked Peter if he was nervous about Harada getting his hands on that type of technology, he assured me that he probably already had. I still haven't decided if I find that comforting.

Either way, I guess it's pretty strategic to let your enemies destroy each other. Maybe someday we'll get lucky and a bigger, uglier bad guy will take down Harada. As for Dr. Silk, no one really knows where he ran off to, but Peter assures me it will take him a very long time to rebuild everything he lost.

I turn to Matt and Ches and take each of their hands in mine, my eyes welling with tears. "I think it's time."

Ches's lower lip begins to tremble as Matt attempts to fan away his tears.

Hugging Matt first, I whisper in his ear. "Call me every day. Twice a day. When Rowan's ready to talk, I'm here."

Rowan was still wrapping his head around the implications of passing out at prom and what that could possibly mean for him. Matt and I both decided the best thing we could do was not to rush him.

"I love you, Faith," he says. "And I can't wait to have an existential crisis halfway through college and crash on your couch in LA."

"I'm counting on it," I tell him.

Turning to Ches, I pull her close to me. "I'm so beyond proud of you. I can't wait for you to be the smartest witch in all of Chicago."

She shakes her head, her tears wetting my T-shirt. "You're the one who can fly," she says. "You're closer to a witch than I'll ever be."

"I'll always need you and your magic to carry me," I tell her before giving her a kiss on the cheek. I reach for Matt and open our hug to let him in. "You too."

My wings tattoo feels like a beating heart on my arm.

"Christmas," Matt says with certainty. "We can make it until Christmas."

Ches nods.

"Christmas," I say, even though I'm not 100 percent certain when I'll be back. Christmas seems like a good thing to shoot for, though.

I get into my car and take one last look at Grandma Lou's house. With any luck, it'll be the last time I see it before new owners take over. Matt and Ches even helped me repaint the trim, and Dakota filled in the flower beds. The place is looking pretty good if I do say so myself.

"Thank you," I whisper silently to the house that has been one of my biggest comforts since Mom and Dad died.

Before I pull away, I notice Miss Ella standing there on her porch, so I roll the window down.

"You watch for speed traps," she says, shaking a finger at me. "And pull over if you get tired . . . but only if it looks safe."

"I will!" I call back to her. "I'll talk to you soon!"

She nods. "I've got your number on the fridge in case anything comes up."

"It's in your phone too," I remind her. "Just like it has been for the last five years."

She waves me off with a laugh and I roll my window back up.

Ches and Matt walk out into the street behind me and wave.

The tears begin to really spill as I watch them in the rearview mirror and they turn into silhouettes before disappearing altogether.

Christmas, I promise myself.

I have one last stop before really hitting the road: Cedar Hills.

After parking in one of the visitor spots, I run toward the entrance and wave to Benji, who's talking to a resident just outside the front doors.

He pauses to wave back and says, "Have a safe trip, Faith!"

After prom and Harada essentially buying out the contents of the Cedar Hills bunker like it was an abandoned storage unit, Benji did some digging and found many not only unsavory, but illegal things his father had done since he began to take over the family business.

Because Benji didn't trust George to be hard enough on his father, he anonymously passed on some of his findings to the FBI, who had already been eyeing his dad for some shady blue-collar crimes, so Benji's information was the fuel they needed to arrest him.

I take the elevator up to Grandma Lou's floor, and when I get off, I peer inside Augustus's—or Dr. Silk's—room.

A custodian with short black hair and light pink lipstick gasps as I catch her in the midst of making the bed with fresh sheets.

"Sorry!" I say. "I just . . . I thought this room was empty and then—"

She grins, still holding her hand to her chest. "New resident moving in today."

"Oh, good!" Even though I can't help but feel a little suspicious. I wanted to move Grandma Lou out of Cedar Hills, but Matt and Ches talked me off that ledge. And hearing that Benji was working on getting his dad out of the family business helped. Plus, I couldn't handle the thought of tearing her away from George. "My grandmother will be happy for some new company."

"Is Lou your grandmother?" she asks.

I nod.

"She's a staff favorite," she tells me with a conspiratorial grin.

My heart swells and I feel just a little more at ease. "Can't say I'm surprised."

I find Grandma Lou in her recliner with Timothy the therapy cat that George gave her in her lap.

"It's the big day!" she says. Her eyes are bright and lively, and I'm so relieved she remembered, but in a way, it might make our goodbye that much more difficult.

We sit for a while, and she catches me up on George and how he's started to join her for water aerobics and that they've begun gardening twice a week. I tell her about the fireworks, and how we sat on the roof last night and watched them. I leave out the fact that I took both Matt and Ches on a little aerial tour of the fireworks show as well.

"George took me out on one of the golf carts, actually," she says. "And we were able to see a few ourselves."

"That sounds like a date, if you ask me," I tell her.

She rolls her eyes, but she can't stop herself from smiling. "All right, enough. It's time for you to hit the road if you're going to make it to your hotel before sunset."

"Okay, okay, okay," I say, hyping myself up for the scariest goodbye I've ever had to say. When Mom and Dad died suddenly, there was no goodbye. There was no anticipation of goodbye. And even though losing them without warning was like having an organ ripped from my body, knowing that this goodbye with Grandma Lou was looming has been its own special kind of pain.

She walks me to the door and says, "You couldn't make me happier if you tried by going out there and doing something, Faith."

"I don't know if this is a good idea," I blurt.

"Oh, Faith. Oh, my darling. The not knowing is the exciting part. Go and find out. Make mistakes. Make memories.

Do it all, because you can."

I nod through the tears building all over again. We share a long hug, which isn't long enough, but I commit it to memory. The crisp clean smell of her favorite bar soap. The soft wrinkles in her skin. The way she tsks at my tears despite her own.

I'll remember it all for both of us.

As I'm waiting in line to drive through the last security check at Cedar Hills before I officially hit the road, my phone chimes.

A text from Dakota.

Dakota: We're both settling in and hope you can visit soon!

Attached is a picture of Bumble in a harness with her leash floating above her as she stands among huge, towering ponderosa pines and mossy rocks.

Looks like you're both blending in, I type back.

After prom and graduation, Dakota and Bumble stayed with me for a few more weeks. Margaret even stayed for a couple of days before she turned herself in to the feds in connection with the warehouse fire.

Margaret's lawyer negotiated a pretty incredible plea bargain for her, so she'll only have to serve two years before being let out on parole, and that's not even considering good behavior. *Vanity Fair* already did a whole piece speculating on what her comeback might look like.

Peter offered to activate Dakota, so she could explore what her psiot ability might be. At first, she said no. The only exposure she'd had to the world of psiots, outside of me, was through Margaret and Dr. Silk. She didn't have any interest in lingering in Margaret's world of drug rings and evil geniuses, but after a few days, curiosity got the best of her, and I'm glad it did, because Dakota's power was the one thing she's spent so many years wishing for: invisibility.

So now, she and Bumble have set up a life for themselves in a small town on the coast of Oregon. She has no plans to hide her identity, but she's also taking full advantage of her newfound gift.

Maybe one day, her path will lead her back to LA, and if so, maybe to me.

But maybe not, and that's okay too. I'm thankful for all that we've shared, and the people we helped each other become.

I take a deep breath and close my eyes, but then the car behind me honks its horn, ruining the moment, so I hit the gas and I go.

I go, even though I don't know if I should or if I can, because not knowing is the most exciting part.

The future is a mystery waiting to be solved, and I'm ready to soar into the unknown.

ONE WEEK LATER

"How's the apartment?" Peter asks as we walk across the parking lot of the dilapidated business park where he asked me to meet him. The melting sun has nearly set below the horizon. The way the sky here looks like summer and sherbert every night is one thing I don't think I'll ever get tired of.

Behind us, something rustles, and I quickly glance over my shoulder, but nothing is there. Sometimes I wonder if I have heightened senses or just PTSD from the wildest senior year of high school ever.

"Probably a raccoon," he says. "A whole colony of them live here."

"Trash pandas!" I squeal. "So cute."

His laughter comes out like a grunt. "Remind me how cute they are when one of them gives you rabies."

I roll my eyes and tell him, "I'll make an animal person out of you yet. And the apartment's okay. The listing said room with a view, but it didn't specify that the view was of the parking lot."

"At least you have a place to park your car," he says as he ducks under a half-rolled-up freight door.

I follow him into the dark shipping warehouse, and for a moment I wonder what the hell I'm doing. I know Peter, but do I *know* him? My internship is great and I love the other interns, but if I'm being honest, the real reason that brought me to Los Angeles was Peter and his promise of a family of psiots—people who might get me on a level I could never quite explain even to Matt and Ches. "Actually," I say, "it's not my parking lot. I have to park on the street."

"I'm not surprised."

At the far corner of the warehouse one of those bright construction lights casts three shadows stretching up the wall. Three people. Like me. People who know there is more to this world than most can even imagine.

As we draw closer, I suck in a deep breath and even though my nerves feel like they're eating me up, my chest slowly begins to fill with a warm sense of calm.

Peter, a few steps ahead of me, holds his arms out as he says, "Faith, meet the Renegades."

ACKNOWLEDGMENTS

Contrary to what I believed as a child, books don't just appear out of thin air. There are so many moving parts and people behind the scenes, and I have some folks I'd like to thank.

Thank you so much to my editor, Alessandra Balzer, for your incredible patience and insight. And to my entire family at HarperCollins, especially Jackie Burke, Shannon Cox, and Caitlin Johnson.

Thank you to Jenna Stempel-Lobell and Catherine Lee for this amazing cover design and to Kat Goodloe for this perfect artwork. I'm so grateful to the managing editorial staff for their patience as I got this one in under the wire. Thank you as well to the best school and library, marketing, and sales teams an author could ask for. I'm always in awe of the Harper audio staff and am so thankful for their work and to Joy Nash for lending us her voice as the audio narrator for Faith.

Thank you to my agent, John Cusick, and the whole

team at Folio Literary Management.

To my whole crew at Valiant Entertainment, thank you so much. I've loved playing in Faith's sandbox and count myself lucky to have played a role in her story. First and foremost, I will always be a fan. Special thanks to Lysa Hawkins and Peter Stern. And, of course, a huge thank-you to the kind people at Aevitas, particularly Jen Marshall, Jennifer Gates, and Erica Bauman.

Thank you to Bethany Hagen/Sierra Simone for your early and encouraging read. I owe a huge, whopping thanks to Natalie C. Parker, who dug in so deep on this project with me and helped me not only thread the needle but also carry it through. I love you and can never say thank you enough.

To my family and friends who have walked with me through one of the most chaotic (and exciting!) years of my career (a web of my own making!), you saved me in many ways. Every hug, chat, and joke lifted me up.

Ian, I love you. Always have and always will. Thanks for always tolerating the late nights, the ups and downs, and for always being the first out of bed to feed our hungry little fur monsters.